SHUT OUT

CATHRYN FOX

Discover other titles by Cathryn Fox at www.cathrynfox.com. Please sign up for Cathryn's Newsletter for freebies, ebooks, news and contests: https://app.mailerlite.com/webforms/landing/c1f8n1

ISBN: 978-1-989374-82-5
ISBN Print: 978-1-989374-81-8

RYAN

I grip the steering wheel tighter, and the snow crunches beneath the tires on my old 1998 Subaru Outback. It's a good thing my buddy Beck recently gave the old girl a tune up and helped me put on my winter tires. Driving from Halifax, Nova Scotia, to Summerside, Prince Edward Island, in the winter is always risky. But right after a heavy snowstorm, now that's a little trickier and slow going—especially when I have precious cargo on board.

Speaking of precious cargo.

I take a fast glance at Alysha and find her clasping her hands tightly, her eyes glued to the white road ahead. I don't normally carry anything so precious in my old vehicle, but this year, I'm bringing Alysha Tiffany home for Christmas. Partly because she doesn't want to go back to the Hamptons —I've yet to find out why—and partly because she sprained her ankle in last night's Christmas performance and needs a friend. Bringing her home with me has nothing to do with the fact that I've had it bad for her for a long time now. Nope, nothing to do with that at all and it's a good goddamn thing, considering she's practically engaged. Which raises the question: if her guy is waiting for her, why doesn't she want to go home?

I want to ask, but it's not my business. Nope, my business is to be her friend, help her with her injury, and enjoy a Christmas where my mother goes all out, using recipes that have been passed down from generation to generation, and presents are made, not bought. It's simple, wholesome and unpretentious and I wouldn't have it any other way.

Alysha though... I like the girl a lot, and while I like the idea of her around our tree and table, I'm sure our humble holiday is a lot different than what she's accustomed to. But that doesn't mean it won't be fun for her. I'm going to personally guarantee that it is. Sure, I get it, she'll never see me as anything more than a friend, but where I grew up, a person helps another when they're in need. Right now, it seems to me Alysha is in need—of a friend.

"Doing okay?" I ask, my gaze quickly moving to her foot, which I insisted she prop up on a few pillows below the dash. She's in a pair of untied sneakers today. Her foot was too sore and too swollen to get into her boots.

She tosses me a wobbly smile, and I try to ignore the wobble it causes in my chest, right around the vicinity of my heart. She's hurt about something. I mean, she has to be, right? Who doesn't want to go home for Christmas? She used to live with my friend Daisy, until Daisy got together with Brandon. Now Alysha is in her own condo. From what Daisy explained, Alysha comes from a great family. Heck, her father just recently bought the NHL team in Boston, although Alysha's never mentioned it.

"I'm okay," she answers quietly, softly. "Are you okay?"

Nope, not okay. Not okay at all. How could I be when the girl who's invaded my dreams for nearly a year now is sitting next to me—coming home with me—her sweet scent filling the car and teasing all my senses, and there isn't a damn thing I can do about it.

"Yeah, good."

She wipes her hand over the frosty passenger side window. "The roads are pretty bad. Maybe we should have waited a day."

"It's okay. I'm used to driving in the winter." She twists her fingers together, and without thinking, I reach out and give her hand a squeeze. Her gaze shoots to mine. "Don't worry. I won't let anything happen to you."

Her smile is warm and grateful, and I think she actually believes me. We've not spent a whole lot of time together—other than the night I slept on her sofa—but I like that she trusts me. That night, though, when I slept—didn't sleep a wink, actually—on her sofa, it took every ounce of my strength not to follow her to her room, to her bed, and just hold her and tell her everything would be okay. I had no idea why she was crying as she walked along the Halifax water-front. But when I came upon her on my way home from a friend's place, and found her shaky and sad, no way was I going to leave her. Daisy wasn't home, so I planted my ass on her sofa and stayed there until morning. Until I knew she was okay.

"Thanks, Ryan...for everything."

My heart pumps a bit harder as she hugs herself, and I jack the heat. "I'd put on the seat warmers..." I tap the dashboard. "...but this old beast doesn't have any."

A smile spreads across her pretty face. "That's okay. I really like your station wagon."

I chuckle. Not too many guys my age drive a wagon, but I don't care. This was my father's car. He bought it the year I was born, and I inherited it when he passed away. I was only twelve, so it sat for a few years before I was old enough to drive it. But I love everything about the old car, just like I loved everything about my old man. Jesus, I miss him.

"You don't have to say that." I wink at her. "Gertie has a thick skin."

"Gertie?"

I rub the dashboard. "That's what Dad called her, and I think it's fitting."

She grins, and I can't help but think how adorable she looks in my big-ass passenger seat. She's so tiny the plush seat nearly swallows her whole. Yeah, it's probably a good thing she'll never be mine. I'm six-four and tower over her. There's no way we'd ever fit together.

"It's a perfect name and I'm not just saying that. I like... Gertie." She shifts and stretches her injured leg out even more. "Look at the leg room." She nods toward the back. "I could even take a nap in the back if I wanted to."

"Been there done that," I say with a laugh. Yeah, in my younger years at the Academy, I slept off a few party nights back there, and well, there were nights I didn't get any sleep either. I'm so past that shit now, though.

"Oh yeah... Wait?" Blue eyes that look big against her tiny face and prominent cheekbones widen as she eyes me. "Do I want to know?"

I snicker as I pull onto the highway. "No, probably not. But if you want to sleep, go ahead and close your eyes. I know you didn't get much last night."

"Neither did you."

"How did you know that? Wait. Did you sneak into the spare room and check on me?"

She shifts, and OMG, she did, she totally did.

"No, I just...well, I had to go to the bathroom and your door was open and you were tossing and turning."

"So you were creeping me." In real life and in my dreams. Although in my dreams, she wasn't creeping, she was nestled beneath me as I put my mouth on her body.

Abort.

Do not go down that path, Ryan. She's practically engaged.

Her phone pings, and she jerks her gaze away, looking grateful for the reprieve. I turn back to the road, but her worry, her angst-ridden anxiety, wraps around me as she slides her finger across her phone and reads the message.

After a moment, she sets her phone down and the radio fills the silence. I toss her a glance. "Thanks."

"For what?" she asks.

"For saying you like my car." It actually means a lot to me. "It was my Dad's."

"Well, he had good taste in cars." I grin, and she asks, "What do you do for fun in PEI?"

"You know the usual. Drag racing, cock fighting...knitting."

When she doesn't respond, I cast her a glance and find her lush lips parted, disbelief mixed with worry in her eyes. "What?" I ask with a laugh. "You don't do those things?"

"No."

I wink at her again. "Don't worry, only one of those things was true."

"God, which one?"

"Knitting."

"You're lying."

"No, I'm not."

She folds her arms, and whatever had her worried a moment ago, is now gone, and I'm happy I can make her forget for a little while. "You knit?"

"You don't?"

Astounded. That's the only way to describe the look on her face. "No."

"Cock fighting?"

She whacks me and laughs. "No, and I'd better not see any of that. I love animals."

"Then you're going to love the farm. We have lots of animals."

She settles back in her seat, a small smile on her face. "Yeah? Like what?"

"Mr. and Mrs. Potato Head."

She laughs at that, her mood lightening, and I let my shoulders relax as I navigate the slushy highway. "Do you play fetch with them?"

"No of course not. They're chickens" I give her a look that suggests she's dense. "I played with Carter."

"Not a chicken?"

"Of course not, he's my dog, of course. Was, I mean. Carter is gone now."

"I had a dog when I was little. One day I came home, and he was gone. Mom told me he went to a big farm. I wonder if it was your farm."

I cast her a sideways glance. "Ah, you know that's just what parents say—"

"Wait, are you telling me that my dog died?"

Shit. I break out into a sweat. "Alysha—"

She whacks me. "I'm kidding. I did have a dog though and Mom did tell me that. Tell me more about your game of fetch."

"Carter and I played, but when he died, I tried turning to Sam."

"Sam?"

"It's not like I could play fetch with Sam. Not anymore, anyway."

"Sam is a dog?"

"Ah, no." She arches a brow, and I make a hissing sound as I wince like I'd just eaten something sour. "Not a dog."

She gathers her long dark hair in her hand, and pulls an elastic off her wrist to tie it up. "So you don't play fetch with chickens, but you play fetch with something that isn't a dog?"

"Did you miss the part where I said not anymore?"

"What did you do, Ryan?" Her voice is light and full of laughter as it wraps around me and squeezes tight.

"Well..." I begin and exhale as I remember our pet pig. Of course, he wasn't supposed to be a pet, and that's why you never name animals on a farm. "There was this incident."

She angles her head, her blue eyes narrowed in on me. "Incident?"

"Yeah, that's how we refer to it now."

She laughs harder. "Oh, God, maybe I don't want to know."

I laugh with her, and turn on my wipers as a truck flies by and covers the windshield in slushy snow. "Goddamn idiots," I say under my breath.

The conversation shifts, the mood in the car changing as she hugs herself again. "I wouldn't want to be out in this in my car."

She drives a tiny little blue Mini that would have been buried under by that truck's spray. It's a cute vehicle and suits her, but useless in the snow. "I'm glad you're not driving back to the Hamptons in this weather."

She gives me that grateful smile again and ignores her phone when it pings. I glance at it, but can't tell who's texting. "What do you do for fun back home?" I ask. Her head dips and she frowns, like she's trying really hard to figure that out. "You must still have friends there." Still no answer so I add, "You and Linc must do a lot of fun things together."

Okay Ryan, way to be subtle.

She nods. "Yeah, we do. We like to go to restaurants, and concerts, and things like that."

"Dancing?"

Wow, did she just physically tighten? How could dancing be a sore spot when it's what she studies and wants to do after college?

"No, not really." She lifts her head, her eyes half closed. She looks at me through dark lashes and asks, "Do you...dance?"

"Sure. I mean It's not pretty. I'm all legs, and I jump around like a cricket in a hot frying pan, but yeah, I dance."

"Wait, you put crickets in hot frying pans?"

"You don't?"

"Ohmigod," she says as she playfully reaches for the door handle. "Tell me you're kidding or I'm jumping."

"Okay, I don't. I'm not that great of a cook, but I can't say other people in my family don't."

"Ryan!"

I laugh. "No, we don't eat crickets in PEI. We eat potatoes. Lots and lots of potatoes."

"I don't usually eat potatoes."

"You will be this holiday."

She shrugs. "Okay."

Wow, that was easy. If I told her she'd have to be beneath me in my bed, would she agree just as easily?

Cut that shit out, Ryan.

Her phone pings again and she picks it up and exhales as she stares at the screen, her brow furrowed.

"Go ahead and text." I stare at the road to give her privacy. "I don't mind."

"It's Linc," she says quietly as she turns her phone over to hide the message and sets it on her lap.

There's no missing the sadness in her voice. I guess maybe he isn't not the reason she doesn't want to go home. I don't know why that guts me. I want her happy, and if Linc makes her happy, then so be it. "I guess it's hard for you not seeing him over the holidays. Is he pretty upset about it?"

Her head moves slightly, the smallest nod I've ever seen. She laughs, but it holds no humor. "It's not like we would have seen a lot of each other anyway."

She snorts, and it holds a measure of frustration and something else, something just below the surface that could be... relief? Does she not want to see her almost-fiancé? I'm not sure, but my interest is seriously piqued.

"Yeah?"

"He's a lawyer. He works for my father, and with the new..." She goes quiet and her fingers tighten on her phone.

"The new team?" I ask. Why does she not like talking about it?

"Right, and so there is a lot of work, which doesn't stop because it's the holidays, plus..."

I go quiet and wait for her to continue. When she doesn't, I reach for my Thermos mug and take a sip of coffee. "Anyway, it's nothing."

Nope, not nothing at all. Just nothing she wants to talk to me about, and that's fine. We're friends, and she doesn't have to tell me anything she doesn't want to.

She reaches over and puts her fingers on the cuffs of my well-worn winter sweater. "Will you show me?"

"Show you what?" I ask, thinking about all the things I'd love to show her and all the things I'd like for her to show me in return.

Jesus, don't go there, Ryan.

"How to knit?"

"Sure."

She sinks deeper into her seat, and says, "Okay, now tell me everything about Sam and the incident that forever changed your game of fetch."

2

___

ALYSHA

___

I sit up straighter as we cross the Confederation bridge and try to see over the sides. "It's really eight miles long?" I ask. He jokes about a lot of things, and I'm never entirely sure if he's kidding or being serious.

"Yup, longest bridge in the world crossing over ice-covered water. It opened a couple of years before I was born, and before that there were only ferries, one from Nova Scotia and one from New Brunswick. That could be slow going, from what I heard."

"I think the ferry would be fun."

"In the summer, not the winter. If you come home with me again in the summer, we can take the ferry." His words bang around inside my head and I sink back into my seat. I won't be going home with him in the summer. Honestly, I can't believe I'm going home with him now. Well, maybe I can, because deep down, I'm a big coward. Pathetic, I know, but that's what I am. I should be going home and facing Linc, but instead I used my twisted ankle as an excuse. I could have flown home instead of driving, like Linc suggested, but I played into my injury, and laid it out like mobility was near impossible. Like I said...pathetic.

"You only have to pay a bridge toll when you leave the island," Ryan says as we reach the other side and drive by a bunch of shops. "That's Gateway Village. If you're thinking about souvenirs, we can stop."

I shake my head. "I'll look for something later." I don't want to be rude, but there is no one in my life back in the Hamptons that would want a trinket from Prince Edward Island. My mother doesn't have anything nice to say about Canada as it is. She thinks all Canadians live in igloos and eat seal blubber. So rude.

But maybe that's why I chose Halifax for my higher education. Don't get me wrong. I love my mother and father, totally, but I needed to get away from the pressure. I want to be a dancer, not a socialite like my mom. She was a beautiful, talented dancer who gave it up to cater to my dad and turn a blind eye to his affairs. A sound crawls out of my throat.

"You okay?"

"Yeah," I say. "I was just thinking about poor old Sam."

"Don't worry, Sam might be bad at playing fetch, but that old pig lived a good life, was spared from the butcher, and no cows were injured during our game."

I grin. "Maybe not, but Mr. Burke didn't fare so well."

He laughs. "Sure, he did. Now if it had been the bull that charged him, we'd be telling a different story, but it wasn't, and he, for all his troubles, now has a lifetime supply of potatoes."

"Blackmail potatoes. He could have sued you." I shake my head and laugh. "I can't believe Sam chased the ball into the cow pen and scared the crap out of them like that."

"Oh yeah, there was crap." He crinkles his nose like he's knee deep in something stinky. "A lot of crap."

Poor Mr. Burke. From the way Ryan told the story, the man was simply walking by when a herd of frightened cows broke through the fence and took off running down the road and bowled him over. I laugh, but it's not funny. Okay, it's sort of funny—if you have a sick sense of humor, like Ryan and I do. Who would have thought we'd have that in common?

"I can't believe he didn't sue."

"We're Canadians. We don't sue over just a cow herd running you down."

I stare out the window and look at the snow-covered fields. I revel in the wide-open space, and can only imagine how lush it must be in summer.

"Are we close?" I ask, suddenly finding myself excited about spending the holidays on his big family farm, even though I'm being a coward. But going home...Mom throwing a big fake party, Dad schmoozing with the guests and no doubt looking for some young thing to take to bed, and Linc...well, I'm pretty sure, when he's not working, he's going to get down on one knee before me. My lungs constrict and a strange wheezing sound catches in my throat.

"Are you okay?"

"I think I need a drink."

He reaches into the back and produces a water bottle. "Thanks. But I'm not sure this is strong enough." He eyes me. "My ankle," I fib. "I think I moved my foot the wrong way."

"Is there a right way when you have a bad sprain?"

"No, you're right."

"We're almost there, and then we can get your foot properly elevated."

I take a long pull from the bottle and recap it. "Are you sure your family won't mind me just showing up over the holidays?"

"It's a farm, Alysha. We take in strays all the time."

"Hey," I whack him, and the second my hand lands on his hard chest and lingers for a second too long he takes a fast look at me, and I can't help but think he liked me touching him as much as I liked doing it. But he's well aware that I have a boyfriend at home and he's definitely not the kind of guy to make a move on a girl who's attached.

What if you weren't attached, Alysha?

Whoa!

I quickly shut that thought down. Heck, Ryan is a good guy and is helping me out. There's nothing more between us, and maybe the heat I spotted in his eyes a second ago was wishful thinking.

Wait...what?

I am not wishfully thinking about anything. I think my sprained ankle is affecting my brain somehow. Or maybe I'm just feeling emotional because every house we pass is decorated for the holiday and while I don't approve of the way my parents live, I still miss them.

"We're here," Ryan says and I sit up a little straighter as he turns into a long driveway. I take in the acres of snow-covered land and all the big red buildings on the property.

"It's huge." I scan the area as he pulls up in front of a big house, a couple of cars in the driveway.

"What were your sisters' names again?"

He laughs. "Lucy is the youngest, Monica is the middle, and Lauren is the oldest."

I repeat the names in my brain as a part of me really hopes they like me. I've always wanted a sister. "And your mom is Patricia and your grandfather is John."

"That's right. You got it."

I reach for the door, and he puts his hand on my arm to stop me. Okay, his touch should not be warming me from the inside out like that. What is going on with my body? Sure, I haven't been touched in a very long time, and the last time I was home, I barely got a peck on the cheek from Linc. He was in the middle of some big negotiation and was working around the clock. The thing is, though, I wasn't really upset about it.

"Let me help."

"I can walk."

"The doctor said to keep it wrapped and elevated, so I'm not letting you walk into the house."

I stare at him. "You are not carrying me."

"I carried you to the car."

We didn't have an audience then. "Yeah, but your family...I don't want them to think you're carrying me over some threshold or that we're a couple or anything." I'm not entirely sure I'm telling the whole truth here. I liked it a lot when he carried me, too much actually.

He goes quiet for a second, and his eyes narrow. I'm not sure what's going through his mind, but I know I'm not going to like it.

"Wait here."

He hops from the car, and I sit still as he disappears around the side of the house and comes back with a wooden sled. He opens my door.

I shake my head as I stare at the wooden slats. "Are you kidding me?"

"Nope."

"I'm not getting on that thing." Determined to walk, I put my legs outside the door, and push up, standing on my good foot. Before I can take a step, he scoops me up and sets me on the sled. "This is ridiculous."

"What's ridiculous is how stubborn you're being. You do want to dance again, right?"

I let out a breath and everything inside me softens. How could I be upset when Ryan cares so much about my career? He's the only man in my life who does.

"I do, but this is kind of embarrassing."

"Nah, it's not." His breath turns to fog in front of his face as he talks. "But I can carry you."

"I'm good, let's go."

He grabs the rope and I brace myself as he pulls me over the snow. He turns to face the house as he carefully negotiates the wooden sled over a bump, and unfortunately for me, the sled goes one way and I go another.

I gulp as I faceplant into the snow and I swear to God, I'd rather stay put until spring—my face buried in the snow—then face anyone who might be looking at my ass in the air.

"Shit, I'm so sorry," Ryan says as he scoops me up. His dark eyes move over my face, and he drops down on one knee, sitting me on his leg as he brushes snow from my face. His lips quirk.

"You better not be laughing," I warn.

"I'm not," he says. "Nothing about this is funny."

"Right, everything about this is funny, and if I didn't have a bad ankle I'd run all the way back to Halifax, or maybe Siberia."

He smiles at me and I shake my head and smile back. "That sled is out to get me."

"It's a pretty mean fucker." He glances at the sled. "One time when I was a kid, that bastard ran me right into a tree. Look." He pulls his hair from his forehead to show me a scar.

I glance at the slats of wood on the sled. "Maybe we could have a bonfire later. Prop him by it, let him know who's boss."

Ryan's fingers graze my cheek as he brushes my damp hair back. "I like the idea of a fire. You didn't hurt your ankle, did you?"

"Nope just my pride." I look around, praying no one saw me. "I don't want to be known as an 'incident'."

He laughs. "We need to get you inside and warm. I'll come back for our bags." As the sky grows darker, the outside Christmas lights flicker on and I might be on a farm, but it feels more like I'm stuck in a Norman Rockwell painting. Mom decorates too. Or rather, she hires out for it, and it's lovely, but there's something a little more real and warm about the lights that aren't in a perfect strand.

Instead of moving Ryan continues to balance me on his knee. "I can stand so you can get your key."

"Key? Where do you think you are? This is Summerside, PEI, Alysha. No one locks their door."

"What if someone breaks in?"

"Then they probably need what's inside more than we do." He nudges the door open with his shoulder, and the sweet scent of cinnamon fills my nostrils.

"Mom's famous cinnamon rolls."

"Ohmigod, that smells good."

He gently sets me down and I balance on one foot as a woman about my height comes around the corner, wiping her hands on a dish towel, a huge smile on her pretty face. "Ryan," she says and he picks her up and swings her around. I smile as I watch. I remember once someone told me to watch how a boy treats his mother and that it was a good indication how he'd treat a girlfriend or wife.

He finally sets her down. "You must be Alysha."

I hold my hand out to shake hers, but nope, she's not having any of that. She pulls me in for a tight hug, and I stand there, soaking in her comfort and trying to remember the last time

I was hugged this hard or this long. Oh yeah, I remember. Never.

She breaks the hug and there's a deep warmth in her dark brown eyes as she threads her arm through Ryan's. As I revel in their closeness—almost a little envious—I chuckle as Ryan hovers over his mom. Is that how I look standing next to him? Probably, and he probably got his height from his dad.

"It's so nice to meet you, Mrs. Potter. Thank you so much for opening your home to me over the holidays."

She waves the dish cloth in a dismissive way. "Any friend of Ryan's is a friend of ours and always welcome, and please call me Patricia." A line forms in the center of her forehead as her gaze drops. "I'm so sorry to hear about your ankle." She taps Ryan's arm. "Why don't you carry her to the sofa, Ryan, so she can rest? I'll bring in coffee and cinnamon rolls."

"I can wa—"

Scoop.

I yelp, and throw my arms around his broad shoulders. Who knew working a potato farm would give a guy such hard muscles?

"Your grandfather and the girls will be home shortly. They went to the store to pick up some groceries for me, and a trip to Cow's was involved."

I grin. Prince Edward Island is known for their award-winning Cow's ice cream. We even have a kiosk on the Halifax waterfront, and I too would suffer through grocery shopping if Cow's was involved afterward.

Ryan carries me to the sofa and sets me down. He puts my legs over his and slowly removes my untied sneakers. I lean forward to take a look. "It looks like the swelling is down a bit."

He lightly touches my ankle as he adjusts my sock. Small goosebumps break out on my skin.

"Are you cold?"

"Yeah. I guess I shouldn't have eaten all that snow, huh?"

He laughs and rolls his eyes. "City girls."

He turns his attention to my other foot and unties my laces. I have no idea what is going on or why I can't seem to take my eyes off his big fingers as he removes my sneakers. You'd think a guy as big and strong as Ryan wouldn't know how to be gentle, or wouldn't be good at all this nurturing stuff.

Needing a distraction, I glance around the living room, but something is missing. "You guys don't put up a tree?"

"Sure, we do." He stands and sets my feet on a pillow. "They were just waiting for me to get home. Dad and I cut one down every year when...well, when he was here. I've taken over the tradition. We grow our own trees at the back of the property."

An almost giddy thrill goes through me. "Are you serious?"

"Yeah, want to come?"

Watching Ryan work an axe. Hell yeah, I want to see that. I frown as he adjusts the pillow under my feet. "I do, but I can't."

"We'll find a way." I open my mouth and he holds a hand up to stop me. "No sleds will be involved."

I laugh. "Or carrying." He arches a brow. "You can't carry me and use an axe, Ryan."

"What's this about carrying you?" Patricia asks, as she comes into the room with a tray. She sets it on the coffee table, and hands me a cinnamon roll.

"Alysha wants to watch me cut down our tree."

"Oh, fun. We'll all go first thing tomorrow after everyone is up. I'll make hot chocolate."

Ryan adds a teaspoon of sugar and a dash of milk to a mug, stirs it and hands it to me. How does he know how I like my coffee? We've all been out together before, but I can't imagine he cared enough to watch. I snort. I'm sure Linc has no idea what I put in my mug, but thoughts of him bring pain to my chest. I'll have to text him before bed, but right now, I just want coffee and treats.

"You'll be sleeping in Ryan's room while you're here," Patricia says, and I nearly choke on the big bite of pastry.

"What?" I glance around. This big old farmhouse must have at least a dozen rooms.

"His bed is much more comfortable than the one in the spare room. I've been meaning to buy a new one, but we don't often have overnight guests and I keep forgetting."

"Oh, okay. I thought—"

"You thought Mom was putting you in my bed with me," Ryan says with a devilish smirk.

Yes, I did think that which is crazy. "Your mom said you don't often have guests, and here you said you often take in strays."

Ryan grins and his mother's mouth drops open. "Ryan, what a horrible thing to say."

"I was kidding, Mom."

Patricia shakes her head. "I'm sorry my son has a strange sense of humor. You are not a stray and Ryan hasn't brought anyone here in a while. Last time was his friends Kennedy and Matt. They were the sweetest couple." Her gaze goes from me to Ryan and back to me again.

Wait, does she think?

"Oh, they are a great couple, but Ryan and I are just friends. He's just helping me out. Travel would be hard." *Stop freaking rambling, Alysha.* "We're not a couple or anything. That would be..." I let my words fall off, because while crazy is hovering on the tip of my tongue, why would it be so crazy. Ryan is a nice guy.

Oh right, it would be crazy because I'm practically engaged.

"Is crazy the word you're looking for?" he asks, and for a split second I think I see hurt in his eyes.

"No, I just mean, we're...friends." Ryan is friends with a lot of girls back on campus. I'm not sure if I've ever seen him on a date, and no girls talk about hooking up with him. That's when another thought hits and I blurt out, "Do you have a girlfriend here, on the island?"

His mother sits back in her chair, her body tightening, and the muscles in Ryan's jaw ripple as he clenches his teeth. Clearly, there's a story here, and it's not a happy one.

"No." His voice is deep and hard, and he turns his attention to pouring milk into his cup. I sip mine, needing to occupy my mouth before I blurt something else out—something that's none of my business. "I'll get the bags."

He disappears and I take a sip of my coffee. "Tell me about your dancing," Patricia says.

"My mom was a dancer."

Her eyes light. "You're following in her footsteps. How lovely." She glances down, a frown on her face as she stirs more sugar into her mug. "Ryan is following in his father's footsteps."

"His father was in the NHL?"

she shakes her head. "No, no. Farming."

Wow, it doesn't sound like she likes that idea at all. Wait, is she saying he wants to move back to PEI? "I thought he wanted the NHL?"

Before she can answer, in comes Ryan with his grandfather and his sisters, tromping through the front entranceway like a herd of elephants. Patricia jumps up as everyone talks at once and hugs Ryan.

"Girls, John, come and meet Alysha."

I shift and put my foot on the floor as his sisters, every one of them gorgeous, come into the room.

"Sorry to hear about your ankle," the tallest one says and the other two agree. Patricia introduces them as Ryan runs the bags upstairs. He comes back, and holds his arms out. "Uh, didn't anyone miss me?"

"We already hugged you," Lauren says and rolls her eyes at me. I grin, loving the comradery.

"How was Cow's?" I ask.

Monica rubs her stomach. "So good."

John comes in and we exchange pleasantries for a second and then he says, "Okay girls, come on, the groceries aren't going to put themselves away and you'll have plenty of time to get to know Alysha." He winks at me. "We don't want her getting sick of us and trying to run off. Although she's not going to get far. Not with that ankle."

After everyone leaves me alone with Ryan, he puts his arm over his shoulder and rubs the back of his neck. "Come on. I'll show you to your room."

I push to my feet and he moves toward me. "Fine," I say and let him pick me up. "I'm sure by tomorrow, I'll be able to put more pressure on it."

He carries me upstairs, and sets me down outside his room. He looks over my shoulder. "Don't be snooping through my things."

"You have something to hide in there. Dirty magazines?" Oh, God, why did I ask that? Heat moves into my cheeks.

He leans in, his body close, as his breath stimulates the shell of my ear. "Don't check under the mattress."

He's kidding. I think. I'm never really sure with him. "Now I have to."

"Oh, you're one of them, are you?"

I turn and glance around the room. Everything about the room feels like Ryan. Warm. Comfortable. Homey.

I spot my bag on his bed, and I turn back to him. "Ryan, I'm sorry I asked about a girlfriend. That's not my business. I shouldn't have asked. I just..."

He leans into me again, his big body eating up the entrance way. He's so close I can smell his skin, the shampoo he used on his hair this morning—my shampoo. He didn't have to stay the night to watch over me, and I told him that, but deep inside, it was kind of nice having him at my place.

"It's okay. It's been over for a while. You can ask me whatever you want."

"Did she…hurt you?"

He takes a step closer, and my body should not be tingling the way it is. "Yeah."

"I'm sorry."

"Nothing for you to be sorry about."

His head dips, and his gaze moves to my mouth. I instinctively wet my lips as my heart pounds a little faster against my ribs. Ohmigod, is he going to kiss me? Do I want that? I must be reading this wrong. Ryan would never try anything with me, not when I have a boyfriend. Right? I guess I'll never know now, because my phone just pinged and Ryan is inching back, scrubbing his hand over his face.

"Linc," I say. I shake my phone. "I should probably…"

He gives a curt nod. "I'm sure he's missing you."

My throat tightens and I force my words out. "I probably wouldn't have seen much of him anyway." He doesn't answer, but his eyes are full of questions. "Like I said, he's one of Dad's lawyers and always working around the clock to make a name for himself."

He nods like he understands, but I'm not sure how he can. "I'm sorry you're missing him."

I stare at his broad back as he turns and disappears into the room across the hall, and before I can blurt out, *I'm not,* I shut my door, lean against it, and wonder exactly why I'm not missing Linc, and why I wanted Ryan to know.

3

RYAN

I wake, and the second reality replaces the dream in my brain, I glance around the room, and stretch as my mind goes to Alysha—snuggled in my bed. Last night it drove me crazy to think she was in there on the phone with Linc. Christ, they were probably sexting, or maybe they were on a video call and she was touching herself as she writhed on my bed.

I groan and roll over, my early morning boner tenting my boxers. I'm just about to take it into my hand but stop myself. I should not be tugging one out while thinking about a girl who is unattainable.

Fuck, I wish I didn't have it so bad for her. Last night, what the hell was I thinking? I nearly kissed her. How could I not want to when she was standing in my bedroom door, looking warm and soft and sexy. It was all I could do not to take her to my bed and crawl in with her. Not that I've ever done that in my family home. I'm the oldest and I'm supposed to be setting a good example, but Christ. I really like Alysha—who is practically engaged. What the hell does practically engaged even mean, anyway? You either are, or you aren't. If I were Linc, I damn well would have put a ring on it a long-ass time ago.

Dishes clang downstairs and I get my dick under control before I kick off my blankets. The cool morning air hits my skin and I tug on my jeans and sweater. Outside, there's a fresh new layer of snow on everything, but it's letting up, which means we'll be able to go get our tree. I make a quick trip to the bathroom, walking past my bedroom door. I stand for a second, and debate on knocking, to see if she wants to come down for breakfast. But if she's still sleeping, I probably shouldn't wake her. I just don't want her negotiating the stairs on her own. I'll listen for her and dash back up to get her when I hear her door open.

I head downstairs and I'm taken aback when I find Alysha seated at the big kitchen table with my mom, grandfather and Lauren, who has both feet on the chair and her big sweater pulled over her knees. I stop dead in my tracks the second I realize Alysha is wearing my flannel pajamas. Wow, who knew I could be jealous of a pair of pajamas?

"I hope you don't mind," she says and toys with the button on the loose-fitting top. My God, I never thought flannels were sexy before.

"No, not at all."

"I forgot to pack pajamas, and I got cold through the night."

"Help yourself to anything in my room."

Myself included.

"Hey kiddo," I say and ruffle Lauren's hair the way she hates. "What are you doing up?"

"Ryan!" she squeals and whacks me. I catch the grin flirting with Alysha's lips.

I turn my focus back to Alysha. Yeah, that's right. I can't stop staring at her. "How's the ankle?"

"Good, actually." She sticks her leg out, and tugs the pants up to show me her ankle. "The swelling is down."

That makes one of us.

"Doesn't hurt quite as much to walk on it," she adds.

"You should have woken me." I head to the cupboard and pull out a mug. "I would have carried you downstairs."

"I went slow, and I used those." I follow her gaze and set eyes on my old crutches. "I found them in your closet when I was searching for something warm to wear. I hope you don't mind."

She must really hate it when I carry her. "Right, I forgot I even had them." I set my mug on the counter. "Sleep good?"

She makes a moaning sound that teases my cock, and Jesus, now is not the time for a boner. "Your bed is so comfortable. I might never leave."

I laugh. "That's why I keep coming back." I grab the carafe and pour a cup of coffee. I hold it out to see if anyone needs a refill, and my grandfather points to his mug.

"Time to hand his bed down to me," Lauren grunts as she fixes her hair. "I saw one on the side of the road last week. Looked good and lumpy."

"Hey, are you saying you don't want me coming home?"

"Not if you're going to mess up my hair."

I pull out a chair and drop down next to Alysha, and as our thighs bump, I try not to react, even though my body is buzzing from her close proximity.

"He won't be coming back once he's drafted," Grandad says before taking a big drink of coffee, and my chest constricts. It's what he wants for me, what everyone here wants—everyone but me. The truth is, I love the game, but my heart is here on the island. Everything I love and want is here.

"Yeah," is all I say as Alysha stares at me, confusion on her face. "What time should we head out to get the tree?"

"Snow's letting up. We can go as soon as the girls are up."

Alysha sets her mug down. "I'm not so sure I can go."

"We'll take the sled," Grandad says, and Alysha opens her mouth, about to protest.

"Not that one," I hurry to explain. "The one the horses pull."

Her brows bunch together as she questions, "You have horses?"

"Yeah, do you ride?"

She smiles. "I used to, years ago."

"Today you can ride in the sled with mom and my sisters. Grandad will drive and I'll take the snowmobile with a different sled attached to get the tree back. Sound like fun?"

"Yeah, it does. I've never been on a sleigh ride."

"It's a lot of fun," Mom says. "And of course, hot chocolate."

"I'm in," Alysha says and lifts her mug in salute. "Oh wait, I don't have boots."

"I have a big pair you can pull on. They'll keep you warm and shouldn't hurt your ankle." Her smile wraps around my chest and squeezes. "Mind if I pop into my bedroom to get clean clothes?"

"No, I'll go with you. I need to get changed too."

She pushes from the chair and uses the crutches to follow me to the stairs and I work hard to stare straight ahead and not glance back at her. I should not be admiring the way my pajamas hang on her body and just how sexy she looks.

I take a fast look over my shoulder, and her head lifts slowly, too slowly, because yeah, I just caught her staring at my ass—and I liked it.

"It's all good?" I ask, my voice coming out rough and strange.

Her eyes go wide. "Ah, what?"

"The crutches, the stairs. You good or do you need my help?" She hesitates for a second, and that's all I need to add, "If you let me help, you might be back to dancing sooner rather than later."

"I can't stop dancing," she says quietly, and I angle my head, because yeah, that's kind of a strange thing to say.

My heart aches at the worry in her voice. "Hey, Alysha, it's just a sprain. I know you can walk, and it's going to get better. I don't mean to worry—"

My words fall off as she shakes her head hard. "No, I know you're being kind. I know I'll dance again. It's my...I want to dance."

"I guess that's why you're a dance student, huh?"

Her laugh holds a measure of embarrassment and I no longer wait for her permission. I slide my hands around her body and lift her. Her arms go around my neck, and I simply love the way she clings to me. She's a girl who's been living on her own, and I know she can take care of herself, but I like taking care of her. Maybe it's because I have younger sisters and have tried to be the man of the family since we lost Dad, but either way, I pull her in a little closer and splay my fingers around her back.

"That was a stupid thing to say. I'm just saying I don't ever want to give it up."

I head up the stairs, and take in the tightness in her face. Not my business but I ask anyway, "Who wants you to give it up?"

Her eyes flash to mine, big and blue and worried, like she'd said too much. "I didn't say that."

"Okay."

She falls quiet as I take her to my bedroom and deposit her on my bed. Her phone pings and she stares at it. I turn to give her privacy and pull open my closet. "Linc wants me to," she says so quietly, I nearly miss it.

I turn back around and find her picking invisible lint off her pajama pants. "Why would he want that?"

"It takes up a lot of my time. We hardly see each other."

"Okay, wait, let me get this straight. He wants you to stop pursuing your passion because he doesn't get to see you enough? Didn't you just tell me he's a lawyer who works around the clock?" She nods. "Then maybe he should give that up." Okay, that came out louder and harsher than I intended. I crouch on the floor in front of her and soften my voice. "I'm sorry, Alysha. I'm not trying to judge anyone here.

It's just..." I scrub my face, and glance around my room, my gaze flitting over all the trophies and medals I won at hockey. "I understand when you want to go one way and those around you are pushing you another."

She lightly brushes my hair from my forehead, and I swear to God if she didn't have a boyfriend, I'd lay her out on my bed and kiss the hell out of her. But she does and I can't. I jump to my feet, walk to my window and stare out at Granddad as he walks to the barn to get the horse ready.

"I just want you to live your own life. Do what you want. I'm sorry Linc doesn't support that."

"My parents want me to dance as a hobby."

"What do you want?"

A smile instantly forms on her pretty face. "I actually want to teach dance. I volunteered at a studio back home, working with little girls. It was so much fun, Ryan."

"You have to live your own life, Alysha, the life you want."

"You say that like it's so easy."

"Nothing is easy," I tell her. Jesus, after Dad died, life was hell and trying to be the man of the house and taking over his role was hard. Mom had Granddad of course. The business was his before Dad took over. In fact, it's been in our family for generations, and I was going to do my damndest to learn every aspect of it, back when I was only twelve, going to school, and playing hockey. "My Dad used to say, work hard to get what you need; work harder and you'll get what you want."

"Ooh, an inspirational speaker and a potato farmer."

I laugh at that. "He would have liked you."

"I'm sorry I never got to meet him, Ryan."

As my chest squeezes tight, I head back to the closet. "Did he want you to make it to the NHL, too?"

"Too?" I ask.

"From what I understand, sounds like your mom and grandfather want you to focus on hockey." I nod. "Is that not what you want?"

"It's what my ex-girlfriend wanted too." Alysha goes very quiet and I wish I hadn't brought up Lexi. There must be a storm coming or something, and it's messing with my brain. Alysha and I don't usually talk about personal things and talking about what happened with my ex still leaves a bad taste in my mouth and a hole in my gut. I still can't believe the extremes she went to, to convince me to make it to the NHL.

"Is she here...on the island?"

"Not anymore." I shake off the memories and lift my chin. "I want to farm," I say pointedly.

She nods, and for some reason, I get the sense that she doesn't believe that. Sure, all boys who grow up playing want to make it into the NHL. But I'm simply not one of them.

I search my closet and pull out a big pair of sweatpants and a hoodie. Alysha must read something on my face when I turn back to her. She studies me for a second and then says, "Kind of a deep conversation on a Saturday morning before your second cup of coffee, eh?"

I grin at the use of Canadian slang, and hold the clothes out to her. "I'm not sure what you packed, but you're going to needs something really warm."

A grateful smile passes over her face. "Thank you. I definitely did not pack for rural PEI. Not that I could have. I don't have the proper clothes, even at home."

"What's mine is yours," I tell her as she brings the clothes to her nose. "Ah, did you just smell my clothes?"

She laughs. "They smell so good. I need to find out what fabric softener your mother uses."

I put my hand over my mouth and laugh as I cough into it. "Freak."

She laughs and throws a pillow at me. But she's not the freak. I am, for counting down the seconds until I see her in my sweats, and wishing I could be the guy to help her on with them—off would be preferable—and really, both thoughts are inappropriate and never going to happen.

I tug out my own clothes, and speaking of tugging. Yeah, it's true, I might just have to tug one out in the shower before we head out into the tree lot out back, otherwise, I'm afraid when I swing the axe, it might hit wood, and I'm not talking about the tree trunk.

4

ALYSHA

Ryan runs downstairs, brings the crutches back to me, and leaves the room to grab a shower. I should probably tear my gaze away from his backside and the hot way his loose jeans are hanging low on his hips. Nothing about that look should be sexy to me, but damned if it isn't, and I can't do anything about it. Maybe that's not entirely true. I could stop staring. He glances at me over his shoulder, and I'm far too slow to lift my eyes. Dammit, I'm pretty sure he just caught me checking him out. Again.

He gestures toward the hall with a nod of his head. "You sure you don't want to go first?"

"Yeah, I'm sure. I have some texts to answer." It's true, I do, but I mostly want to sit on his bed for a moment and get my head on straight. I can't believe I told him about Linc or my parents, or that he told me he doesn't want to go to the NHL. Maybe he made that up because he felt he needed to tell me something personal. He seemed sincere enough, and maybe there's a part of him that really believes he doesn't want it, but like his family, I think the NHL is a dream that might seem unattainable to him. Most of his friends have been drafted already, and while he's an excellent player, maybe he just doesn't think he's good enough.

He looks like he's about to protest, so I snatch my phone off the nightstand and scroll. The door clicks shut and I throw myself on the bed. My hair flares, and I blow a strand out of my mouth as my mind goes back to last night's conversation with Linc—and my mother.

They both want me home, not that I'll see much of either one of them. Mom will be too busy with her charities and her parties, and Linc will be working day and night. I'm almost positive he's going to propose at the Christmas party. There were a few things Mom let slip and when I started piecing them together, I figured he was going to drop to one knee. The thing is, why does he want to marry me? Yes, we've been together for years, and my family loves him. But does he love me?

Do you love him?

Heck, I'm not even sure I know what love is. I think I might describe our relationship as comfortable, familiar...a relationship that makes my family happy. Last night on the phone, in order to appease him, I promised him that if I felt better, I'd try to get home for the Christmas party. I told Mom the same thing and she threatened to fly here in the family's private plane and bring me home herself. I'm not sure she'd go through the trouble if a proposal wasn't at stake.

If I do say yes, then what? I have no doubt dancing will eventually get swept to the wayside and I'll be throwing parties for him and supporting his busy career. I am a good dancer—not the best by any means—and I get the feeling that in his eyes, being a prima ballerina, a position worthy in his eyes, is something he might get behind. A children's teacher? Not so much.

I shoot off a text to our circle of friends to let them know we're in PEI and my ankle is healing. A few responses come back instantly and I check to see if Linc texted me. Things didn't end so well last night, and he was a little surprised to find out I was on a potato farm in PEI with a guy. At first, he had his back up, and I thought he might be jealous. He wasn't. Apparently, he's so secure in our relationship, a potato farmer/hockey player from Prince Edward Island doesn't worry him. Not that it should. I am not a cheater, and he knows that. But Ryan is a great catch. Why again has no one caught him?

The shower turns on in the room beside me and I refuse to think about Ryan's hard naked body all lathered up. That's right, I'm not a cheater, so instead of picturing him running his hands over his firm muscles, I turn on some music, close my eyes and choreograph a dance in my brain.

Just then my phone pings, and since Linc has his own special ring tone, I don't need to look to know it's him. My stomach tightens, anxiety gripping me by the throat as I slide my finger across my phone and read his text.

Linc: Your mother said she'd send the private plane to get you. It can be there by tonight.

I swallow hard, and consider my response. I don't want to fight, but I don't want to go home, either. God, I wish I wasn't such a coward. If he is going to propose, I'm going to have to deal with it. I can't hide forever. Right? Ugh. I glance at my ankle and roll it.

Me: I don't really think I should be traveling.

Linc: There's something very important we need to discuss.

Me: Can you just text me?

I stare at the phone, watching the three dots appear and disappear. The shower turns off in the next room, and even though Ryan's bedroom is a bit chilly, I break out in a sweat.

Linc: If you don't come home...

I bite my lip, my gaze glued to the phone, waiting for more to come in. When his threat remains hanging, I text back, even though I'm not sure I want him to finish his sentence.

Me: What?

Linc: Then you can consider this relationship over.

The room closes in on me. Holy shit, did he really just go there? I gulp and stare at the phone. While tears prick my eyes, my heart thundering in my chest, I can't quite figure out if I'm sad, or...relieved. I understand my parents will be devastated, and I'm still not sure what I want in life—I just know I am not ready to be engaged—so I choose my next words very carefully.

Me: I hurt my ankle and you're giving me an ultimatum. An injury like this could ruin my career. I can't take chances.

Linc: You're being ridiculous.

You know what? It's possible he's right. But going home, being there mostly by myself and putting on a happy face at the Christmas party? I don't know if I have it in me anymore. I'm about to text back when three dots appear.

Linc: When we get married, there won't be time for silly dancing.

Silly dancing?

Silly-fucking—dancing?

I resist the urge to respond with: Why don't you tell me what you really think.

Me: Didn't you just say we were over?

Linc: I guess that's up to you now, isn't it?

Knuckles rap on my door, and I lift my head, staring at the blurry image. "Come...in."

The door yawns open, and I take a few gulping breaths as Ryan takes one look at me, and goes still. "Alysha."

A garbled laugh crawls out of my throat. I lift my phone and give it a little shake. "Looks like Linc and I are through."

"Holy shit," he swears under his breath and comes to me, dropping to his knees on the floor. He puts his hands on my thighs. "I'm sorry. Are you okay?"

How horrible would I come across if I said *yes, perfectly fine.* The truth is, I'm not perfectly fine, but for the first time in a long time, the knot in my stomach begins to loosen.

"I...I'll be okay."

"I'm so sorry." He leans in and pulls me into his big body. His arms hold me tight and I breathe in the fresh scent of his skin. We stay like that for a long time, and I take comfort in his strength and concern. Neither of us speak, just holding one another, and it's insane how nice it is to be hugged. After a long moment, he inches back, and his dark eyes move over my face, a careful assessment.

His hands go to my thighs as noises in the big old farmhouse penetrate the quiet between us. Stairs creak and doors open and close as the rest of the household comes to life. I wipe my hand over my eyes, needing to pull myself together. Today is a special day for the Potter family and I'm not going to bring it down.

"I should get ready." I need to move, but I can't seem to pull away from him. There's something so comforting in the way he always drops to his knees in front of me, putting us eye to eye.

"Do you think you should go back home, talk things out?"

"No," I say far too quickly, judging by the way Ryan's eyes just narrowed in on me. "I mean, I think we both need time apart. Do you want me to go?"

"God, no." He swallows, glances down for a second, like he has a million questions on his brain. His thumbs move along my thighs and holy, he might as well be touching me between my legs. "Did you break up with him?"

"He gave me an ultimatum. I go home or it's over." My phone rings, and I steal a glance at it. I figured Linc would have called my mother by now. I ignore it and stare at Ryan.

He shakes his head. "Wow." He looks at me again. Is he reading it all over my face? Reading that I don't want to go home, that maybe I'm okay with this breakup?

"So...," he begins, removing one hand from my thigh and it's crazy how fast I miss his touch. He scrubs his face, deep in thought and his breath is warm, minty when he speaks. "Not practically engaged, then?"

Omg, is that heat in his eyes? "No, not practically engaged," I manage to get out, my voice a bit shaky.

"Okay," is all he says as he stands and pulls me to my feet. I wobble as I balance on my one good foot, and my body bumps his. Did he just moan? He puts his hands on my shoulders to stabilize me as he says, "We should get moving." I'm about to move, but he continues to hold me, his big body blocking my escape as one hand leaves my shoulder to lightly touch my hair. His head dips, and once again I think he's going to kiss me. This time, however, I'm not practically engaged. "I know this isn't easy and I want you to know I'm here for you. Whatever you need."

Oh God, what do I need? Right now, my body is vibrating, letting me know in no uncertain words it wants to be touched. But I'm not certain that's what he has in mind. I don't come from a family that hugs, and maybe all this physical contact is messing with my mind, making me think things I shouldn't be thinking. "You're a good friend."

He nods as I put pressure on my sore ankle. "Want me to carry you?"

Do I want to feel his arms wrapped around me again?

Honestly, I'm a hot mess and I don't know what I want—except I don't want to get engaged. Until I know what I want my future to look like, maybe it's best I stay out of his embrace. I nod toward the crutches. "The bathroom is just right there. I'll be okay."

He moves to the side, waving his hand for me to head to the shower. I gather up the clean sweats he gave me and walk on wobbly legs, not because Linc just gave me an ultimatum, but because I still feel the effects of Ryan's hands around me, on my thighs. God, now that I'm not practically engaged, it means he could kiss me, if I wanted that.

Do you want that?

Oh, God, I really don't know what I want, and I really hope my mother isn't boarding the family's private jet and flying to Prince Edward Island. Not that she knows where I am, exactly. Although that wouldn't be too hard to figure out. I gave her Ryan's name, and how many potato farmers are there on the island anyway? Probably a lot, but still, I don't think she'll just show up.

My phone continues to ring, and I hit the decline button. I'll have to call her back, but I'm going to need a hot shower and a few more cups of coffee first. The room is still steamy and warm as I strip off and turn on the water. The scent of Ryan's body wash fills my senses. I climb in and squirt a generous amount into my palm. As I rub it over my body, my nipples tightening as I spend an extra minute washing them, one question—do I want Ryan to kiss me—keeps dancing in my mind.

Oh God, I think I might actually know the answer.

RYAN

Jesus, she's no longer off limits.

Oh, but she is, Ryan.

She's sad and suffering from a breakup, which means I can't kiss her or put my hands on her, no matter how much I want that.

But goddammit, she's no longer practically engaged.

Yeah, but it would be wrong to swoop in. That would make me her rebound guy and that shit never works out, and I'm pretty sure she's still in love with Linc.

Which is why I should stop picturing her naked in the shower.

As I sit on my bed and battle back and forth with myself, Lucy pokes her head in. "Hey, how's Alysha's ankle?"

I nod and work not to sound as distraught as I feel. "She's good. Made it downstairs and to the shower on her own."

"I like her. She's nice."

"Yeah."

Lucy eyes me. She might be fourteen and the baby of the family, but damned if she hasn't always been able to read her big brother. She spins. "Maybe she'll show me some dance moves."

"Her ankle, remember?"

"That's why she's here then, her ankle?"

Shit, I should have known she was baiting me. "Yes."

"The only reason?"

"What other reason would there be, Lucy?" I push to my feet, making my annoyance evident in my tone.

"Oh, I don't know. Maybe the fact that you like her."

"Of course, I like her. We're friends."

"Sucks she has a boyfriend."

"Why would that matter to me?" She gives me that annoying knowing grin of hers. "And how do you know she has a boyfriend, anyway?"

"It came up when she was talking to Mom and Granddad this morning."

"You weren't even there." Her grin widens and I shake my head. "Right, gossip spreads faster than potato warts around these parts."

"Eww, don't compare us to warts."

"Out," I say and point as the bathroom door opens.

"Ah, did you call your sister a potato wart?" Alysha asks, as she comes around the corner, looking warm and sexy in my sweats. She grins at me as she towel-dries her hair, and that pink flush on her face... let's just say it's a flush I want to put there myself.

"Don't ask."

"Okay, I won't." She crosses the room and I breathe in the scent of her skin. Fuck, she used my body wash. She bends and I stifle a groan as she roots through her suitcase and mumbles under her breath. "I forgot my brush. Do you have one? Honestly, I was so upset when I packed it's a wonder I put anything of use in here." She pulls out a crop top. "Although I don't think this is of use."

"Not if we're outside, but you can wear it inside, by the fire. Be right back." I go to the bathroom, tug open the drawer and pull out my brush. She's sitting on my bed, giving her phone the death glare when I come back.

"Linc?" I ask.

She shakes her head, a few strands of wet hair sticking to her mouth. Unable to help myself, I reach out to remove them, and find myself—stupidly—brushing my thumb over the soft swell of her lower lip. A little gasp catches in her throat and I tear my hand away.

"Hair," I explain, pretending I was removing it from her lips. Lame, I know.

"It's my mother. I should call her back. She's not going to be too happy about the breakup. They adore Linc and want him in the family."

"You have to do what's best for you, Alysha."

"I know."

She glances down and her sadness is like a punch to my gut. "I'll give you some privacy. Take your time and come down when you're ready. No one is in a hurry."

"Thanks."

The kitchen is empty when I enter and I grab a bowl of cereal. Mom steps in as I shove a big spoonful into my mouth. She kisses my cheek as I chew and swallow.

"Did Alysha eat?" I ask.

"She had some toast with us. Her ankle seems to be doing a lot better."

I nod and shove more cereal into my face. "Maybe she'll be able to make it home after all. Not that we mind having her here. She's a lovely girl."

I debate on how much to tell Mom and decide on nothing. "Yeah," I mumble.

"I can't imagine not having you around for Christmas. Although I guess I'll just have to get used to it, if you choose the NHL path."

The milk in my stomach sours. Why is she—along with Granddad—always pushing the NHL? Don't they want me here? Fuck, being here for my family is the most important thing in the world to me. Being there for anyone I care about is important. Not being wanted—needed—is equivalent to being gutted with the sharpest sword. I miss my dad, and stepping into his shoes was hard, but it was also the most rewarding thing I've ever done in my life.

Alysha appears in the doorway, and her smile is forced as she greets my mom. I set my spoon down and eye her. She's put on a tiny bit of makeup, making her big eyes look even bigger. Is she trying to hide the tears she shed after the breakup?

Mom pours another mug of coffee. "I'll gather up the girls."

"Everything okay?" I ask when Mom disappears. She nods, but the sadness in her eyes gives it away. "Is your mom upset about the breakup?"

She snorts. "Oh, yeah."

I pour her a mug of coffee, and add the milk and sugar. "What can I do to make it better?"

She grins. "I love how you just ask questions like that. I'll be okay, Ryan. I think a sled ride is exactly what I need today."

I arch a brow. "And maybe some Cow's ice cream. Unlike Halifax, the creamery is open all year round."

She laughs and the happy sound wraps around me. "Rebels."

"That's a yes?"

"Depends. Will this ice cream have a cherry on top?"

"Is there any other way to have ice cream?" I ask, and try not to think about cherries, or how I'd like her on top. Fuck me sideways.

She takes a sip of her coffee and I rinse my bowl and put it on the rack to dry. "Now let's find you boots and a big coat." I walk slowly and she follows me into the walk-in coat closet. I pull out one of my old warm coats, and fit her with a pair of big boots.

She lifts her arms and lets them flop to the side. "I feel like a potato in a big sack."

I laugh. "You look adorable." Her cheeks flush. "I'll make a potato farmer out of you yet." Her smile runs away from her face. "I'm just kidding. You'd be a terrible potato farmer." She angles her head, clearly offended.

"Why do you say that?"

Oh, because she's a city girl, one meant to dance, and a life on a farm would likely bore her to death and kill her creativity. Like I said, this place isn't for everyone. Since that scenario is never going to happen, I say, "Instead of running the equipment, or sorting potatoes, you'd probably be out in the field dancing, getting zero work done, and the poor animals would starve." She opens her mouth and I put my hands on her shoulders. "You should always dance in the fields, Alysha. Leave the farming to me."

She chuckles. "For the record, I'd never let an animal go hungry." Just then there's a scratch at the door, and a bleating sound. "What was that?" Alysha asks, her eyes big.

"Probably Billy."

"Who's Billy?"

Instead of answering, I pull on my coat and find us each a hat and pair of mittens, knitted by none other than me. "I made these." She holds her hand out to take them and I put them on her. The scratch comes again.

"Shouldn't we let Billy in? It's cold out and he sounds kind of funny."

"Yeah, you're right."

I open the door and in trots Billy, looking indignant that I took so long. I pet his head and he runs his horns over my legs. I take in the surprise on Alysha's face and laugh. "Alysha, meet Billy. Billy, this is Alysha, she's staying with us for the holidays."

"You have a…"

"Goat," I say. "He's actually a therapy goat."

She puts her hands on her hips, her jaw open as her dubious eyes challenge me. "There's no such thing as a therapy goat."

"You need to get out more often, my friend."

"Hey Billy," Monica says as she comes bounding into the front entranceway. She bends to pet Billy and he bleats at her. "Now that Ryan is home, he'll take you in to see the kids."

"Children's hospital," I inform Alysha.

She shakes her head. "You're serious?"

"Yeah."

"I know the guys from the team visit the children's hospital in Halifax, I didn't realize you did it here, or with a…"

"Goat."

"Right a goat. Hi Billy." Billy turns to her and she holds her hand out, unsure of how to pet him.

"Like this." I take her glove off, and put her hand on Billy's head. "Soft," she murmurs, and then her hand goes still. "Wait, you don't eat him, do you?"

Both Monica and I laugh. "You can't eat anything after you name it," I tell her. "That's why Sam lived to a ripe old age."

"Billy is an angora goat. We make sweaters and things from his mohair."

"Oh, nice." She examines the scarf I put around her neck. "This?"

"Yup."

Bells clang outside. "That's Granddad. Ready?" She nods and Lauren and Lucy come with blankets and Mom has a picnic basket. I walk slowly as Alysha negotiates the steps, and I help her onto the sleigh. She sits on a pile of hay and as the girls all settle in, I circle the house, toss a chainsaw and rope into the sleigh attached to the snowmobile and start it up.

It revs to life and I take off into the open field ahead of Sugar Bear, the big Clydesdale named by my baby sister. I glance over my shoulder and see that Alysha is in good hands and seems to be content with my family, so I play around on the snowmobile, swishing from side to side and jumping over piles of plowed snow. It's nice to get outside after a hard term of schoolwork and hockey, and no I'm not showing off for Alysha, who is no longer practically engaged. Well not much, anyway.

I reach the tree plot and slow to a stop. My breath turns to fog in front of my face as I stand and wait for the others to reach me. When they finally do, Alysha has a big smile on her face, everything about her like a kid on Christmas morning.

"Fun?" I ask.

"Yes, I love it." She glances at the rows of trees. "Did you pick one out?"

I glance at Mom. "Any preference?"

"How about we let Alysha pick one this year. Apparently, she's never had a real tree."

Alysha's eyes go big, almost fearful. "I can't pick out your family tree. I have no idea what's good and what isn't. I don't want to mess it up."

I lift the chain saw. "Tell me which one you like."

"Um..." Her gaze darts around, and she points to the biggest, tallest white spruce. "That one."

"It's perfect," Mom says, and Alysha's face lights up. My granddad secures Sugar Bear, and hops down to help me as Mom opens her basket. I turn my attention to the gigantic tree. Will this even fit in the house? I'm not sure, but if this is the tree Alysha wants, this is the tree she gets and who the hell had never had a real tree before? That's all about to change.

Grandad and I go to work on cutting the tree, and securing it to the sled behind my snowmobile. I'm warm by the time I'm done, my muscles tight from the heavy lifting.

"She's big," Grandad says, and shakes his head.

I shake mine right along with him. "City girls."

He laughs and I slap his back. "Come on, I think we both deserve hot chocolate after that." We both jump onto the sleigh and it doesn't go unnoticed by me how everyone moved around so I had no choice but to sit beside Alysha. She lifts her blanket and covers me as I sink into the bundle of hay. I instantly sneeze and a round of 'bless you' follows. I note Alysha's rosy cheeks.

"Are you warm enough?"

She snuggles into the blanket more, and I move closer, until my body is touching hers. "My God, your body is so hot," she says.

"Thanks," I reply deadpan as I take a sip of my hot chocolate. My family, who are used to my antics, just roll their eyes at me.

Alysha stares at me for a second, and her eyes widen when she realizes what she said. "Wait, I didn't mean..."

Before she can finish, I get a fistful of hay to the face, compliments of my youngest sister, it's followed up by another clump and a violent round of sneezes.

"I suppose I deserve that," I say, when I finally get my allergies under control.

Granddad climbs to his feet. "Come on, let's get back."

I'm about to follow him but, unable to help myself, I lean into Alysha and whisper, "I think your body is hot, too."

I still can't stop thinking about what Ryan whispered to me on the sleigh, or how his warm breath, and body, sent shivers skittering through my veins. My God, it's hours later, and I'm still feeling the effects. I take a lick of my ice cream cone, not caring that I'm in a big winter coat and it's cold outside, and turn to glance Ryan's way.

His whispered words haven't come up, and I'm not sure if I want to address them. I realize he's a kidder, but nothing in the way he spoke to me felt like he was joking. We walk along the quiet streets of downtown Charlottetown and the touristy shops on the boardwalk are pretty much closed for the winter. Waves lap against the shore, and in the distance, a dog barks.

"Pretty," I say. He has a mischievous look on his face as he opens his mouth to respond, but I hold one gloved hand up to stop him. "I'm talking about the boardwalk, not you."

He laughs, and I add, "I bet this place is so gorgeous in the summer."

"Bustling with tourists, but you'll see it. You're coming back on the ferry with me."

He says it so nonchalantly, I almost believe it's true, even though I didn't agree to it. I can't help but think about it, though. I'd love to see the fields full of potatoes and the production in full swing.

"What's it like where you live?" he asks.

"It's nice. Private, ocean view." I nudge him. "We do lock our doors, but we're close to the city and theaters and restaurants."

"How are the potatoes?" He takes a lick of his brownie explosion ice cream with a cherry on top, and I realize he's serious.

"Like I said, I don't eat a lot of potatoes."

"Right. I'm sure they're not as good there anyway. You like living in the city?"

"It's okay. I like Halifax. It's a lot smaller than where I'm from, and I'm beginning to think country living might grow on me." I nudge him again. "Like a potato wart."

"Here, try this?" He holds his ice cream out.

"I've never licked anyone's cone before."

"You can lick mine."

Oh, God, now I'm thinking of licking...his...and I'm not thinking about ice cream. A car creeps down the street and I momentarily think about throwing myself in front of it, but it's going so damn slow, it probably wouldn't injure me.

"I won't tell if you don't."

I laugh and take a big lick. "Ohmigod, that is so good."

"Can I lick yours?"

Jesus.

I hold out my cone and he leans down. "I don't know anyone who gets orange pineapple."

"It's good. Take a lick."

If I asked him to take a lick of something else, will he not tell anyone about that either? He hesitates for a second, and I can't help but wonder if the same thought is going through his head, but my brain stops working the second his tongue slides across the cold cream. My entire body heats, imagining what that tongue would feel like—between my legs.

He puckers his lips. "Not bad. I like mine better."

I pull my cone back. "Then eat your own."

"You don't have to be so mean about it."

I laugh. "I like your family, Ryan." We turn and walk very slowly down Queen Street, toward the regular shops, which are open and bustling this Saturday afternoon. Christmas is only a week away, so I guess that's to be expected.

"They like you too."

Ryan keeps glancing at me. "What?"

"I think you've been on your feet too long, you're walking funny. We should head back."

I laugh. "It's because I'm in boots that are eight sizes too big."

He looks hurt, but so damn adorable when he says, "I just thought—"

"You thought right. These are better than my tight shoes and I want to see a few more things before we head back."

"We don't have to do everything today. You're here all week. Unless…"

His words fall off. "I'm not going back," I say, and keep to myself that I'm a big ol' coward who's trying to avoid a marriage proposal from a guy any girl would likely fight for.

I tug on his coat. "Come on." I finish my ice cream and peer into one of the windows and see the cutest pair of pajamas with lobsters on them, but who would I bring anything back for? I know! Myself. I'm sure I'll never be back here again, and I think I want something to remember it by, something more than Ryan's whispered words.

"Come on." I step up to the door and pull it open and I'm immediately greeted with the scent of cinnamon, coming from the candle burning in the window. "Does all of PEI smell like cinnamon?" I ask.

His grin is so adorable it's all I can do to stop myself from going up on my toes and pressing my lips to his. "Some of it smells like potatoes."

"Do potatoes even have a smell?"

"Yeah, I like it. Come out to the storage barn, and I'll show you."

I run my fingers over a dish towel with little foxes on them. "Actually, I'd love a tour of the farm."

Ryan finishes his cone, and shoves his hands into his pockets. I sense he's not much of a shopper. "Not much to see in winter, but I can show you the storage sheds and the equipment. Exciting stuff."

I grin, because he's not being sarcastic at all, and this time I know he's not kidding. He does think the sheds and equipment are exciting. "I'd like that." I pick up a wig from Prince Edward Island's famed book series, Anne of Green Gables, and examine the pig tails. Ryan takes it from me and puts it on my head.

"Perfect." He turns me so I can see in the mirror and I laugh as I smooth out the red pigtails. "I've never had red hair before."

"Suits you."

It doesn't. "I've never read an Anne of Green Gables book, either," I say. "Have you?" He looks away, but damn, there's no way I'm going to let him be embarrassed by his choices. Hell, we all just found out Brandon was a romance author and I love everything about that. "You have, haven't you?" A pause and then, "You can tell me, Ryan."

"Maybe."

I grab his coat and tug him back around. "There is no shame in reading what you want to read. I kind of like it that you have."

"I don't think you can grow up here without reading at least one, and in summer, Charlottetown has shows, and Cavendish has a museum with a fiction house styled like the farmhouse where the author Lucy Maud Montgomery spent time as a child." I love that he knows all this. "That's who Lucy was named after by the way."

"Maybe I can borrow one to read while I'm here. Can we see the house in the winter?"

"Sure, I can take you by, but the books." He looks like he's in agony as he scrubs his face. "Mine are kind of collector items now. I'll get you your own." He grabs a few books beside the stack of wigs, and takes the wig off my head. "You're getting this too."

I gasp. "Ohmigod."

"What?"

"You have an Anne of Green Gables fetish, don't you?"

He looks blatantly shocked for a second, then he gives a fast shake of his head. "No." A beat passes and he laughs. "Well, I might have had a crush on her when I was a kid. I'm not a kid anymore."

I pick up another wig and twirl it around my fingers. "So you've never made any of your girlfriends wear this wig when you were...you know." I playfully wag my brows at him, and can't believe he's actually blushing.

"Why, are you offering to wear it for me?"

Okay, I wasn't expecting that comeback.

"I'm not your girlfriend," I point out.

He steps into me, his big body crowding mine and warming me from the inside out. "If you were, would you wear it for me?"

For the briefest of seconds, I consider the scenario and imagine that I am his girlfriend. It's not an unpleasant thought by any means, but I just had a breakup—I think— and I need to get my head on straight before I get involved with anyone. Besides, it's not like we could have a future. I'm a city girl. He's a country boy who wants to farm, or be in the NHL. I'm really not sure. Nevertheless, getting involved right away after a breakup is never a good idea. The next person is usually nothing more than a rebound, and Ryan is a good friend, and I don't want to ruin that.

What about a no-commitment, friends with benefits holiday hookup, Alysha?

I gulp as that thought jumps into my rattled brain and can't help but wonder if that's something he could get behind.

"Is that a yes?" Ryan asks, his head dips as he turns the tables on me.

Before I can answer, and I'm not even really sure how I would —it would probably be a yes—someone behind us clears their throat. Ryan steps back, like he suddenly remembered we're out in public.

"Is there anything else you want?" he asks.

Oh, yes, yes there is. "No, and I can buy the books."

"Christmas present."

"I thought you said you all made presents."

He shrugs, his big shoulders drawing my attention. "New traditions."

I laugh, and it's oddly weird how I like the idea of making traditions with Ryan. He grabs a box of Anne of Green Gables chocolates to add to the pile.

"My God, between the potatoes you're going to make me eat and the ice cream and chocolate, I'll be as big as your potato barn by the time I leave here. Then I'll never be able to dance."

"We'll find a way to work the calories off."

I gulp. Is he suggesting what I think he's suggesting? Do I want that?

"There's always work on a farm, even in the winter."

"Oh."

"What?"

"Nothing."

He eyes me. "Did you think I meant something else?"

"Um, maybe."

His dark eyes grow darker, a storm brewing in their depths. He opens his mouth, but before he can speak, someone clears their throat again. "Fuck," he murmurs under his breath. "Let me pay for these things and we can get out of here."

The bell over the door jingles, and I step back. "Okay."

"Sweet fuck," Ryan hisses under his breath when he turns around. I follow his gaze and spot a pretty girl behind the cash register, her intense gaze locked on Ryan. His entire body stiffens, and my heart stops beating. I'm not sure what's going down, all I know is the girl who's just turned her focus to me, means something to him. I put my hand on Ryan's back, and he takes a step forward. "I'll be right back."

Okay, he obviously doesn't want me following him to the cash register, so I don't. I do, however, mill about the store and keep a close eye on Ryan, and the stiffness in his body. He drops his things onto the counter, and exchanges a few words with the girl serving him. I can't hear what they're saying and while I'd like to get closer, I stay back and give him his privacy.

After he finishes paying, she bags his things and there's a hardness about him that I've never seen before and he stalks toward me. "Let's go."

I nod and follow him out, but he's walking a little too fast for me. I get it, he's upset about something and trying to blow off steam, but I don't want to hurry and risk hurting my healing ankle. As if realizing I'm not beside him, he stops and curses as he turns back around. His shoulders sag.

"Fuck, I'm sorry, Alysha."

"It's okay." Instead of waiting for me to catch up, he hurries back to me, and puts his arm around my waist, pulling me close for support.

"I shouldn't have been walking so fast and you probably shouldn't have been on your ankle this long."

"The swelling is down."

"Let's head back, okay?"

I nod and he stays quiet, lost in thought as we walk to his car and he opens the car door for me. He hands me the paper bag, and I stare at him as he circles the front of the vehicle, and slides into the driver's side. He grips the steering wheel, his knuckles white, and I have no idea who that girl was, what she meant to him, or the words they exchanged, but there's a difference in him. A hardness...a hurt. My heart pinches tight, and I reach out, and put my hand on his.

"Hey."

Without looking at me he says, "If your ankle is better and you've changed your mind and want to go back home, I can take you to the airport. I know I sort of gave you no choice but to come home with me after you hurt yourself." I stare at him. Does he want me to go? Before I can ask, he reaches over, puts his hand on mine and says, "I just want to do what's best for you, Alysha."

Okay, what the hell happened back there?

"Right now, I don't know what's best for me, Ryan. Until I do, I'd like to stay here. If that's okay?"

His jaw clenches as he stares straight ahead, like there's a war going on inside him. He finally breaks the quiet, turns to me, and says, "It's more than okay. I like...having you here. I just don't want you...." He sighs. "I just don't want you to stay here and regret it. I mean, your family..."

As I stare at him, take in the scruff on his face, the mess of hair from the wind, and the way his big hands are gripping the steering wheel, I'm beginning to believe the only thing I might regret is not getting naked with him.

7

RYAN

My ex-girlfriend is the last person I thought I'd run into downtown. Although I don't know why. This is a small island, and I figured she'd be home for the holidays. What I hadn't expected was to find her working in one of the shops, giving Alysha the death glare.

After our bad breakup, she hooked up with Owen, a fellow hockey player who ended up going to college and playing in Quebec. Why he'd trust her after what she did to me is beyond my comprehension. But he did and she left the island to go with him. I'm not surprised. Her only goal in life was to get out of the country's smallest province. What can I say, some love it, some hate it. She was definitely in the latter group.

Her dad is an RCMP officer and her mom is a teacher and they wanted what was best for her. All she wanted was out. And she was going to make sure that happened, using anyone and any means—including lying—to make it possible.

So apparently, according to Lexi, Owen cheated on her and they broke up. Since she could barely make rent, she came back home. I'd feel sorry for her, if she hadn't been so goddamn cruel to me. I pull onto the street, and we're both quiet as I head back home.

After a long while, I turn and find Alysha staring at me. I'm not sure how much to tell her, but she should at least know why I'm upset.

"That was Lexi. She's my ex."

"I kind of had a feeling it was something like that." She goes quiet for a second, like she doesn't want to probe or bring up past memories, but then she quietly says, "Things don't seem very good between you two."

I snort. "That's an understatement."

Her eyes hold all kinds of warmth, sincerity, and sympathy as she looks at me. "A bad breakup?"

"Yeah." Everyone knows it, so I might as well tell her too. Not that we speak about Lexi in the house, but if I run into old friends, someone is bound to bring her up. We were a couple for a long time.

"Do you...still have feelings for her?"

It's a fair question, considering my reaction to seeing her. "No. She moved to Quebec. She wanted out of PEI. I was just surprised to see her, actually."

"I'm sorry she hurt you." I narrow my eyes and take in the warmth in her gaze. I never said she hurt me. I guess she can read that all over my face. She's intuitive like that.

"Thanks." I swallow against a scratchy throat. "This island isn't for everyone. It's full of tourists in the summer and the winter months can be long and isolated." I pause and add, "I almost married her."

I slow at the light and when Alysha doesn't say anything, I turn and find shock on her face, her eyes wide as she stares at me.

"I had no idea you were engaged before."

"I was moving, heading to Halifax for college. We weren't getting along, we were fighting all the time in the end, and I thought it was time to go our separate ways."

"How did you end up engaged, then?" The paper bag crinkles as she adjusts it on her lap and shifts a little more to face me.

I snort again, and grip the steering wheel. "She told me she was pregnant."

Alysha takes a deep breath as she puts it together. "She wasn't."

It's a statement, not a question, but I answer anyway. "That's right. She lied about it."

"How did you find out?"

"I was home, and my buddy Jesse called me to tell me Alysha was out with friends and was pretty drunk. I was worried about the baby, you know. When I found her, she told me she'd lost the baby. She cried so hard, and I held her for hours." My stomach twists. "It was really awful, Alysha," I say quietly, my voice catching in my throat. I go quiet for a moment, as my chest rises and falls erratically. "I wasn't ready for a child, but the idea was growing on me. Anyway, I took her back to her home, and that's when I found her birth control pills on her nightstand. She was still taking them and when I questioned her, she lied some more. But I knew in my gut something just wasn't right. I pushed for answers, and eventually the truth came out. She was afraid I was going to leave her behind, and she did what she had to do to prevent that."

"God, I'm so sorry, Ryan. What a horrible thing to do. I'm glad you found out before it was too late."

"That makes two of us."

"I guess you never knew that side of her if you were going to marry her, even though things weren't working out?"

"I didn't and I thought marrying her was the right thing to do." Alysha gives a slow shake of her head. "What?"

"I don't know. I guess I just don't think it's the right thing to do. You both would have been miserable, and it wouldn't have been great for the child."

She almost sounds like she's talking from experience here. "There was no child, but if there was, I wasn't going to abandon it."

"That's honorable, Ryan."

"When I found out she was lying, using me to get off the island, I was completely through with her, but she really did a number on my head."

Her hand reaches out and she touches my arm. The little squeeze of support helps push back those painful memories. "I always want to be there for the people I care about."

"Like running the farm," she says quietly, turning to look out the front window.

I nod. "I'm studying agriculture, so I can learn new technologies and implement them into the farm. I want to keep it in the family for many more generations."

"So your ex—"

"Lexi."

"You said she moved."

"Hooked up with my buddy, also a hockey player. She didn't just want off this island, she wanted a guy who was going to make it to the NHL."

"She didn't know you wanted to run the farm?"

"Yes, but after she told me she was pregnant, she pushed me toward the NHL, saying the baby would need more than a farmer could give it."

"Um, isn't potato farming a major industry?"

"Yeah, we supply potatoes all around the world. If you've eaten French fries from any fast-food restaurant, they probably came from our farm."

"Oh wow, what a small world." She grins. "Now I'll always think of you when I'm eating French fries."

"Being a farmer's wife wasn't something she wanted. Now she's back here. She said Owen cheated on her."

"I hate cheaters," she practically spits out.

My heart thumps. Christ, if her ex cheated on her, hurt her like that I might just have to hunt him down. "Has Linc…"

"Not that I know of. I just know…a cheater." I'm not sure why, but from the pain on her face, I sense it's someone very close to her. "I'd feel sorry for her if she wasn't so cruel to you." I stare at her, and she angles her head and asks, "What?"

"I had those exact same thoughts just a few minutes ago."

She opens the paper bag and pulls out the chocolates. "The only thing to wash that whole encounter from our brains is chocolate." She tears the plastic off the box, pulls out a chocolate and says, "Open."

I open my mouth and she plops it in. "Mmm."

"That good, huh?"

"Oh yeah."

She stares at the box and sighs. "I'm going to be a potato when I leave here."

I laugh. "Eat it, already."

She puts it in her mouth and moans as it melts on her tongue. "So good."

"More," I say and she plops another into my mouth. With my mood a thousand times lighter, I jack the radio and Alysha sings along as we head back to the farm. I pull into the driveway, and both Granddad's truck and Mom's car are gone.

"Doesn't look like anyone is home," I note.

"Someone's home," Alysha says and points to Billy. "If you take him to the hospital, I'd love to come along."

"Really?"

"If that's okay."

"Yeah, sure." She packs the chocolate back into the bag, and I exit the car, walking around to her door to help her out. "Ankle still feel okay?" She nods and I take the bag from her, pulling the Anne of Green Gables wig out to plunk on her head.

"Maybe one day you could dance in the musical here."

"Maybe," she says, and I get it. Prince Edward Island is not the place for a girl from the Hamptons. I'm not about to fool myself into thinking she could make a life here. She'd likely be bored by the first winter snowfall.

We walk up the plowed path, and I open the door. Warmth falls over us, and the scents from the tree fill the house, and bring back memories of my childhood. God, I miss my dad. I wish he could see what I was doing, the education I was getting and all the ideas I have for the farm.

Alysha inhales deeply. "That smells so good. Mom used to put this fake pine scent on ours." Her face twists. "It always reminded me of a car air freshener."

"You're going to help us decorate it, aren't?" I ask.

"I don't want to intrude if it's just a family thing."

"All strays eventually become family," I tease, and she whacks me.

I kick off my boots, and she sits on the bench and unties her boot laces. I drop to my knees before her and help her with them, carefully removing them one at a time. I lift my head and she's smiling.

"You spend a lot of time on your knees with me." As soon as the words leave her mouth, she pales. "I didn't mean it like that."

"You didn't mean it sexually?" I ask. Do I tell her that's exactly what I'm thinking right now? Maybe not, because I think she already knows.

She covers her face. "Ohmigod, Ryan."

"Come on." Giving her a break, I say, "Let's go see the tree."

I stand and pull her up with me. We step into the living room, and glance at the gigantic tree. It's a good thing we have twelve-foot ceilings.

She takes the Anne of Green Gables wig off, sets it on the coffee table, and plants her hands on her hips. I take in her body, and the tight yoga pants shaping her barely-there curves, and I try not to stare or think about how I'd like to shove her hands away and put mine on her hips—among other places—instead.

"Okay, what do we do first?"

I walk around the tree, needing to occupy myself. "You've never decorated a tree before?"

She looks almost embarrassed when she answers, "Nope."

"Well then, the first thing we do is put on music, and make hot chocolate."

"More chocolate?"

"Are you saying there's a limit on how much chocolate you're allowed to have?" Before she can answer I say, "It's the holidays. Calories don't count over the holidays."

"You are very bad for me, Ryan."

I laugh. "Come on, we need to go to the attic and get the decorations. We have to wait until everyone is here before we decorate, though. But we can get things ready." She takes a step and I put my hands on her shoulder. "No, wait, what am I thinking. You sit here. I'll go to the attic."

"No, I'll help."

"I don't want you climbing up a ladder."

"I can walk up a ladder, and if not, you can pretend you're a firefighter and carry me."

I nod my head and grin at her. "Ah, and now I'm getting insight into your fetishes."

She laughs and whacks me. "I do not have a firefighter fetish." She crinkles her nose. "Okay, maybe a little. Hey, maybe I can wear the Anne of Green Gables wig when you carry me. Two birds, one stone sort of thing." I stare at her, and her cheeks flush. "I don't know why I said that."

"Thinking about firefighters is messing with your brain."

"Something like that."

I just laugh and head to the stairs. "Go ahead of me. If you stumble, I'll catch you."

She nods and heads up the stairs very slowly. At the top, I head down the hall, reach up and tug on the string to pull down the stairs leading to the attic

"You sure about this?" I ask.

She grips the ladder, and tests it. "They look more like stairs than a ladder."

"It's still a ladder." She puts her foot on the bottom rung. "Go slow, and I'll be behind you."

She nods and starts up and while I don't think this is a good idea, I am enjoying the view from behind. Carefully negotiating the steps, she reaches the top and wobbles a tiny bit as she puts her foot on the attic floor. I reach out, cup her backside and help stabilize her.

"Good?" I ask, working very hard not to squeeze her cheeks in my palms.

"I'm good."

She's breathless and I can't help but wonder if it's from the climb or my hands on her ass. I stand in the attic and move to the stacks of labeled boxes all stored on shelves.

"Everything is so organized," she points out and starts reading the labels.

"Christmas stuff is here." I reach up, grab a box and pull it down.

"Oh, Ryan, can I look through this one?"

I turn and find her pointing to the box labeled Ryan's elementary years. "No."

She laughs. "Come on, one little peek." She reaches up and I move in behind her, my chest to her back as I grip her extended arm, pull it back down and circle my arms around her so she can't move.

"Too many blackmail pictures in that box."

"Were you a big nerdy guy or something?"

"Yes."

She laughs hard. "All the more reason for me to look." I let her go and groan and she claps her hands because she knows I'm going to give in to her.

"Why do I always want to please those I care about?"

She turns, all humor gone from her face. "You care about me?" she asks, her voice a little quieter.

"Of course, I care about you, Alysha. That's why you're here, with my family and me for Christmas."

Her smile is a bit shaky. Is she not used to people caring about her, showing affection? If that's true, that really sucks, but she has me, and I'm always going to try to do what's best for her. You know, like holding her ass to balance her.

Christ.

"Okay, the box." I reach over her, grab the box and set it on the floor near the old sofa. As she sits and opens it, I gather the rest of the Christmas boxes and put them near the ladder. She chuckles and I shake my head.

"What?"

"You were so cute."

"What do you mean were?"

"Always fishing," she teases and pats the sofa and I stomp across the floor, and drop down next to her. "Look at this one. You're taller than every kid in your class."

"Yeah, I was gigantic, I know."

"Who is this guy beside you?"

"That's Jesse. We've been friends since we started kindergarten."

"Oh, the guy who called you about Lexi drinking." I nod and she continues. "He really saved your butt, didn't he?"

"Yup."

"Is he here, on the island?"

I nod. "Yeah, he's actually going to veterinary college here. His mom and dad are both veterinarians and he'll work with them and take over when they eventually retire. He was a much better student than I was."

"What are you talking about? You're a good student."

"If it's something I'm interested in, like agriculture."

She nods, and goes quiet, like she can't quite wrap her brain around that, and I don't think most can. I know Mom and Granddad sure are pressuring me to go a different route. I'm not going to just abandon them, and it's what I want. My stomach tightens. Sometimes I get the feeling they simply don't need me around.

"Will you be seeing Jesse while you're here?"

"Normally a bunch of us meet up for a beer, but I probably won't be going."

"Why not?"

"Because you're here."

She shrugs. "No reason not to go. I could even go with you. If you wanted."

I arch a brow, a bit surprised. "Yeah?"

"Why do you say it like that?"

"I don't know. I didn't think you'd be interested in meeting my friends."

She laughs. "I bet they have great stories about you."

"Oh, God, you really are looking to blackmail me, aren't you?"

"Just don't not go because I'm here."

"I'll message Jesse later, see what he has planned for a meet-up."

She snuggles into the sofa. "Good. Now let me have a better look." She reaches into the box and pulls out an album and starts going through my hockey pictures. "My God, you were the cutest. You don't even have front teeth here." She narrows her eyes. "Wait, why do you have a patch over your eye here?"

I put my hand on hers and close the album. "Okay, you've seen enough."

"No, I'm not done."

"Fine then, when I visit you, I get to look through your albums, and make all kinds of comments."

"Deal."

"I had a patch because one eye wasn't as strong. You were probably always beautiful though, and not a big cross-eyed dork like me."

She swallows and that's when I realize I just called her beautiful. Oh well. What can I say. She's gorgeous, and I can barely take my eyes off her. She shifts closer, our legs touching, and when she opens a different album, my hand lands on her thigh. Her head lifts, and a ray of light shines in through the window, casting a soft glow over her. The air in the room seems to change, become volatile...sexual, if I'm reading things right. I gulp as my pulse jumps in my throat, and my cock jumps to life between my legs.

"Ry..." she whispers her gaze moving over my face. "You think I'm—"

"Yes, Alysha. You're beautiful."

"I think you are too."

"I've been called a lot of things, but beautiful was never one of them."

She chuckles. "For what it's worth, you weren't a dork. You were the cutest kid, lazy eye or not," she adds with a grin, one hand going to my hair to mess it up. "Now, you're all kinds of..." she pauses like she's trying to think of the right word.

"Hot," I provide, and she laughs.

Unable to help myself, my eyes drop to her sweet lips, and when she wets them, my cock thickens even more. She leans in a little closer, heat arching between us. I spread my fingers on her thigh, the only thing separating my palm from the warmth of her flesh is a pair of thin yoga pants.

"Aly..." I whisper back, my voice rough and fractured.

She practically vibrates as she drops her gaze to my hand, and sets the album beside her. "It's been a long time since I've been...touched," she admits quietly.

My hand stills and as much as I want to continue, I ask. "Do you want me to stop?"

She gives a slow shake of her head. "No."

I brush my thumb back and forth and she sucks in a breath. "Do you like it, Aly...?"

God, I need her to like my touch more than I need air right now.

Her gaze moves back to my face and that's when I see the want shining brightly, blatantly. "I like it."

Everything about this is wrong—she's still reeling from a breakup—but goddammit, the need in her body, her eyes, her voice does something to me. I should walk away, run even. I like this girl but she's hurting right now, confused. She'd only just told me she didn't even know what was best for her, which means, putting my hands and mouth all over her, probably isn't going to help her figure it out anytime soon. I need to get my shit together and be the responsible one, the one to make good decisions.

Okay, dude, get the fuck out of the attic. Right now.

"Tell me what else you'd like, Alysha."

Well, fuck...

8

ALYSHA

The second his lips touch mine, I forget every reason why this isn't a good idea. I forget that I just had a breakup, and I'm confused. But nothing about this feels confusing, and my God, I'm not sure I've ever had fireworks go off in my brain quite like this before.

My entire body vibrates with a kind of excitement that is new to me, and while I don't want to compare Ryan to my ex, Linc's kisses were never like this. But maybe that had more to do with me than him, because our relationship lacked a certain spark, a certain intimacy.

I know we're only kissing here, but it feels far more intimate than anything Linc and I did together. Ryan groans, and all thoughts of my ex dissipate. I honestly don't want to be thinking about him right now. Nope. I only want to be thinking about Ryan, and how one big hand has circled around my neck, holding me to him like he's afraid I might flee.

"Is this what you need, Alysha?" he asks, breaking the kiss to put his mouth on my neck. He peppers my flesh with hot, wet kisses until my entire body is tingling, from the top of my head to the tips of my toes.

"Yes," I whisper.

"Rebound…" he mumbles. At least that's what I think he's saying.

"Ryan?" I ask, and cup his face, bringing his eyes back to me. They drop to my mouth, and the hunger flaring there practically scorches me. What was I going to ask? Oh right. "What did you say about rebound?"

"You need to be touched, which means you need a rebound guy." He cups my face, his eyes dead serious. "I want to be there for you. I want to be whatever you need me to be."

I touch his shoulders, and his eyes close for a split second as he sucks in a breath. God, I love the way this big strong guy reacts to my little hands on his body, and while I want them there, I do realize he's a guy who has a deep-seated need to be there for others, maybe even a guy who puts his own well-being last.

"But what do you want?" I ask.

He angles his head, confused. Has no one ever asked him what he wanted before? "I want to be that guy for you." I wait for a second, and he adds, "I want you, Alysha."

With that, his lips find mine again, and this time the kiss is deeper, harder, filled with so much hunger that I let go of all my worries and give in to what I'm feeling. I run my hands over his shoulders, his chest, and being bolder than I ever have before, I grip his sweater and tug. He breaks the kiss and my heart leaps. Did I go too far? Did he come to his senses and realize this probably isn't a great idea?

He grips the hem of his sweater and peels it off, along with the T-shirt underneath, in one smooth movement.

"Ooh," I breathe out quietly as I take in his hard chest, and rippling abs. This guy is cut, his muscles born of hard work on a farm. I lift my gaze and find him smiling. I should be embarrassed by my reaction, but for some reason I'm not. "Nice," I tell him.

"Alysha," he moans.

"Yeah."

"Touch me." I put my hands on his hot body and his groan of pleasure curls around me and encourages me to examine more of his body—with my mouth. I lean in and press a kiss to his chest, and his mumbled curses bring a smile to my face. It's evident that he needs to be touched just as much as I do.

As I press my lips to his skin, skimming them over his body, goosebumps appear and his fingers go to my sweater. He tugs at it, and I sit up and lift my arms over my head, to make it easier for him.

"Fuck yeah," he groans, as he peels my sweater off until I'm sitting before him in my yoga pants and bra. He swallows as he stares at my breasts, which are rather small, but from the pleasure on his face, I'd say they were just perfect for him.

"You're gorgeous," he murmurs, and cups my breasts. They disappear beneath his big palms and he leans in for another kiss. It's a bit softer this time, as he touches my breasts gently, treating my body like it's a treasured possession.

One hand goes around my back and with a flick, he unhooks my bra. It falls from my shoulders, and I let it slide off my body. His eyes are wide, his face elated as he gazes at my hard nipples, like he'd just won the world's biggest lottery. No man has ever looked at me like that before.

He puts his hands on my bare flesh and exhales. I'm beginning to think he'd been holding his breath for a while now. His thumb brushes my nipple, a slow easy sweep and I toss my head back and lean into the touch. I love everything about this.

"I knew it," he whispers.

"Knew what?"

"That you'd be perfect." He gulps and that's when he realizes what he's said—what he admitted. He's been thinking about this for a while. Believe me, I totally understand.

"Ry..."

He doesn't take his eyes off my breasts. "Yeah."

"Still want to know what else I like?" He nods, like his voice is no longer working. I take his head and guide his mouth to my nipple, and he groans as he takes the hard bud between his lips. The heat from his mouth seeps into my skin and warms me from the inside out. A moan I have no control over crawls out of my throat and seems to urge him on. He sucks hard and rolls my nipple between his teeth, and his groans of pleasure take me to a whole new level.

He turns his attention to the other breast and offers it the same delicious treatment, until I'm squirming, wanting his mouth somewhere else. He shifts, pushes the photo album off the sofa and moves me until I'm beneath him. God, is this really happening?

Yes, yes it is, and I'm reveling in the sensations.

He kisses a path down my stomach, moaning as he breathes in my skin. His teeth nip at the band on my yoga pants and when I lift for him, eager for him to remove them already, he chuckles and shifts backward.

His gaze meets mine, holds for a second and I read the question in his eyes. "I want this," I tell him and he tugs on my tight yoga pants, dragging them down my legs, far too slowly for my liking. With the utmost care, he works the legging over my injured ankle, and carefully sets my foot back on the sofa.

A growl rumbles in his throat as he slides his hands up my legs, his focus on the needy spot between my quivering thighs. I expect him to remove my panties, but instead he presses his lips to my sex, the thin cotton separating his mouth from my flesh. He licks me through the fabric, and my clit swells as I take the back of his head, run my fingers through his hair and press him harder to me.

His growl grows louder as he slides a thumb under the thin material and strokes my clit with the rough pad. My hips lift, and I bang against his face as his slick thumb circles my aching nub.

"God, yes," I cry out and rock against him, so damn needy and not afraid to show it. I love being touched by Ryan. As I think about touching his hardness in return, putting his cock into my mouth, moisture breaks out on my body. "I want you in my mouth," I say without shame. I'm not usually so vocal when it comes to sex, and I'm not sure I ever asked what I wanted.

He lifts his head. "You will, when I've had my fill of you." With that, his head dips and he tugs my panties down and tosses them aside. Gripping my thighs, he spreads me wide, putting me on full display, and I begin to pant. "So pretty," he murmurs, and the next thing I see is the back of his head as he slides his tongue all over my pussy, licking and sucking until pleasure is the only thing I know.

I move my body, and grab my breasts, pinching my nipples and reveling in the dual pleasure. He inserts a thick, deft finger, and strokes the hot bundle of nerves inside me. Wow, that is fantastic.

"Ry," I murmur and go up on my elbows, loving the way his head moves between my legs. My throat dries as heat sizzles through my veins, and I want to hang on, want to make this moment last, but it's been too long since I've been touched, and for some reason, this man knows exactly what my body needs.

He licks my clit, and strokes me deep and I flop back down as white hot pleasure centers between my legs.

"Ry, yes, just like that."

Using his tongue, he applies more pressure to my clit and that's when my entire body ignites. Pleasure floods in a whoosh and a keening cry spills from my throat. I clench around his finger, and he moans like it's pure torture—like he's desperate to put another body part inside me. Dammit, I want that too.

I rock against him, and he stays between my legs, wringing out every pulse and drawing out the pleasure. I put my hands on his head, needing to touch him and he glances up at me. I'm sure I'm smiling like an idiot, but I can't stop myself and I really don't care. I want him to know what he's done to me.

"Exquisite," I murmur.

As my spasms subside, he gives my pussy one last lick, a slow, leisurely swipe of his tongue that sends pleasure shooting through me again. His mouth is wet as he climbs up my body and presses his lips to mine. His cock presses against my leg, and I want to free it from his jeans.

"I need to touch you," I murmur as he kisses me with hunger.

"I need that too."

He shifts to the side and I slide my hand down, rubbing his cock through his jeans. I reach for the button, and go completely still as voices rise up to meet my ears.

"Shit, they're back," he grumbles.

"Ohmigod." Panicked, I try to shimmy out from beneath him.

He puts his hand on my stomach to stop me. "It's okay. No one is coming up here. But we should get dressed."

I nod in agreement, and before he lets me up, he kisses me again. "I really liked making you come, Aly..."

I grin. "I probably liked it more."

"Oh, it's a competition, is it?" He shakes his head and laughs. "I always knew you were competitive."

He sits up and I put my bra on. "When I put your cock in my mouth, who do you think is going to like it more?" I'm teasing him, just playing around and being silly, but he goes completely still, and I'm unable to read the strange expression on his face. Wait, does he not want his cock in my mouth? Don't all guys like that?

His jaw is clenched when he asks, "Are you telling me you're going to like my cock in your mouth?"

I tug on my shirt, and snatch my yoga pants off the floor. "It's exactly what I'm telling you."

"You don't have to say that or do that, you know."

"I know." What the heck is going on here? "Do you not like that?"

He laughs, tugs on his shirt, and tries to adjust his pants over his still hard cock. "I'm a guy. I like that." He steps closer and I put one arm on him to stabilize myself as I put on my pants. "Lots of girls don't like doing it, though."

I take in the honesty on his face, and want to be honest with him too. "I've never really loved it. Linc..." I begin and he puts his hands on my shoulders.

"You don't have to talk about him."

"I just want you to know that sex between us wasn't really great. It's strange. It was always rushed, and it was like his thoughts were always elsewhere." I purse my lips. "I don't think he liked having sex with me."

"I can't imagine anyone not liking sex with you, Alysha."

"He didn't really...make any sounds. It all seemed rather clinical and emotionless." I shrug. "I guess I didn't make sounds either."

He brushes hair from my face, and takes my chin between his thumb and finger. "You made lots of sounds with me."

"You did too. I think that's why I felt like I could."

He presses his lips to mine. "You can do whatever you want with me."

Footsteps sound on the upstairs hall, and I lean in and whisper, "Even moan when I take your cock in my mouth?"

"Jesus, Aly," he moans and tugs on the front of his jeans. "Keep that up and I'll never be able to get out of this attic."

I grin. "Maybe we can sneak back up here later."

"Trust me, there's a lot we're going to do later..."

9

RYAN

I fix my clothes, and give Alysha a once over—twice. I probably should keep my eyes to myself. Walking downstairs with a boner, yeah, no one wants to see that. But I wanted to make sure she was put back together. She'd be embarrassed if anyone knew what we were doing up here, and I don't want her to feel anything but happiness and pleasure this holiday season. Not an easy task, after that asshole Linc broke up with her. While one part of me is happy about that, there's the other part that doesn't want her hurting.

"All set?" I ask, as she finger combs her mess of hair.

"Do I look okay?"

"Good enough to eat."

Her face flushes more and she whacks me. I snatch her hand, bring it to my mouth and kiss her palm. A moan crawls out of her throat and I like the way she reacts to me. I let her hand go, and she wobbles a bit.

"Let me help you down." She nods, and I wave my hand for her to make her way to the ladder but she turns and snatches the photo album off the old sofa first. "Really?"

She chuckles. "Yes, really."

I shake my head at her. "You owe me a look at your pictures."

"Sure, when you come to the Hamptons, you can look." She walks to the ladder, and my stomach tightens, because honestly, there's no way I'll be going to her place in the Hamptons. I can't imagine her parents would be too pleased to know she was hooking up with a potato farmer, not when they want her with Linc. It does make me wonder how much influence they have over her, and if that influence will lead her back into Linc's arms.

I go down the ladder and wait at the bottom to help her. Once she's secure, I head back up and grab the boxes we need. Everyone is in the kitchen making hot chocolate by the time we get downstairs, and I drop the boxes in front of the tree. Billy is inside and starts nipping at the tape.

"Back off, Billy," I say and he bleeps at me and trots to the kitchen. I turn to find Alysha grinning.

"I still can't believe you have a therapy goat. Farmers are strange."

"Hey, watch it, or you'll be sleeping outside with him."

"He looks quite snuggly. Maybe that wouldn't be so bad." She's smiling, but my heart clenches, well aware that Alysha hasn't been hugged, snuggled or treated properly by those who love her. Well, I plan to do all those things while she's here.

"Thanks for getting the boxes, Ryan," Mom says as she comes into the room carrying a tray. She sets it on the table and the smell of chocolate reaches my nostrils. She turns to Alysha. "Did you have a good time in town?"

"I loved it. I even got a new Anne of Green Gables hat and a couple books."

Mom laughs as my sisters and granddad come in, and Lucy puts on Christmas music. I glance at Alysha, who has a strange look on her face. I walk over to her, and hand her a mug. "You okay?"

"Are you sure it's okay for me to be here?"

"Absolutely. Come on, you can help unpack the boxes."

I hold my hand out to help her up, and she crosses the room and sits on the floor beside my sisters. They all start digging into the boxes and Alysha's hand stills when she pulls out my father's Christmas stocking. She runs her finger over the embroidered letters spelling out Jack, and as understanding dawns, her gaze darts to mine and I put my hand on hers, giving it a little squeeze to let her know it's okay.

"We still hang it," I tell her, and she nods. "Stockings were Dad's favorite things at Christmas."

"That's sweet, Ryan," she says quietly.

"He might not be with us, but he's still with us..." I put my hand over my heart. "In here." I tug the rest of the stockings out of the box, and hang them on the mantel. Alysha has a warm smile on her face as she takes in the seven stockings, and I get the sense that maybe she never had one.

"Look at this," Monica says and hands a ball to Alysha. She laughs as she turns it and finds my baby picture on it.

"This is adorable."

Monica shows her the others. "We all have a first Christmas ball with our baby picture. Mom made them."

"You guys were so cute." She eyes the ball.

"They were all one month old in the pictures."

"Ryan, what is going on with your hair?" she asks, trying not to laugh. "Why is it sticking straight up like that?"

"Give me that." I snatch it from her and put it on the tree as Granddad works on the lights. That's his favorite part and he does it every year.

"Troll," Lauren whispers.

I glare at her. "I can hear you, and it's not my fault my hair grew straight up."

Mom laughs. "It defied the laws of gravity."

"Okay, can we pick on someone else?" I ask, even though Alysha seems to love the way my family is making fun of me. I run my hand through my hair, knowing it's probably still sticking up. Not because it defies gravity, but because Alysha had been running her fingers through it earlier. Although I can't think about that right now.

Needing something to do with my hands, I take a mug of hot chocolate and swallow a mouthful. "Aww, don't be mad," Alysha says. "It doesn't stick up anymore." She angles her head. "Much."

I grin at her. "You really want to sleep out in the barn with Billy, don't you?"

She laughs and as if hearing his name, Billy comes running into the living room. He starts nibbling on the tree, and Mom shoos him away.

He trots over to Alysha and drops down beside her. She rubs his back after emptying the boxes, and once Granddad has the lights on, we all start putting on the Christmas ornaments.

"You have some gorgeous decorations," Alysha says.

"Some of them are pretty old." Mom holds out a ball and shows it to Alysha. "This one belonged to John's mother."

I notice that she doesn't touch it. "Wow, that's old."

"Hey," Granddad teases. "Who are you calling old?"

Alysha grins. "No one."

Granddad drops into his favorite recliner and stretches out. "Not resting because I'm old. Resting because my work here is done," he teases.

"Oh wait," I say and dart upstairs. I come back down with Granddad's favorite chocolate bark from a shop in Halifax. I can only get it at Christmas and he absolutely loves it. I hand him the box and his eyes light up. "Did you think I forgot?"

"Nope, just wondered what was taking you so long to hand it over." He eyes Alysha. "But I guess you had your hands full with other things."

"John," Mom chides him, and he chuckles, pops a piece of chocolate into his mouth and closes his eyes.

Monica covers him with a blanket and kisses his cheek. In return, Grandad gives her shoulder a squeeze, and Alysha watches the exchange of affection with sheer delight. I drop down next to her, our legs touching, and she turns my way.

"Hey," I say.

"Hey," she responds, and with everyone working on the tree, I put my hand on her back, and run my finger down her spine. She visibly quivers, and her lips part as she searches the room to make sure no one is watching.

"Having fun?"

She nods. "I am." There's a hitch in her voice as I continue to run my fingers over her back, and my heart beats a little faster as tension bubbles around us. "I never knew decorating a tree could be so fun."

"We can do a lot of fun things while you're here."

She takes a quick breath, knowing exactly what I'm talking about. "Yeah?"

"Sure, we can go skating, sledding, and dancing."

"Um, bad ankle, remember."

"Oh, right. I guess we'll have to do things that keep you off your feet."

"Sounds like you're talking about bed rest."

I lean into her, my mouth near her ear and her quivers goes through my body, coming to rest between my legs. "Bed yes, rest no." She gasps and glances around again, but my family are all chatting and working on the tree. "I mean, if you want to do all those things again, it's the only solution."

"The only solution," she agrees, and gives me a small grin.

I realize I've set myself up to be her rebound guy, and that's never a good thing, but I want to give her what she needs right now.

"What do you think?" Mom asks as she stands back to admire the tree.

Alysha gasps as the lights flick on and glisten on the balls. "I think it's gorgeous, Patricia."

"Do you want to help me hide the pickle?" I ask, and a sound crawls out of Alysha's throat as her eyes go wide.

"Ryan," she croaks out, her body tight.

I laugh, and jump up, pulling the pickle ornament out of my stocking, where we safeguard it every year. I hold it out to show it to her, and she stares at me in complete confusion. "It's an old family tradition," I explain. "I hide it on the tree the night before Christmas, and the first person to find it gets a special gift."

"Oh, I thought..." Heat floods her cheeks and that's when I realize my blunder. I asked her if she wanted to help me hide the pickle, right after telling her I wanted her in my bed.

"Sorry, I always think everyone knows this tradition."

"I've never heard of it."

"It's an old German tradition," Mom says. "Jack used to do it every year, and after he passed, Ryan took on the responsibility." Mom looks at me with a mixture of sadness and pride. I know she still misses Dad.

"I'd love to help you hide it this year," Alysha says. I put the glass pickle back into my stocking for safe keeping, and laugh when Granddad lets out a big snore, shaking himself awake. Mom shakes her head.

"On that note, I think I'll get started on dinner. Girls, do you want to help?"

"I can help too," Alysha offers.

"No, I think you should rest your foot." Mom's eyes narrow as she puts her hands on her hips and examines Alysha's ankle from a distance. "Why don't you go on up and put a pillow under it. I'll give Ryan some ice to put on it."

She looks like she's about to protest, so I pipe up. "Come on. If you want to go with Billy and me to the hospital tomorrow, you'll need to rest right now. You walked enough today as it is."

She nods. "Okay, but once it's better, maybe I can make a meal for the family. A little something to thank you for taking in the stray."

Mom laughs. "That sounds lovely, and maybe Ryan can help you."

"You do want it to be edible, don't you?" I ask in mock horror.

"I'm not eating anything he makes," Lucy calls out. "You remember the 'incident'."

"Shut it," I yell and Alysha grins at me.

"Incident? Is there more than one?"

"Something like that."

I nudge her to get her moving up the stairs. "Do tell."

"Nope."

"Don't worry, Alysha, I'll tell you later," Lucy calls out with a laugh.

"How did I end up with three sisters who are all out to embarrass me?"

"I like them," Alysha says.

"Of course you do. They side with you and you enjoy it when I'm embarrassed."

"Do not." She chuckles when I raise my brow. "Okay, maybe a little."

We make our way to my bedroom, and she walks to the bed and drops down. Fuck, seeing her like that, it's more than my dick can take. I clear my throat. "I'll be back with the ice."

I hurry down the stairs, taking them two at a time. I hope Mom gives me a big bag full of cubes. I might need to toss a few down my pants.

In the kitchen, everyone is fussing about. Mom hands me a wet dishtowel, with a bag of ice inside. "Twenty minutes on, twenty off."

"Yup." I, of course, already know this from my own injuries over the years. "Dinner in an hour. I hope Alysha likes potatoes," Mom jokes.

Back upstairs, I step into my room, just in time to see Alysha's sweet ass in the air as she changes out of her yoga pants and into a pair of my pajama pants. "Whoa," jumps from my lips and I practically skid to a halt. She falters a bit as she spins to face me, and I guess a part of my brain didn't register that she'd closed the door after I left to get ice.

I take in her panties, and I know I just had my mouth all over her, but ogling her without her consent, feels wrong, I turn around, to give her privacy. Her soft chuckle curls around me.

"A little late for that, isn't it?" she asks, her voice soft, and if I'm not mistaken, seductive.

"Are you saying I can turn around and stare?"

"Is staring what you want to do?"

I adjust my thickening cock as it strains against my zipper. "Tip of the iceberg, babe."

She laughs. "You can turn, and please close the door."

I turn, kick the door shut with my foot, and as she tugs on my pants and ties them at the waist, I know one of two things must happen tonight. I'm either going to tug one out or wait until everyone is asleep and sneak in here with her.

I'm pretty sure I know which one I'm going to do, and yeah, everything about Alysha being here is messing with my brain. What was it that I said earlier about making good decisions? I guess they sort of flew out the window when I put my mouth on her and decided I'd be her rebound guy. Sure, I'd do anything for those I care about, even putting my own well-being last.

I guess I'll deal with the fallout later when she figures out what's best for her and that it's not the life I'd like to give her.

10

ALYSHA

I roll over in Ryan's bed, the moonlight shining in through the cracks in the curtain. Restless, I roll the other way, unable to get comfortable. Even though Ryan had spent before and after dinner putting ice on my leg, my body is still burning hot. Probably from the hungry way he was looking at me all night. Even when he dug into his potato casserole, his eyes remained on me, and each time he moaned or licked his lips, I had the feeling he wasn't thinking about or savoring the food in his mouth. Thank God no one noticed, and maybe it's just my imagination, although after what we did in the attic...

Honestly, I still can't believe what we did up there, or how he offered to be my rebound guy. I'm not sure I'd call him that, but I guess technically, if I'm fooling around with him within a day of a breakup, that's what he'd be. I'm not sure why he'd want that label, but then, maybe like me, he just wants to have a friends with benefits hook-up—something fun to help pass the holidays. He did say this place could get isolated in the winter months. We're both now single, and I guess there's nothing wrong with that, as long as neither of us get the wrong idea about what's really happening here.

I mean, a no strings hook-up is all I want, right?

I snort because my brain is buzzing and I don't know what's best right now. All I know is that I'm craving Ryan's touch, and despite being a hot mess, there's no way I'd be able to deny myself if he offers it again. I kick my blankets off and throw my legs over the edge of the bed. Maybe a drink of water or another cold shower—I had one before bed—will exhaust me as it puts out the flames, and then I can finally get some sleep.

I begin to debate my actions as I tiptoe to my door. Will the running water wake everyone up? I wince as I open my door, and the hinges groan in protest. I'm about to change my mind and take a step back when a tall figure comes into view. I open my mouth, about to gasp, but the sound is stifled by a large palm. The second I realize it's Ryan, I relax.

He eyes me, and I read the look on his face. I nod and he slowly removes my hand.

"You scared me," I whisper.

"Sorry. I didn't mean to."

"What are you doing out here?" He puts his big arm around me, and backs me up until I'm in the bedroom. He carefully closes the door and locks it. The sound shivers down my spine, and that's when my rattled brain becomes fully aware that Ryan was outside my room because he had every intention of sneaking in.

"What were you doing?" he asks, and puts his arm back around my waist, tugging my little body to his. I really don't know how we fit together so well.

"I was going to take a shower."

"You already had one."

"It's...hot in here."

His mouth is near my ear as he chuckles, and the sound stimulates my aching clit. "This old farmhouse is never hot in the winter." His hand slides under my T-shirt. "Ah, I see the problem."

"There's a problem."

"Yes, it's not the house that's hot, it's you. Your skin is on fire, babe."

"Do you think I'm coming down with something?" I ask and it's followed by a moan as he lightly runs his callused hands along my back. The man really is a gentle giant.

"Definitely, and we probably need to get you straight back to bed."

He scoops me up, like he's done a dozen times before and carries me to the bed. He sets me down and a groan crawls out of his throat as he stands back and takes in my body, bathed only in the moonlight.

"I think we need to cool you down."

He tears off his shirt and it takes all my power not to moan. "Do you think it's contagious?"

He crouches between my legs, and I do love the position he always puts himself in. "Yes, but it's okay, I think I already have it." He puts his hands on my legs, and lifts himself up to his full height and I can't help but notice how close his crotch is to my face. Before I can do anything about that, he sits on the edge of the bed, takes my hand and puts it on his hard, hot chest. I spread my fingers and a shiver goes through him. "Are you tingly all over too?" he asks, his voice serious and laced with concern, as he vibrates beneath my fingertips.

I revel in the play of his muscles beneath my fingers. "I am, is that bad?"

"Oh yeah, for sure." He narrows his eyes, like he's going through a mental check list. "Having trouble sleeping?"

"Yes."

"Same." He puts his hand on my chest, and my heart thumps faster. "Higher heart rate too, I see." Frowning, he shakes his head at the diagnosis.

"How about your skin? Is it sensitive?"

"Yeah."

He slides his hand down, brushing over my nipple to dip into my oversized pajama pants. "Tell me, when I touch you like this, does this make it better or worse?" He brushes his finger over my slick pussy, and I moan.

"Better," I murmur. "Much better."

"Then we have no choice."

He pushes me back until I'm flat and climbs onto the bed. He positions me until I'm in the middle and he slides between my legs, widening them with his big body.

"No choice?"

"I'm going to have to get you out of these clothes and cool you down with my mouth and fingers..." His head lifts, dark, intense eyes lock on mine. "If that doesn't work, we'll have to go one step further."

"We'll probably have to do that."

He chuckles at my enthusiasm. "You don't even know what it is yet."

"Oh, right."

He tugs on my pajama pants to expose my pussy. His big thumb rubs my throbbing clit. "I'm probably going to have to put my tongue right here."

"This will help both of us?"

He scrubs his chin like he's in deep thought. "If it doesn't, we'll have to try and try again."

Loving this little game we're playing, I ask, "These symptoms, this infliction, does it have a...have a name?"

"Yes, of course. It's something that happens in rural Prince Edward Island, in the isolated winter months. It's called nooky-itis."

I cover my mouth to stifle a laugh. "That sounds very made up, Ryan."

"Nope. When these symptoms happen, a person requires very special attention and care." He holds his hands up, to show me exactly how he plans to give me that attention and care and a thrill races through me.

"Maybe I should check with Daisy to see if she's heard of it."

"I doubt it. Like I said, it's a local condition."

"Does it only happen to people in rural Prince Edward Island during the cold winter months or does it happen to the crops too."

He inches back, his face playfully twisted, like I might have just offended him. "Hey, what a farmer does to save a crop is between the farmer and his crop."

"No judgement here." I laugh, a little too loudly—God what is wrong with me? Why am I so giddy? Oh, probably just the fact that I haven't been touched in ages and he's promising to do just that. He puts his hand over my mouth to muffle the sound. I go quiet, not because he's stifling my voice, but because everything about his intensity and need is taking my arousal to a new level, and I definitely have nooky-itis, too because I definitely need to be touched.

"But nooky-itis isn't all bad."

Really? I'd have to say it seems all good to me but I stay quiet to let him finish—besides he still has his hands on my mouth so I can' t speak anyway.

"You see," he continues. "It's an affliction on farms, but what we need to do to cure it also helps us work off the calories from all the potatoes we eat."

His hand leaves my mouth and his lips come down for a hard, hungry kiss, and I moan as I spread my legs to wrap them around him. He devours me with his mouth, and I grow hotter, a desperate need building between my legs.

His lips leave mine, and his gaze moves over my face. I can't see him well in the dim light, but I get the sense he's checking in on me. Either that or he's having second thoughts about being my rebound. That's the last thing I want, because if he doesn't continue to touch me, I'm pretty sure I might spontaneously combust. So I need him to know that I'm not looking for more.

"So nooky-itis, a no strings hook-up is the cure, right?"

I hear his throat as he swallows. "Yes."

"Okay." I put my hands on his face. "Touch me."

He continues to gaze at me, and then he slides down my body. He positions himself between my legs again, and I lift my hips for him and he tugs my pants down and off my legs. He tosses them away, and lightly runs his finger over my soaking sex.

"Babe, you're in bad shape."

I lift myself up, desperate to touch him in return. I put my hand over his cock. "This swelling, it's caused by the same affliction?"

"Yeah," he murmurs and throws his head back as I squeeze him. With a desperation I've never felt before, I tug his boxers down. His cock springs free and hits my eye. I ignore the sting and take his girth into my hands, and he practically trembles as I say, "This seems serious?"

As my warm breath falls over his stretched skin, he puts his hand around the back of my head and guides me to his crown. I lightly lick the cum pooling on the end, and he growls, like he's struggling very hard not to make noises and wake the household.

I take him as deeply as I can, until I chokes and he inches back when I make a sound. "Easy," he murmurs. He shifts backward and I lift my face up to find dark eyes full of warmth and affection staring back. My stupid heart misses a beat as he takes my chin between his fingers and lifts it, until my mouth is poised open, his for the taking.

He kisses me again, and I close my eyes, losing myself in the sensation. But I'd be wise not to do that and to remember this is just about sex. "Ryan," I whisper, and put my hands on his back. He quakes, and it makes me wonder when he's been touched last. "I need."

He grabs my hips and tugs until I'm flat on my back, and I love the way this gentle giant moves me around so easily. His hot lips go to my neck and sensations rocket through me as he presses hot, open-mouthed kisses to my scorched skin. My nipples tighten, desperate for his mouth and as if reading my thoughts, he pulls my T-shirt up, and lightly licks my nipples, one at a time, moaning as he savors them individually.

I tear the shirt off and put my hands around his head and pull him harder against me, and he shifts, his cock straining against my leg. My God, I can't wait to feel him inside me. I somehow know it's not going to be a quick in and out, and done and gone home, leaving me aching for so much more.

His teeth clamp gently around one nipple and the sensation rockets straight to my sex, and a small wave ripples through me. I can't believe how close I am to letting go. There must be something in this fresh country air, because I don't climax fast...or at all. I mean, I have, but it's always taken a lot of work, on my part.

He drags a finger down my body and slides it between my legs. As soon as he dips it inside me, his head jerks up. Knowledgeable eyes meet mine as my muscles tremble. He's well aware what his touch is doing to me, and that I'd climaxed with him only a few hours earlier. But yeah, I'm that turned on.

"I need to taste you," he murmurs, his voice deep and low— full of want. God, I love seeing this strong hockey player, strong farmer, losing it a little. He shimmies low on the bed, and puts his mouth over my throbbing sex. I grip the bedsheets and bite down on my lip to keep myself from crying out as his hot mouth envelopes me.

His tongue teases and tortures my clit and I writhe against his mouth as he works a second finger into my quivering body. I gulp air, reveling in the sensations yet trying to fight them off at the same time. I want to climax but I don't want this to end.

"Come for me, babe," he murmurs. "Come all over my mouth. I like when you do that."

Oh, God. The honest and open way he talks to me pushes me over the edge. Of course, his tongue on my clit and his fingers inside me also help. I shut down my brain and go up on my elbows to watch him pleasure me, but what's really turning me on is that he blatantly loves eating me. The moans, the way his body is squirming, it's all so expressive. He's not holding anything back and I love the freedom in the way we're having sex.

He changes the pace and rhythm and it sucks the air from my lungs. "Ryan," I whimper as the last of my control crumples and my body gives into the pleasure. I break around his fingers, heat gushes from my sex and soaking me and him and the bed. My chest rises and falls erratically, and I reach for his hair, run my fingers through it.

"So good," I cry out as I ride out each powerful wave until my body is nothing but a hot, depleted mess. He pulls his thick fingers from my body, sits back on his ankles and licks them clean. He's positioned perfectly for what I want to do.

I sit up and take his cock back into my mouth, and he grunts as his hips jerk forward. He swells even more in my mouth, stretching my lips, and I love everything about it. I cup his balls and lightly massage them and from his rapid fire breathing I sense he's hovering on the edge. He moans and groans some more and the sounds are music to this dancer's ears. I move with the music he's making, matching the rhythm with my mouth and I'm certain he's seconds from exploding when he grips my head and eases me off him.

"Alysha," he breathes out heavily. "Jesus."

He's in total and utter pain. I make a move to suck him deep again, and he shakes his head to stop me. "No, I want to be in here." He reaches between my legs and lightly strokes my clit. "If that's what you want too."

"I do," I say quickly and firmly. It brings a smile to his face, although it appears a bit twisted, considering how much pain the man is in.

"Condom." He stands, kicks his boxers all the way off and grabs a condom from his nightstand. "I hope these aren't expired."

I kind of like that he hasn't used condoms in a while. Then again, he hasn't been home in a while, either. He tears into it and quickly sheathes himself and I can't take my eyes off his gorgeous, hard body, lit by the moonlight as he climbs back between my legs. I put my hand on his chest.

"Your body is amazing," I say, as I once again find myself saying and doing things in bed, that I never have before.

"You're the amazing one, Alysha," he counters and presses a kiss so soft and tender to my lips it somehow makes it all the way to my heart and leaves a little imprint.

He falls over me, his cock nestled between my spread legs, and it's insane how this all feels so right, and comfortable, and natural. He kisses my mouth, my nose, my cheeks and my chin.

I'm not sure if he's reconsidering, or is giving me time to reconsider, worried I might have regrets but I want him to know I want this, so I say, "Remember you wanted me to tell you what I liked?"

"Yeah," he says, the vibrations in his voice as he kisses my neck strum through my body and stroke my clit.

"Well, I'd like your cock in me now please."

He growls, puts his hand on either side of my head and stares into my eyes as he slowly pushes into me. He's big and I'm small, and we breathe together as he offers me inch after inch until he's seated high inside my body.

I grin at him. He grins back. When was the last time I ever felt this happy? I'm not sure but I don't want the feeling to stop.

"Feel good?" he asks.

"Oh yeah." I lift my hips and lower it. "Feel good?"

"Fuck yeah."

We both chuckle and the next thing I know, his mouth is devouring mine again and I'm clawing at him as he starts moving his hips, sliding in and out of my tight core and creating beautiful, pleasurable friction with each thrust. We kiss, touch, take and give, neither afraid to express ourselves. My entire body grows hot, the sensations rocketing through me almost too much to bear. I want to cling to them, I want to push them away...heck, I don't know what I want. His pelvis grinds against my clit, and his deep, needy grunts are like a lover's primal symphony.

As I hold on tight it occurs to me that Ryan fucks with passion and rhythm. His movements are smooth and effortless like a beautifully choreographed routine, felt and performed straight from the artist's heart. It touches me deep, on a level I had no idea existed and brings a smile to my face because maybe we do have some things in common. My art is performed on a dance floor, his is performed in bed. Together we're creating a masterpiece.

I close my eyes to revel in it and as my body follows the journey to completion, I cry out Ryan's name, and come all over his pistoning cock. His mouth finds mine, hushes me with a kiss and a second later, he pushes high inside me, and my body absorbs his hard pulses as he too lets go. He nibbles my bottom lip, his breath hot and heavy as he depletes himself in me, and once he's done, he collapses on top of me being careful not to crush me, and I do appreciate that.

He rolls to the side, and pulls me with him. With his arms around me, my body tucked into his, barely and inch of my skin is exposed to the cold night. He holds me for a very long time, and just when I think he's fallen asleep, he speaks.

"I think I liked it more." I lift my head to see him. What on earth is he talking about? Wait, is he grinning? "When you put my cock in your mouth, I'm pretty sure I liked it more."

I chuckle, remember the conversation about competition that we had in the attic. "I kind of liked it too."

"Not as much as me," he says with a laugh, and runs his finger over my bottom lip. His smile is soft and sweet when he adds, "Just so you know, sex with you is pretty amazing."

"Um, what's the protocol? Do I say thank you to that?"

He laughs. "No." I wince a bit as he turns me and he makes a face. "Let me get you some ice."

"Actually, my hair was caught under your shoulder. My ankle is feeling quite a bit better." I lift my foot. "Maybe it's the endorphin high."

He chuckles. "While I'm happy about that, I don't want you walking on it during this endorphin high and hurting it again. I'd never forgive myself."

"I think it's much better now, Ryan."

He nods and looks down, a strange kind of sadness about him. "What?"

"If it is better and you want to go home—"

I touch his face, bring his gaze to mine. "Hey, this isn't the first time you tried to drive me to the airport. I'm starting to think you don't want me here."

"I want you here," he says. "I'm just worried..." He goes quiet and my throat tightens. Is he worried about me wanting more, and him not being able to give it? I mean, I explained that this was just sex. A grin plays with his lips, his mood shifting. "Boner-itis," he explains.

I laugh and kiss him. "I'm not worried, you seem to have the cure." He grins, and my mind fills with crazy ideas, ideas I wouldn't dream of speaking to Linc. "You know what, maybe we do need that ice."

His smile crumples. "Really?"

"Yeah, but not for my ankle."

RYAN

I move my leg as I begin to wake up, and hit something cold and wet. What the hell? I slowly peel my eyes open and glance at a sleeping Alysha beside me. I instantly smile, but when water starts running in the bathroom down the hall, I realize I'd fallen asleep, and the wet spot was from the ice cubes we were playing with before I sank back into her warm wet heat.

Shit.

I sit up and try not to wake Alysha as I glance around and search for my boxers. I find them in a pile beside her pajama pants and my T-shirt. The tap turns off and footsteps sound outside my door. I wait a second, tug on my boxers and walk to the door. When my ears are met with silence, I slowly open the door. I slip out, and quietly pull it shut behind me and nearly jump out of my boxers when I turn to find Lucy standing there, a big grin on her face.

She pushes her long curls from her face, and sleepy eyes full of mischief lock on mine. "Morning, brother."

"Ah, hey, morning."

Her lips twist. "Whatcha doing?

Oh, Jesus.

I jerk my thumb over my shoulder. "Just checking on Alysha's ankle."

"Dr. Potter..."

She eyes me, and yes.

Yes, I know I'm in nothing but my boxers and judging from the gleam in my sister's eye, she's well aware of it too.

She chuckles. "Awfully early for a house call isn't it. Or rather, a bedroom call."

The floorboards creak in the room down the hall—my parents' room. I growl. "What do you want, Lucy?"

She holds her hand out. "Twenty bucks."

"Obviously, I don't have it on me right now."

"Fine, I'll collect later." Her smile dissolves. "You like her, huh?"

"I told you I liked—"

She puts her hand on my shoulder. "I like her too, so I get it." A beat and then, "Just be careful."

"What's that supposed to mean?"

"She's a long way from home, and she's just come off a bad breakup. He broke it off with her."

I swallow against a suddenly thick throat because my wise younger sister is absolutely right. "I know what I'm doing," I say, but from the dubious look on her face, she knows I don't. Just like I know I don't. Her face softens, a sympathetic warmth in her eyes.

"You're my big brother. I don't want you to get hurt..."

Her voice falls off and she doesn't have to finish the sentence for me to know she dropped the word...again. Alysha might be nothing like Lexi, but it takes a special person to want to live in rural Prince Edward Island and farm. Alysha is special, and I shouldn't even be entertaining that thought. I made it clear to her that I'd be her rebound, and she solidified what we were when she came right out and clarified that this was a no strings hook-up. Besides, a big part of me expects that she'll end up back with her ex. They've been together for years. But I don't want her going back, and giving up dance. Nothing about that is right.

"Use that power wisely," I say to Lucy and give her a nudge on the cheek. She grins and heads down the hall. I dart to my room, and walk to my window to check out the fresh layer of snow on the ground. A sense of peace, a sense of home and hearth wrap around me as I glance at the fields in the distance. I'm never more content than when I'm back home on the family farm. But obviously, it's not for everyone.

As the house comes awake, I tug on some clothes and head to the barns to take care of the animals. The responsibility lies with my sisters or granddad when I'm not home, but when I'm here, I like to do it. By the time I'm finished, I head back inside to find Billy snuggled next to Alysha in front of the fire in the living room. My heart jumps in my chest as I take in her warm, flushed cheeks, and the clothes on her body—my clothes. Obviously, she likes being in them as much as I like seeing her in them.

"Hey," I say, and wish I didn't sound like my mouth was full of potatoes, but she looks warm and comfortable and so damn fuckable it's messing with my brain.

"Someone has a crush."

I turn at the sound of Monica's voice, my throat tightening. Christ, is it that obvious to everyone? I mean, I might not be in the performing arts like our good friend Sawyer, but I thought I was playing it cool.

"What?"

"Billy," she says with a nod. "He's crushing on Alysha." I swallow as I turn back to them. Alysha rubs Billy's back, dragging her fingers through his hair and for the first time in my life, I'm jealous of a goddamn goat. Needing a distraction, and something to do with my hands before I drag Billy away and take his place on her lap, I walk to the tree and adjust a few balls.

"Sleep well?" I ask Alysha and her cheeks turn a brighter shade of pink when I glance at her. My cock instantly thickens and I swear to God Billy has a shit-eating grin on his face. Little bastard.

"I can put him outside if he's bothering you."

She stretches and reaches for her coffee. "No, it's so nice and cozy in here for him, and he's so relaxing to be around. I can see why he's a therapy goat."

"Right now I think he's an asshole," I mutter under my breath.

"What?"

"Nothing.

She has a soft, contented smile on her face as she gazes at the tree. I put the lights on for her and her smile widens. "That's so pretty."

Her phone pings at almost the exact same moment mine does and sadness envelopes her entire body. She glances down. "It's Mom," she murmurs under her breath. "She's messaging that she wants to talk."

"Do you want to call her?" I glance toward the kitchen. "I can leave."

"Maybe later." Her fingers fly over the phone as she sends her mother a text and then tucks her phone under her legs—legs I parted last night and buried myself between.

Jesus.

I pull my phone from my back pocket. "It's Jesse," I say and her face brightens. "Everyone is hitting the pub tonight."

"Fun."

Before I respond, I angle my head. "Are you sure you want to go?"

"I'd love to go."

"It's not fancy or anything, and—"

"I'd love to go," she says again.

"Okay, I'll let him know." I shoot off a message to Jesse that I'll be there and that I'll be bringing a friend. I'm about to tuck my phone away when it pings. Assuming it's Jesse responding, I glance at my phone and my blood runs cold.

"Ryan?"

Fuck.

I ignore the message from Lexi and shake my hands to get my blood running again. "So what do you think, should we grab something to eat and then visit the children's hospital with Billy?"

She looks like she's about to probe—I did just go from smiling to angry in seconds flat—but instead she nods, and pushes to her feet. "Sounds like a plan."

Billy follows us into the kitchen and chaos ensues as the family gathers and everyone begins to talk over one another. Alysha sits, and I almost expect her to curl up into a ball at the commotion—she is, after all, an only child and is probably used to quiet—but she's smiling and glancing around, trying to take it all in.

"Wait a second," she says to Lauren. "Did you say tractor racing?"

I just shake my head. If she didn't think we were country bumpkins before, she sure is going to now, but I have to say, I love the tractor racing in the snow as much as the rest of us do.

"Yeah," Lauren responds, and the room grows quiet as everyone turns to take in a confused Alysha.

"You race tractors..." She glances outside to take in the fresh layer of snow. "In the winter."

Everyone starts talking again, and I lean into her and say, "It's sort of a tradition, done to break up a long winter."

"I get to drive this year," Lauren says. "You told me." She turns to Mom. "You told me If I had a clean year of driving, I could race."

"You have a tractor's license?" Alysha asks, like she's still trying to wrap her head around all this foolishness.

"Of course. We all do."

Alysha grins and shakes her head. "Right, stupid question. But don't you have to be sixteen?"

"Nope, fourteen."

"I learn something new every day here." She takes a sip of coffee. "If you like driving tractors so much, are you planning on going to college and then coming back to run the farm, like Ryan is?"

Instant. Silence.

Is anyone even fucking breathing? Wow, who knew such a simple question could shut down my entire family. Oh, just me. What the fuck, though? When they act like this, it makes me feel unwanted—unneeded and that is the worst feeling in the world.

"Ryan here is going to play in the NHL," Granddad pipes in.

"Granddad," I begin, but as usual he cuts me off, not wanting to hear of me giving up a chance to play for the NHL.

"And Lauren, she wants to study political science. You're looking at Canada's future Prime Minister there. Lord knows she'll never lose a debate," he adds almost under his breath. We all chuckle and he continues with, "She just wants to drive the tractor to impress Colin, from Red Sand Farms down yonder."

"Granddad," Lauren cries out, her cheeks turning red, and he shrugs.

"Just calling it as I see it, is all."

I take in the way Alysha keeps eyeing me. Does she too think I should play for the NHL? Heck, her father owns a team. Does she think I'm too much of a coward to try? That I'm taking the easy way out by simply joining the family business? Could Granddad be right, and that if I don't follow my skills, I'll be throwing away a chance I'll never get again—a chance very few are offered. But I'm skilled at farming, too, and that's where my passion lies. I want to be here for my family and someday want to fill this old farmhouse kitchen with my own noisy kids.

My phone pings again, and too afraid to check it and find out it's Lexi messaging, I walk to the toaster. "Bagel?" I ask Alysha.

"Sounds great."

"Same," Lauren says, followed by Monica and Lucy.

"You three can get your own. Alysha is a guest."

They grumble, and don't bother moving, so of course I go ahead and grab three more bagels to toast.

"Alysha, tell me what it's like to be a famous dancer?" Lucy asks, a look of longing in her eyes, but she has the coordination of a newborn baby deer trying out its legs for the first time, so I don't see a future in dancing, but hey, one can dream, and one should never give up their dreams.

Alysha laughs, "First, I'm not famous."

"Not yet," Monica says. "But you're going to be a star."

"What makes you say that?"

"Ryan. He told me that."

I turn and eye Monica. "When did I tell you that?" I don't recall having a conversation with Monica about Alysha's dancing since I've been home.

"When you came home for the summer. You were telling us about the year-end recital, and how your friend was an amazing dancer." Monica spins in the kitchen, nearly losing her balance and crashing into the stove. I catch her and balance her, even though I'd like to strangle her. "Don't you remember?" she asks as she rights herself.

"No, I don't."

Okay, maybe I do now at the reminder, and I don't normally blush, like ever, but Alysha is biting her lip after my sister let the cat out of the bag that I'd been talking about her, and now I'm fucking embarrassed. Then again, I let her know I'd been fantasizing about her when I got her naked said I knew she'd be perfect.

"So what about that tour of our potato barns?"

"Eww, what do you want to see that for?" Lucy asks.

Alysha shrugs the comment off. "When in Rome, but I thought we were going to the hospital."

"Yeah, we are." Billy bleeps, as if to remind me as well. I turn to the bagel after it pops. I really just want to get away from my family before they embarrass me any more.

"I'd like to hear more about the tractor races," Alysha says. "Are they this week? I'd love to see them."

"Yeah, early on Christmas eve, before the sleigh rides, exhibition hockey game and community potluck. Mom is hosting it this year, here at the farmhouse."

"So I'll get to see it?" There's so much enthusiasm in her eyes that my heart has a hard time keeping a steady beat. I thought I was going to have to work at keeping her happy while she was here, but she's just so easy to be around, and seems to find excitement in the smallest of things. I like that about her. She's from a high maintenance lifestyle, and it's rude of me to even think she might have been hard to entertain because she comes from the Hamptons.

As my sisters tell her all about the events, I toast everyone's bagels and hand them out. I chow mine down and sip coffee as I watch Alysha listen intently. Once we're all done eating, I glance at her. "Are you ready?"

She nods and I turn to the girls. "Since I made breakfast, you three can clean up."

They grumble as I stand, but get to work on tidying the kitchen as I lead Alysha to the door and help her into my big pair of boots again. Her ankle really is a lot better, but I think the extra room is still a good idea.

I leash Billy, and open the door to head to my car, and I note the odd way Alysha is gazing at me, a half smirk on her face.

"What?" I ask.

"So you talk about me, huh?"

12

ALYSHA

I'm feeling a bit worn out, but also excited to meet Ryan's friends by the time we reach the pub—I think it might be the only pub—in this small town. As Ryan circles the lot, I stifle a yawn. I think all this fresh air is doing me in. Either that or our morning spent at the hospital. It was heartbreaking to see so many sick children, but when their faces lit up, as Billy traipsed around it was so moving.

I'm not surprised at how good Ryan was with the kids. He has younger sisters, but the hockey team at the academy also do volunteer work at the local hospital. They carry a puppet and I have to say, I'd love to see Ryan in action with it. I'm sure he's hilarious. After the hospital, we drove around the Cavendish, and he showed me all the touristy sites, and the Anne of Green Gables house. Everything is closed down for the winter of course. I didn't say anything, but I'd secretly love to come back in the summer when the place is bustling. Ryan grumbles about the tourists, as a local would, but they keep the economy going.

He finally squeezes the big wagon in between two huge trucks and shoves it into park. "Ready?" My heart leaps when I turn to him. Is he getting better looking by the minute? I'm not sure, but the mere sight of him does weird things to me.

I try to sound casual, and not like I want to skip the pub and climb into the back seat and have my way with him when I answer with, "Yup." I reach for the door.

His hand lands on mine and my gaze jerks back to his. Has he read my mind again? He does seem very good at that. "I'll come get you."

"I can get out. I'm not in your big boots anymore." While I appreciated the boots when my ankle was bad, I was walking like one of those pups whose parents put shoes on it, and then recorded the insane way it walked. Yeah, I was that bad.

"No wait, I don't want you to slip."

I roll my eyes at his overprotectiveness, but secretly adore it. "Then you'll never get rid of me."

He makes an exasperated sound. "Exactly."

"Strays," I tease. "They never know when to go home."

Chuckling, he comes around my side. While I'm not in his boots, I'm in his big coat. Apparently, my stylish coats aren't really appropriate for the cold weather tonight. Not that I think we're going to spend much time outside.

Music trickles from the door when someone exits and Ryan grabs it to hold it open for me. I glance inside to see a band playing in the corner, a few people dancing, while others fill tables or play darts in a back room. I don't think I've ever played darts. An instant warmth and comfort comes over me as the server walks by.

"Grab a seat anywhere, luv."

"Did she just call me luv?"

"Yeah, that's Denise." He smiles at Denise as she gives him a wink before dropping a couple of drinks at a table. He puts his hand on my back, and I love the sensations that rocket through me. We begin to walk and my steps suddenly slow.

His head dips, and his brow furrows, and he looks like he's seconds from scooping me up and carrying me. "Alysha?"

"What the heck, Ryan?"

His body stiffens, and the line in his forehead deepens. "What?"

"You told me to wear something loose and comfortable."

"Yeah."

"Then why are all the girls here in tight skirts, pants and dresses."

He glances around, and nods as he takes in the girls having fun on the dancefloor. "I was thinking about your ankle. Something for you to move around easily in." My gaze drops to the baggy sweatpants his youngest sister lent me, and the loose knit sweater he dug out of the back of his closet. Apparently, it was one of the first things he knitted when his grandmother taught him all those years ago. While I like being wrapped up in it, I also feel completely out of place. At least I have a T-shirt on underneath and can peel it off If need be.

I catch the way he keeps turning from me. "Hey, what's really going on here."

"Nothing, I just wanted you to be comfortable."

"I was comfortable in my yoga pants," I mutter. "Next time I come back here, I'm wearing something cute."

"I think you look cute."

"Okay, something sexy," I counter.

His head dips lower. "I think you look sexy."

Heat rushes up my spine at the hungry way his eyes move over my body. Clearly he's been studying and playing hockey too hard if he thinks I'm sexy in clothes that resemble potato sacks. Then again, he does love potatoes.

With his mouth near my ear, so I can better hear him over the music he says, "Do you mean next summer?" He inches back to see my face, which is twisted in confusion. "When you come back next summer on the ferry. Is that when you're going to wear something sexy?"

My heart thumps at his closeness and before I can answer, before I can tell him next summer will likely never happen, he pulls himself up to his full height. That's when I realize some guy just slapped him on the back.

"Jesse," Ryan says and the two guys hug, patting each other on the back, like guys do. They say a few words and the second they break apart, Jesse turns and smiles at me. I instantly like him. Islanders seem to be very warm and welcoming people, with the exception of Lexi. She looked like she wanted to toss me into the cold Atlantic waters.

"Hey," he says and holds his hand out. "I'm Jesse. Ryan told me he was bringing a friend, but he didn't tell me she was beautiful."

"Down, boy," Ryan says, clapping Jesse on the back. He's laughing and being playful, but there's something there, just below the surface. Is it jealousy? Possessiveness. Nah, couldn't be. It's not like we're a couple, but Ryan does protect those he cares about and he does care about me. He told me so.

"Nice to meet you, Jesse. I'm Alysha."

"Ryan's best kept secret, obviously." He turns to Ryan and grips his shoulders. "Dude, no wonder I haven't heard from you."

"Alysha and I are friends. She needed a place to stay. I'm just helping her out."

"Oh, so she's not your girlfriend? I can buy her a drink?"

Ryan scrubs his face and I laugh at them. "I'm actually coming off a bad break-up, and how about I buy a round for everyone?"

Jesse throws his arm over Ryan's shoulders. "Jesus, I like her." He leans toward me. "Sorry about the bad breakup. Guys are assholes." He pats Ryan's chest. "Except for my buddy, Ryan. He's one of the good guys."

"You don't have to sell him to me. I know he is."

I smile in agreement, and Ryan starts leading us through the pub. We find a table, away from the music so we can chat, and I order a pitcher for the table. Denise brings it, and Ryan pours for us.

"Are you from Halifax?" Jesse asks.

"No, actually. I just go to the Academy. That's how Ryan and I know each other. We hang out with the same group of friends."

Jesse takes a sip of beer and waves to someone in the distance. "Where are you from?"

"Um...The Hamptons, actually." He angles his head and I don't know why I'm suddenly uncomfortable. Maybe I just don't want to talk about myself.

"You look familiar. Have we met?"

"I think we're past pickup lines, Jesse," Ryan teases, purposely putting his hand on my leg beneath the table. My gaze flies to his as his touch seeps under my skin and settles deep in my core. God, I really hope he sneaks into my room again tonight.

Jesse laughs. "Asshole."

Just then two more people join us at the table, and Ryan stands to hug them. I smile as I watch. He's obviously well liked in hometown, and why wouldn't he be? He introduces Dillon and Sam, and when he tells them who I am, unlike me, he uses my last name. That's when Jesse's jaw drops to the table.

"Is your dad Brian Tiffany?"

I squirm, suddenly uncomfortable.

"Want to dance?" Ryan says, even though he knows I can't.

"I, ah..."

"Shit, your dad is the guy who bought the NHL team in Boston, isn't he?" Jesse says and the other two guys who'd joined all turn my way.

"Yes, that's my father."

Whistles reach my ears, and Ryan reaches beneath the table to give my leg a supportive squeeze. It's not something I like to talk about. I don't like coming across as privileged and I don't want anyone thinking I can pull strings and get them on the team. Not that anyone has tried.

Ryan leans into me. clearly picking up on my unease. "Want to get out of here?"

I shake my head no. He's not seen his friends in a while and I'm a big girl. I can handle myself. My dad bought an NHL team. It's just one more thing he owns. No big deal, right?

"That is amazing." Dillon whacks Ryan. "Hey Ry, are you going to play for his team?"

"No," he says sharply.

The three guys turn my way again, and start asking a million questions. I shrug. "I'm sorry. I don't really follow hockey."

More questions follow and Ryan looks like he's about to put a stop to them, when a female voice sounds from behind him and the entire table goes quiet. I'm grateful that no more questions are being directed my way until I turn and see who's standing behind Ryan.

"I have to hit the boys' room," Dillon announces and jumps up. His chair scrapes back and nearly topples over. He makes a quick exit and Lexi drops down into his seat. I glance at Sam who pushes to his feet and takes off too.

"So what were we talking about?" She smiles and toys with the straw in her drink as her gaze moves around the table. Wow, her smile is sugary sweet when it lands on me. A very different greeting than yesterday.

"Nothing," Jesse mumbles and takes a big swig of beer, putting his hand up to call Denise over for another pitcher.

"Want to play darts?" Ryan asks.

"Love to."

"Wait, I just got here," Lexi says. "We weren't even introduced yet. All I heard was something about your father owning an NHL team." She takes a pull from her straw as my stomach tightens. She offers me a pitiful smirk. "That makes sense," she says under her breath. At least I think that's what she said, and I assume she means that's the only reason a guy like Ryan would be with me.

I inch my chin up. "I'm Alysha," I say and put my hand around my beer glass to give it a squeeze. I hate her, and how she hurt Ryan, and I refuse to give her any kind of satisfaction by letting her think she's getting under my skin.

"Let's play darts." Ryan stands, and reaches for my hand to help me up.

I take it and push to my feet, and another glance full of pity fills her face as she takes in my baggy clothes. Fuck you, Lexi.

I could explain, but she's not worth my breath. Ryan keeps my hand in his as he leads me to the darts.

Ryan shakes his head, like he's still suffering the effects from her abuse. "Sorry about that."

"She's something."

"She's nothing," he corrects.

I grin at him. "Yeah, she's nothing."

"Doubles?" Jesse says, bringing the pitcher, and Sam carrying clean glasses. They both look a little shell-shocked as they glance at Ryan, checking in on him like good friends do.

Jesse pours the beer and we all clink glasses before taking a drink. Dillon comes back from the boys' room.

"Damn," is all he says, and grabs the beer Jesse poured for him. "Damn," he says again and takes a big drink. Everyone laughs and it lightens the tension in the room.

"Okay," I say. "I have no idea how to play. I just want to put that out there before we pick partners."

Ryan nudges me. "You're my partner."

"Did you not hear what I just said?"

"You're my partner."

Okay, wow, that possessiveness I thought I spotted earlier is back in his eyes, in every cell in his body, and dammit, I kind of like it.

"Fine, how do we play?"

He puts a dart in my hand and stands behind me, his chest pressed against my back, and how he expects me to play darts and not put an eye out when he's crowding me like this, is beyond comprehension. Now I'm glad I have big clothes on, otherwise his friends would see the hardening of my nipples.

"It's easy." He holds his hand over mine as he goes over the rules and moves my hand back and forth to help me zero in on the red dot in the middle.

"Shoot."

"Don't worry. That was just a practice shot."

"I get to go again?"

"Yeah." He picks up my dart and hands it to me. I concentrate and take a shot, surprising myself by actually hitting the board this time. My gaze flies to Ryan, and my stomach swirls when I find him smiling at me.

He nods and as he stands there, leaning against the wall, his legs crossed at the ankle, it's all I can do not to throw myself at him. "Nice."

Jesse takes his shots and kills it, and it's obvious these guys have played a lot of darts in their day.

"All right, step back," Ryan says and rolls up his sleeves. "Let me show you all how it's done."

I laugh and move back, taking his spot on the wall. He hits the red dot first shot, and turns to wink at me, but his smile falls dead before someone steps in front of me, blocking Ryan from my line of sight.

I take in the tall, broad guy who just blocked Ryan from my line of sight, and stand up a bit straighter.

"Hey, you new around here?" the guy says, as Ryan's curses curl around the stranger's body and reaches my ears.

●13

RYAN

What the fuck is Owen doing here, and why the hell is he cornering Alysha like she's Little Red and he's the motherfucking wolf? I take a step toward them, no longer able to see Alysha as he hovers over her small frame. I don't have anything against Owen. Hey, if he wanted to be with Lexi after I broke up with her, that's on him. I had no hard feelings toward him. It's not like he took my girl.

I move in beside Owen and put my arm around and pull Alysha to me. "Your turn," I say. I glance at Owen, and nod. "Owen."

"Hey Ryan," he says cheerily. "Didn't know you were back."

"Yeah, I'm back."

"I'm back too."

I resist the urge to say no shit and hand Alysha the darts. I stay close to her, putting my body between hers and Owen's in a possessive way. I protect those I care about, and I don't think Owen would hurt her, but there's something else bugging me here. I'm just not sure what it is right now.

"I heard her dad owns the NHL team in Boston."

And there it is...

"Yeah, so."

I fold my arms, and stand tall as he nudges me. I don't budge. "Nicely done, buddy."

"What the fuck is that supposed to mean?"

"It means, way to get yourself in with the owner's daughter. You're sure to get a spot on the team now. Sweet deal."

I stare at Owen, who isn't even bothering to keep his voice low. Did he take one too many hits to the head on the ice or something? Alysha is standing right here, and he's being a disrespectful asshole.

"You've got it all wrong, dude. Alysha and I are friends."

His face changes, a new kind of lightbulb going off in the back of his brain. "So you two aren't—"

What we are and aren't doing is none of his business. "We're friends. Good friends." I glare at him, sending home the message that I protect those I care about, but he already knows that. Everyone in my home town does.

He looks at Alysha again and slaps me on the back. "Good seeing you, buddy." He steps away and Alysha turns to me. Her fingers are almost shaky as she tucks her hair back.

"What was that all about?"

"That was Owen," I tell her.

She narrows her eyes. "Lexi..."

"Yeah, the guy Lexi latched on to after me."

"You don't like him?"

"I didn't like the way he was looking at you, or that he insinuated I was getting with you to get on your father's team." She glances down, and I touch her chin, bring her eyes back to mine. "Alysha?"

"It never occurred to me that people would think that."

"The truth is, I'm with you to get into your pants, not on your dad's team."

This makes her laugh out loud. "I don't think my pants will fit you."

"Let me make this perfectly clear. I don't want to wear your pants. I want them on the floor beside me when I bury my face between your legs."

She gulps, her eyes wide and a strange sound crawls out of her throat. Once she realizes people are looking, she clamps her hand over her mouth.

"The truth also is this. You're beautiful and guys want to get with you because you're fun to be around, you're a nice person, and well... there's the flexibility thing you have going on, too," I add as a joke.

She laughs and whacks me. "On that note." She shoves me. "I'm making a trip to the little girls' room." I watch her go, a grin on my face, but it drops into my stomach when Lexi pushes up from the table she's at with friends and follows her.

"Fuck."

"You okay?" Jesse asks.

"Lexi just followed Alysha to the bathroom."

"Your girl is causing a lot of commotion around here."

I'm about to open my mouth and tell him she isn't my girl, but from the way he's looking at me, I'd be wasting my breath.

"Yeah."

"Is she really coming off a bad breakup?" I nod, and he just bobs his head. "I know," I say.

"As long as you know."

"Do you think I should go in there?"

"I think your friend can hold her own."

I grin, liking that he thinks Alysha is tough. She's small but she's mighty, and I don't think too much scares her—other than going home this holiday season. I never did find out why and I don't think she wants me to know, so I'm not pressing.

"You know, I think she can too."

"I know you're not with her to get on her dad's team, but how cool would it be to play for Boston?"

I eye Jesse. He knows I want to farm, so why is he asking me that? I guess maybe he's thinking if Alysha and I were serious...holy shit, wait.

I snort. "A farmer would never be good enough for the little girl of a man who owns numerous billion-dollar businesses, a sports team being one of them, huh?" He exhales and is about to speak. I put my hand on his back. "It's okay, Jesse. I know you, you're not being a prick. You're just grounding me in reality, but I'm already grounded. Alysha and I are just having a holiday hook-up."

I turn back toward the hall, waiting for Alysha to emerge, and that's when I spot Amy, Lexi's younger sister. What the fuck is she doing in here. She's Lauren's age and is too young to be at the pub, looking like she's...drunk.

"Fuck."

I cut across the room, and when Amy sees me, her smile goes wide and she throws her arms around me. The smell of alcohol makes me wince. "What are you doing, Amy?"

"Partying."

I take a look at her friend who is also underage and I curse as I search for the bouncer. He's nowhere to be found. "How did you guys get in here."

"We have ID," her friend says and produces a little plastic card. I glance at it, read her name and hand it back. It's as fake as my teammate Blair's replacement front teeth. "Come on, Amy, you too, Jessica. You're both going home."

"No, we're not."

"Yeah, you are. You both had enough and those ID's are fake."

"Are you taking my sister home?" Lexi asks, catching me off guard as she saunters up behind me, putting her tits against my back. I step away.

"They're drunk and nothing they are doing here is safe."

"I was watching out for them."

I note the dilation in Lexi's eyes. Yeah, she's had one too many too. I look over her shoulder. "Did you see Alysha?"

She leans into me, like she wants to kiss me. "Oh yes, we had a lovely chat in the bathroom. Prince Edward Island is a dreadful place to bring a girl from the Hamptons, Ryan." She snorts. "Especially in the winter. Do you hate her or something?" Her laugh is almost maniacal. I spot Alysha coming down the hall, and I put my hands on Lexi's shoulders to sit her down.

"I'll be right back."

I hurry across the room, and take in Alysha's curious eyes. "Lexi's younger sister is here and she's drunk. I couldn't live with myself if I didn't see to it that she and her friend got home safely." Alysha looks at the table with the three girls.

"Will Lexi be going with you too?"

"Yeah, I think so." I slide my hand down to capture hers. "Let's get out of here."

"I honestly don't want to be stuffed in the car with them. How about I wait here and you come back when you're done."

I frown. "Are you sure?"

She nods toward Jesse. "I'll hang out with Jesse and Dillon. I'll be safe, don't worry."

"They can all sit in the back seat—"

"I'd rather not spend another second around Lexi."

I nod, totally understanding the feeling. "Okay, I won't be long. Sit tight, have a drink, and then we'll get out of here when I come back."

I'm about to leave, but she puts her hand on my chest and in a public display of affection, after we told everyone we were just friends, she goes up on her toes and kisses my cheek. "You're a good guy, Ryan."

"Yeah, I know," I joke. "And good guys come in last."

"Are you in a competition with someone?" she asks.

I stare at her for a moment. Not sure if she's just playing or not. "No, but when I compete, I compete to win." She smiles at me and pats my chest.

"Drive carefully."

I stand and watch her for a moment as she walks back to Jesse and Dillon. They grab a table, and I walk over to Lexi. "Let's go."

The two underaged girls groan reluctantly, but Lexi jumps up and slides her arm through mine. "What are you doing?"

"I might have had a little too much and I'm a bit wobbly." I turn and glance over my shoulder, meeting Alysha's eyes. I shake my head and so does she. I get all these girls into my car, and back out of the parking lot.

"I can't believe you still drive this," Lexi says with a laugh. "Remember back there." She gestures with a nod toward the back hatch area. I shake my head. I am not going down memory lane with her. I'm seeing that she gets home safely and then I'm going back to Alysha.

"She doesn't seem like your type."

Don't engage, dude. Don't engage.

"We're friends."

"Friends who fuck," she states and I grip the wheel harder.

"Listen, Lexi, I'm not getting into this with you. I'm giving you a lift home and you should never have allowed your sister or her friend get into the pub with fake ID's." It does make me wonder if Lexi has any friends anymore. Maybe her sister is the only one who will hang out with her these days.

"All I'm saying is she doesn't seem like your type."

"Why because she doesn't lie, doesn't try to make me into something I'm not?"

Fuck, why did I engage?

Angry with myself, I tighten my hands on the steering wheel. Lexi recoils and puts her arms around herself like my response was like a slap to the face. I shouldn't have said anything. Fuck, the past is the past and I'm not interested in hurting anyone, not even Lexi.

I turn the music on. "Let's just listen to the radio."

"You're throwing your life away, Ryan. You can be a great hockey player. Why you're choosing the farm is beyond me."

"It's not your problem anymore." I've told her far too many times that farming is my life, it's in my blood and soul, and brings me peace. I don't need the fame that comes with the game. I want a simpler life.

"If *she* wanted you to do it, would you?" She spits out the word *she*, like it's full of venom.

"Alysha would never ask me to do it."

Okay, I really need to stop engaging. I've said enough as it is. I turn the radio up louder and Amy moans from the backseat.

I adjust my rearview mirror. "You okay, Amy?"

She puts her hands around her stomach. "I think I'm going to be sick."

"Fuck." I pull the car over, jump from the driver's seat and help her out. Lexi stays inside the warm car and so does Jessica, as I hold Amy's hair back and she vomits all over the sidewalk. "Get it all out," I say quietly.

She stays crouched for a bit, and when she finishes, I help her to her feet, and tuck her hair behind her ears. "Thanks," she murmurs and wipes her mouth with the back of her hand. "Ry..."

"Yeah."

"I think you'll be a good farmer."

I chuckle, make a fist and lightly nudge her. "Do you now?"

She nods. "I do."

"Okay, kiddo, let's get you home."

I help her back into the car, and stay silent as I take them home. I ease into their driveway and the house is quiet. I help them all from the car and up the walkway. We reach the landing and I'm about to open the door when it pops out in front of me.

"Ryan," Lexi's mother says, shock all over her face. Shock and embarrassment. "What..."

Her words fall off as Amy stumbles forward. "I think I'm going to be sick again." Mrs. Baxter puts her arm around her daughter. "Thanks," is all she says, and I walk away. Not my circus, not my monkeys. Not anymore, anyway.

The car reeks, so I roll the windows down as I drive to the pub. I park and hurry inside, and the second I spot Owen seated far too close to Alysha, it brings out some sort of caveman inside me. I stomp across the room, and meet Alysha's eyes. I telegraph a message that it's time to go and she stands when I reach her. Without thinking—okay, maybe I am thinking and I want to mark my claim—I pull her to me, and plant my lips on hers.

She's shocked at first, but then her body softens in my arms. I break the kiss and turn to Owen who is staring at us, anger in his eyes. "I thought you said you weren't fucking."

"What we are and aren't doing is none of your fucking business, but yeah, we are, so keep your fucking eyes and hands off her."

Jesse chuckles and Alysha is looking at me like she's not sure what to do or say. "Let's get out of here," I say.

She goes up on her toes. "What was that you said earlier about getting with me to get into my pants..."

14

ALYSHA

Ryan gives me a grin full of promises and his fingers tighten around mine. His head lifts and he nods to his friends. "Catch up with you guys another night."

"Sounds good," Jesse says and Dillon nods.

He gives my hand a tug and practically drags me through the gawking crowd. I guess Ryan isn't one to lock lips in public with his girl. Not that I'm his girl. I'm not. Okay, I am for this holiday season, but that's it.

While I hated the idea of him having to 'handle' Lexi and her sister, I am glad I stayed here. I enjoyed talking to Jesse about veterinary school, and Dillon and Sam about their plans for a destination wedding next year.

We reach the car, parked in a different spot of course, and he opens the door for me to slide in. "I think Dillon and Sam make a great couple."

"Yeah?"

"I loved talking to your friends. Will you be going to their destination wedding next year?"

"If they invite me."

I laugh. "You're invited. They just haven't gotten that far along in the planning. Dillon still has to finish pharmacy school and Sam is doing his master's in business." I turn to him, put my hand over his. "I think it's pretty cool that they have plans to open and run their own pharmacy."

"Now if only we can get more doctors on this island."

"Talk to Daisy. Maybe she'll come."

He nods, like he's really considering that, but then he shakes his head. "I'm sure this place is too small for her."

"You'll be here, and your whole family. They'd love her and Brandon can write anywhere." I glance into the night. "Long winter nights by the fire. It all sounds cozy and romantic."

"Until you have to do it."

"Hey, you say it like it's a horrible thing."

"It is for some," he responds, and flips my hand so he can hold it.

"That was some kiss back there."

He chuckles. "I hope that was okay. Owen was pissing me off."

"Wow, I should provoke him more often."

"Are you saying you liked it?"

"That's exactly what I'm saying." I lean forward and eye him. "Is that not computing? Have you taken a hit to the head or something?"

"Cut it out." He shakes his head. "

Fine I'll kiss the hell out of you every time we're out if you like it so much."

There's a beat of silence and then I break it. "Why was Owen pissing you off so much?"

"I didn't like the way he was sitting so close to you."

"Yeah, and I didn't like the inquisition."

The car begins to slow. "What? Did he say something to upset you? I'll turn this car around right now and go straighten him out."

I bite my bottom lip. Ryan is a pretty quiet, easygoing guy, but wow, when provoked, look out.

"No, it's fine. He was just asking about Dad's team, and if you were being scouted."

"He should mind his own business." He squeezes my hands. "Sorry. We don't have to go back there."

"I'm pretty sure no matter where we go, we'll be running into your friends. It's a pretty small town."

"I wouldn't consider him my friend." He flicks on his signal light with far too much force and I worry he's going to snap it off in the old vehicle. "Not anymore."

"I can see why he and Lexi hit it off."

My statement seems to catch him by surprise. His head jerks my way. "Why would you say that?"

"She followed me into the bathroom."

"Yeah, sorry. I saw that. I should have asked."

"It's okay, a lot went on tonight."

He casts me worried glances. "Did she say anything to you?"

"Basically she said you were with me because you wanted to get on my father's team, and once that happened, you two would be getting back together."

"She's out of her mind, and jealous of you."

"Of course she is." He arches a brow. "Look at you, you're a real catch. Everyone should be jealous of me." He chuckles and I go serious and add, "You deserve way better than she was ever going to give you, Ryan."

"Aly..."

"Yeah?"

He scrubs his chin, his eyes narrowed, deep in thought as he stares at the dark road ahead. "Your parents would hate me, wouldn't they?"

"Why would they hate a guy who took me home when I was injured and is going out of his way to make this a great trip for me?" He smiles, but I get exactly what he's saying. I exhale. "I don't think they'd hate you, Ryan. I just think they love Linc, and have a certain vision of what married life would be like for me." He goes so quiet my chest starts to constrict. "Not that they'll ever meet you and if they did and didn't treat you right...let's just say I wouldn't stand for that."

Why then did I stand for four years letting them push Linc and me together?

Oh right, coward.

But the thoughts of them disrespecting an amazing, hard-working guy like Ryan... that would likely push me over the edge of sanity. I guess it's okay when they push me around, and really it's not, but if it came to pushing Ryan around, someone I really like, no way.

Quiet once again surrounds us, and I stifle a yawn as I listen to the radio and the warm air blasts against my face. With our windows still cracked, cool wind blows inside and swirls around me. I hug myself.

"Can I close this window?"

"I wouldn't recommend it. Amy was sick. I'll have to take it to the car wash tomorrow for a scrub and vacuum."

"How, uh, awkward was all that for you?" I'm using the word awkward, but realize it could be switched out for painful. Maybe I should have gone with him.

"It was okay. I just…hate that she's not protecting her younger sister, you know."

"Amy's lucky you were there."

"Yeah," he says quietly like he's a little lost in his own thoughts. We drive through the quiet night, and I let the wind blow my hair into a big mess. The house looks quiet, everyone in bed by the time we get back, and he eases old Gertie into the driveway. My phone pings and I expect it to be Mom or Linc, and a little sound of surprise catches in my throat as I read Dad's message. Okay things at home must be really bad if Dad is messaging. He's always too busy to get involved in my little problems.

"Everything okay?" Ryan asks. "Linc…your mom?"

"Dad, actually. It's the first time he's reached out."

"Must be serious."

I laugh. "Yeah, when all else fails they bring in the big guns, aka Dad."

"Is that because you usually listen to him?"

I can't help but wonder if he's talking about my relationship with Linc, and if it was set up by my father. He'd be right, of course. "Yes," I answer quietly.

"Are you going to answer him?"

"Maybe later, after a drink or two. He has a way of talking sense into me."

"You don't think what you're doing makes sense?" I'm hiding from a marriage proposal and that doesn't make sense, but Ryan doesn't know that. When I don't answer, he continues with, "Dads are like that. They have a lot of worldly advice and a lot of influence over our decisions. Even when they're not here."

I take his hand in mine. "Your father would be proud of the man you are, Ryan." A beat of silence. "But..." I let my words fall off. I'm not sure how to say them without upsetting Ryan and it's not my business anyway.

"But...?" he asks.

"I don't know. I guess I was just...I can see that you want to fill his shoes and make him proud. Keeping this farm in the family, being there for those you love. Those things are important to you." I glance around the old homestead. "Is this what you would have chosen if you hadn't lost him when you were so young?"

The muscles in his jaw ripple, and I know I've hit a sore spot. "Farming is what I was born to do."

"According to some, so is playing in the NHL."

"According to some, dancing isn't what you should be doing."

He's not being mean, he's just making a point. But I didn't have someone I love and admire die, leaving a big responsibility on my shoulders at such a young age. "I guess I'm just asking, would you have given the NHL a shot if you didn't feel like you had all this responsibility? Would your father have wanted that? What would his advice to you have been and would you have taken it?"

He sighs and glances into the night. "I don't know, Alysha. My dad did die before he could give advice and yes, I probably would have taken it, but this is the path I'm on, and I have no regrets."

I nod, accepting his answer. There is a part of me that wonders, though. Is he too afraid to try, or too afraid to let down his family...his father. All I want for Ryan is the best, and I don't want him ever regretting not taking a chance at the NHL when he had it.

Maybe he's doing what he wants and I'm only projecting because I'm the only coward amongst us.

"Why don't you head inside and get warm. I'm going to check on the animals."

"Can I help?"

"It's cold and dark. Are you sure?"

I nod, even though he can barely see me in the dark. "I never did get to see the barns."

"Okay, come on."

We both slide from the car and within a second he's by my side and we're walking around the big old farmhouse. Off in the distance, the ocean laps at the shore and I love the sound.

"I'm sure they're all taken care of, I just like being the last one out here at night. It just gives me a sense of peace and security after double checking that everyone under my care is all warm and tucked in for the night."

"Does that mean you'll check on me later."

He laughs. "Of course it does." I can't even describe the warmth that thought generates deep in my soul. I've never met a man quite as protective as Ryan before. The snow crunches beneath our feet and my breath turns to fog as I exhale and glance up.

"I don't think I've ever seen such a clear night or so many stars." A motion light clicks on and I smile at him as we pass under it. "I can see why you love it here."

He makes a sound. I'm not sure what it really means, and by the time we reach the barn, it's forgotten about. He picks up a big flashlight and we walk through the horse barn, and I stand back as he talks to them and checks on food and water, and blankets.

"Does it ever get too cold out here?"

"It gets cold, but we have heat."

A bleeping sound comes from one of the stalls and I turn toward it, but can't see much in the dark. "Does Billy sleep in here?"

"Billy sleeps wherever the hell he wants. He thinks he owns the place."

"The kids sure loved him. That little girl, Cassandra, she was totally smitten."

"Billy is a real Casanova," he grunts as he closes the stall door and secures it.

I chuckle. "If I didn't know better, I'd think you were jealous of a goat."

"Don't think I didn't see the way he was snuggled up on your lap this morning, Alysha. It was all I could do to stop myself from telling you two to get a room."

I stare at him, he's being dead serious, but then the corner of his mouth twitches and I laugh, startling the animals.

"Oops, sorry."

"Do you want to see anything else or do you want to head inside?"

"Is it weird how this ambience feels...cozy and romantic."

"Yes, it is. We're in a stinky horse barn." He captures my hand. "Come on."

"I don't think I'm ready to go inside just yet." We step out into the night and the wooden doors creak as he shuts them and secures the barn door.

"We don't have to." We walk away from the house instead of toward it and I close my eyes as he leads me, simply wanting to take in the quiet and the gentle, soothing sounds of the ocean lapping.

"I might sleep with my window open tonight, just to hear the ocean."

"I thought you lived on the water."

"Your water is different."

His laugh carries in the night. "Things on Prince Edward Island are better, huh?"

"Yeah, even the food tastes better."

"That's because we put love and care into all our produce. Sustainability and providing the highest quality potato is very important to me."

I shake my head. If I heard that statement from a guy Ryan's age before I really got to know him, it would make me laugh. It's not laughable, though. It's commendable.

We start past a huge old barn, and I slow. "What's in there?"

"Nothing now. It's where we used to keep the sheep. But with me gone, sheep are a lot of work, so we sold off the flock. Someday, maybe years down the road, I'll invest in them again. A couple of years ago, Granddad had pneumonia, and my sisters were younger. It proved to be a lot of work. Mom and I decided to lessen the load on the farm."

"Can I see inside?"

He shrugs. "Sure, if you want. Not much to see, though."

He lifts the big board that holds the doors together and they creak open. The aroma of wet wood, and musty space fill my senses, but it doesn't bother me much. He holds the flashlight up and we step inside. I pull my phone out and my heart beats a little bit faster as I step into the space. I have no idea, like zero, what's suddenly come over me, but there's a happiness bubbling up inside me.

I briefly close my eyes as my footsteps echo around us and I walk to the window, and run my finger along the old rolled glass, probably the original from the early nineteen hundreds. Ryan remains quiet and still behind me and I start walking again, music in my mind as my footsteps fill the silence.

"Aly..." I turn to Ryan, and he holds the flashlight up.

"This space," I say, my voice full of light laughter. I turn my attention back to my phone, and turn on my music. It fills every corner of the barn, and Ryan laughs as I spin around, on my good ankle, of course. "This place was made for dancing."

He takes a couple big steps until he closes the distance between us, and wraps his arms around my waist. "I'm not a great dancer, but I'll dance with you, anytime, anywhere, even in this freeze-your-ass-off barn."

I chuckle as he holds me to him, and I know his grip is tight to prevent me from putting too much pressure on my bad ankle. He's so damn sweet like that, it almost hurts my heart.

I hum along, as we move together. He's right that he's not a great dancer, but the fact that he's trying because it's important to me means more than he could ever know.

"I never knew," he whispers, his lips close to my mouth. Good God, is he reading my thoughts again?

I inch back and lift my eyes to his. My heart does a strange little flip as he smiles down at me. "What didn't you know?"

"That this barn was made for dancing."

I laugh and for the first time in a long time, it's light and airy, and ...happy. A complete and utter sense of contentment falls over me, which has everything to do with this man, and that my friends, is a bit scary. We did say this was a holiday hookup only, right?

15

RYAN

I hug Alysha tighter as the wind whispers around us and sneaks its way in through the cracks in the old barn. I breathe in her sweet scent, and for the briefest of moments I gift myself with a vision I probably shouldn't let rise to the surface. But images of Alysha in this barn, dancing with me at night, fills my soul with happiness. It's crazy, I know, and would be nothing short of a miracle. She'll be back with Linc come the new year, even though I hate everything about that. But it's Christmas time, a time for dreaming, and if one can't believe in holiday magic, what can one believe in?

She blinks up at me and I dip my head, and press my lips to hers. I kiss her deeply and her hands go around my back, tugging me to her even harder. The outside world fades around me, and the only sounds I hear are our heated breaths. As our kisses grow more heated, I inch back.

"Let's get inside."

"I like it out here," she murmurs, not budging.

"I do too, but if I strip you off out here, you're going to freeze to death."

She giggles, and the sound wraps around me. "Oh, well, I didn't know that was on the agenda."

I rub my hands up and down her arms to create heat. "Do you want it to be?"

"More than anything."

"Are you sure?" Just a few minutes ago, she'd told me what she was doing didn't make sense, and I get it, she's coming off a breakup and doesn't know her way, but dammit, it makes sense to me—probably because I like her so much.

She angles her head and I think she's going to question me, but instead says, "Positive."

"Good, me too." I take her hand and walk to the barn door. Wind whips over us as I open it, and secure it behind us. "Let's hope everyone is asleep."

"If they're not?"

"It's going to be torturous waiting to sneak into your room. I might have to tug one out."

Snow crunches beneath our feet and the sound mingles with her laugh. The air grows colder as we trek back to the house. I push open the front door and tug Alysha inside. She drops down onto the bench as I close up behind us, and the second I see her sitting there, I drop down between her legs. It's a position I like very much.

She smiles at me and I listen for sound in the house as I help her off with her boots. I check her ankle again, but as far as I can tell—and I'm no doctor—it's much better. She stands and shrugs out of her coat and I do the same. After kicking off my boots, I lead her to the stairs, and when we reach the top, Mom calls out.

"Did you have a nice time tonight?"

I wince. "Yeah, we did. Sorry, I didn't mean to wake you."

"You didn't. I was just reading. Goodnight, Ryan. Goodnight, Alysha."

We both call out good night, and I nod to my bedroom. "Go on in. I need a shower anyway." I want to wash all remnants of Lexi and her intoxicated sister from my skin and brain. I put my mouth close to her ear and love the way her body quivers. "I'll shower and wait for all the lights to go out before I sneak in."

"God, I feel like I'm back in high school."

I chuckle. "Oh, you snuck boys into your room in high school, did you?"

She frowns. "Actually, no. Linc was my..." She pauses and narrows her brow, like she said too much. I run my thumb over my face. If she wants to talk about him, she can talk about him, even though it's like a razor to my heart. "Well, when I was a senior in high school, he was in law school and had his own place."

What the fuck? "How much older is he?"

"Six years."

My stomach cramps. What the hell was a high school girl doing with a guy six years older than her? Better yet, why would her parents want that? The more I learn about her family, the less I like.

"Go on in," I mutter before I say what I really think. I don't want to insult her or her parents. It's not my place. She's about to turn, but I bend and steal one more kiss. As her lips meet mine, a knot tightens in my throat. Should we really be doing this? Everything in her body and eyes tell me she wants this as much as I do, but I also know she's a little lost at the moment.

She inches away a playful grin on her face as she gives me a little finger wave and mouths the words, 'see you soon'. A part of me deflates. I want that too, but now I'm beginning to question my logic. Am I doing right by her? She's trying to figure out what's best for her, and me being in her bed probably isn't helping with that.

Why the hell didn't I keep my hands to myself?

As her door clicks shut, I make my way to the bathroom, and strip off. My phone buzzes and my dick jumps when I read the message from Alysha, telling me her skin is sensitive and she can't get warm, all symptoms of nooky-itis, which makes me laugh.

Jesus dude, what the fuck are you doing?

Maybe a cold shower will help me get my head on straight. I jump in and nearly shriek as the icy water falls over my already cold body. I manage only ten seconds before I switch it to hot. I quickly wash my body and hair, and as I picture Alysha in my bed waiting for me, I take my throbbing dick into my hand. My heart beats fast, aching to be with her, as my mind struggles with what's right and wrong.

By the time I get out of the shower, I've come to the conclusion that I'm doing wrong by Alysha and there is no way I can sleep with her again. Ending this now, until she figures out what makes sense to her, is the right thing to do. I toss my dirty clothes into the hamper, wrap a towel around my waist and step into the hall. With every bedroom light turned off, I flick on my flashlight app and head straight for...my bedroom.

Fuck me twice.

So much for that self-lecture on what's right and wrong. I slowly twist the knob and push the door open. Rustling sounds on my bed reach my ears as I quietly click the door shut, and lock it behind me. A low moan fills the silence and my dick thickens.

"You sound like you've got it bad."

"Nooky-itis," she whispers. "Did you bring the cure?"

I turn my flashlight app off and as my eyes adjust to the dark, I walk to the bed. She sits up, her mouth inches from my tented towel. "I brought it," I whisper.

She unhooks my towel, and a little gasping sound erupts from her throat as she frees my raging cock. "Yeah, you did." She leans forward and I bite the inside of my mouth to stop myself from groaning as she takes my cock to the back of her throat.

"Fuck, that is good," I mumble, and grip the back of her head, letting my hand follow the sweet movement of her head. She moans, because she likes it too and that just makes me harder. She cups my balls and pre-cum drips from my slit as she lightly massages them. She drinks me in, little sounds of delight in her throat. I move my hips, wanting to come down her throat but I need my mouth on her sweet pussy first. I need the taste of her on my tongue when I go to sleep tonight and when I wake up tomorrow, and if we could do it without consequence, I wouldn't use a condom so I could fill her with my come.

My dick grows thicker, and as I near the point of no return, I tug on her hair to pull her mouth off me.

"Babe," I whisper.

She smiles up at me. "The thing I like best about this cure," she begins. "Is it works and it tastes good."

I nearly laugh out loud at her playfulness. "Oh, is that right," I ask and nudge her until she's flat on her back. I gaze at her nakedness, loving that she stripped off and was waiting for me. I can't even believe I was thinking about not doing this. Christ, she needs this and I'd do anything, help her any way I can.

Yeah, like this is all about her, dude. Good try.

Okay, it's true. I fucking need this more than I care to admit.

I move her in the bed and stretch out beside her. Using the tips of my fingers, I begin at her jaw and lightly caress her skin. "Goosebumps," I say. "A new symptom."

She arches into my touch as I lightly circle her breasts, brushing the pad of my finger over her nipples. "Hot and swollen. I'm going to have to do something about that."

"Yes, I think so too."

I lean toward her, and brush my tongue over her nipples. "Is this helping?"

Her hands slide around my head and she holds me to her. "I don't think so. You'd better keep trying." I chuckle and her entire body vibrates. I pull her nipple into my mouth as my hand trails downward and her little whimpering sounds wrap around my dick and squeeze tight. I reach her pelvis and her hips come off the bed. She writhes and shifts and tries to maneuver my hand between her legs.

Fuck, I love how much she wants this—wants me.

I give her what she wants and slide my hands between her legs. I dip into her dripping wet heat and nearly shoot off on her leg as her muscles lightly clench around my finger.

"Ry..." she whispers, and spreads her legs even more, and I pull my mouth away from her delicious nipple and shift until I'm flat on my back.

"On my face, now," I say and she gasps as I tug at her. She sits up and turns to straddle my mouth and her sweet, swollen clit brushes over my hungry mouth. I suck on it and her keening cry wraps around me and hugs tight. Fuck, I love the taste of her, and when this is over—Jesus, I don't want it to be over— I don't know how I'll ever taste another without comparing her to Alysha.

She rocks her hips and shuts down my brain, and she slicks easily over my face, her hot juices searing my flesh. I push my tongue inside her and fuck her with it, and she moans and wiggles and grinds against me.

"Come in my mouth, babe," I command in a soft voice, and she presses down harder, stimulating her engorged clit and a second later, she bursts in my mouth. I lap her up greedily, wanting all her cum on my tongue and she whimpers as I suck and lick and revel in every delicious drop.

Once I lick her clean, she shifts lower, and lifts herself up until she's on her knees, and my rock hard cock is inches from her opening. All I have to do is grab her hips and tug her down and I'd be able to bury myself high inside her. I'm about to do just that when one working brain cell kicks me in the nuts. I grip her hips, ready to move her off me so I can grab a condom when she stops me.

"Ry…" her voice is low, full of need and urgency.

"Babe, what is it?"

"I don't…I don't want to use a condom. I want to feel you cum inside me."

I gulp, because yes, I want that too. "I want that too, but—"

Her eyes go wide, something in my words pushing back the lust and clearing her brain. "Right, no, I get it. You had a pregnancy scare before. I'm on the pill, I just thought—"

I put my fingers on her lips to hush and assure her she's not done anything wrong. "I know you're not trying to get pregnant, Aly." She goes still, her eyes locked on mine. I blow out a breath and add, "I know you're running away from something, but I also know you're not trying to get pregnant to avoid whatever it is you're dodging. I know you don't have an agenda, like…" I don't need to finish that sentence for her to know I'm talking about Lexi.

"My only agenda is avoiding…home," she says quietly.

"Okay." I nod, already knowing that. She's yet to tell me why she's avoiding home, and I'm not going to push. She'll tell me when she's ready and that might be never. She doesn't owe me an explanation. We're not a couple. "I've never had sex without a condom before."

She shakes her head, like she's embarrassed by the whole thing. "It was stupid."

I touch her face, running my palm over her cheek. "No, actually. I think it was the best thing I heard all day."

A grin flirts with her lips. "Really?"

"I want to be inside you, no barriers, Aly. I love that you trust me enough to even ask."

"I do...trust you. I'm on the pill, and I'm clean. I haven't been with anyone in a long time."

I realize she's talking about her 'almost fiancé' here. "You haven't been with anyone in a while either."

I cock my head and grin. "Keeping tabs."

Embarrassment floods her face. "No, I just...we all run in the same circles and I haven't seen you with anyone in...ages."

I push her hair from her face. "It's true. I haven't been." The reason I haven't been is currently straddling me, but I can't come right out and tell her that. I don't want to scare her off. "I'm clean, Aly, and I trust you too. Trust is very important to me."

I put my hands on her hips again, and slowly bring her down. Her mouth falls open as my crown breaches her opening and stretches her wide. I glance down between our bodies, and my heart jumps as her sweet swollen lips spread around my cock.

"Jesus," I say, and she follows my gaze to take in the way her pussy is swallowing my cock. "It feels so good like this." Then again, maybe it's only because it's with her that unprotected sex feels good. I mean, we're protected, she's on the pill.

"Ry," she murmurs and wiggles as I slowly fill her. Her hands go over mine as my fingers dig into the soft flesh of curves and her gorgeous breasts call out to my mouth. I lift myself up and take her nipple into my mouth as I slide in another inch. My dick swells even more, and now I'm not so sure sex without a condom was a good idea, considering I'm going to have to do mental math to keep myself from climaxing before I've even given her every inch.

She wraps her arms around me and I bury my mouth in the hollow of her throat, licking and tasting the saltiness of her skin. God, I could lose myself in her if I'm not careful, and guess what, I'm not being fucking careful at all.

She rocks into me, her nails dragging the skin on my back, and the sensations curl around my balls and tease my orgasm. I lie back down and tighten my hold on her hips as I lift my hips and bury every last inch inside her tight, hot sheath. I grumble under my breath and she laughs and pants at the same time.

"Are you counting sheep?"

"Don't ask," I grumble, and she laughs some more.

"Seriously." She chuckles. "What are you doing?"

"I'm counting sheep," I admit.

"Isn't that what someone does when they're trying to fall asleep? Are you trying to fall asleep, and I'm keeping you up?"

"Oh, I'm up, all right." I pump into her and her eyes roll back as I hit her cervix.

"Then why are you counting sheep?"

"Math," I confess. "I have to count, otherwise I'm going to explode, babe, and I'm not ready for that."

"Oh. Then we should go slow." She lifts up and lowers her body, her sweet cunt squeezing around my thick cock, and I know I'm a goner.

"Slow might be worse."

She takes over, moving her body and lifting and lowering herself on my cock, and I lay there as she takes what she needs from my shaft and tortures me in the most deliciously painful ways. Fuck, I love everything about this.

I curse and try to count more sheep, but my entire body begins to vibrate, and I can no longer catch my breath, but goddammit, I want her to come first. She grinds her clit against my pelvis and the second I hear her little whimpering cry and feel her flood of heat coating my cock, I grip her hips, hold her still and splash my seed high inside her.

Fuck. Me.

I grunt, and I'm sure there's nothing pretty in the faces I'm making, but from the way she's watching me through satisfied eyes, it makes me feel like the most important guy in her life. It's wishful thinking, but right now, I'll take it.

"Babe," I say and cup her face, bringing her lips to mine. "How do you feel?"

"Amazing," she whispers and kisses my mouth and cheeks.

"Same."

"Did it feel better for you without a condom?"

"Yeah, it was unbelievable. Can we keep doing it that way?" I ask, childlike enthusiasm in my voice that brings a laugh to her throat.

"Of course. We can't go back now." She lays her head on my chest and circles my nipple with her finger. After a moment, her head lifts. "Do you think it will come back?"

I glance at her and smile when I take in her playfulness. Knowing exactly what she's getting at, I say, "Nooky-itis always comes back. As long as you're here on the island in the winter, it's hard to escape."

"Hard," she murmurs playfully. "Does it happen in the summer too?"

"It can. The only way for us to know for sure is for you to come back."

She shifts, completely content. "I'd like to come back in the summer."

I try to quell the rush of happiness. Right now, she's feeling the high of an orgasm, and probably isn't thinking straight. Despite that I say, "You're always welcome." I go to my side and go up on my elbow. "There's nothing stopping you, is there?"

"I graduate."

"I know, I do too." I run my finger around her nipple. "Do you have work lined up?"

"Actually, the studio I worked at in Halifax said they could take me on part time."

"That's amazing. I didn't know that."

"That's because I'm not sure. I didn't accept yet and I don't know if I want part time, or to work for someone else. Plus, I don't know what next year will look like."

I'm aware she's talking about Linc, and I don't want his name on her tongue after our lovemaking, so I say, "Have you thought about opening your own studio?"

Her face lights up. "I have. A lot."

"You should do it."

Her smile falters. "Yeah."

"Hey, you can do it if you want to."

"There are dance studios on every corner back home."

"Then open one somewhere that's not back home."

"I'd have to secure loans. I don't think my parents would help out, especially if…"

"If you don't follow the path they want you to follow." Which includes Linc, clearly.

She nods, sits up a bit straighter and tucks the blankets around us, looking very much like she has something on her mind. I wait, and she finally turns to me and says, "My mom gave up dancing for Dad."

"You said something about that. Did she give it up for him, or was she ready to do something else?"

"She loved dancing, but he needed a wife who was involved in charities, and was available to accompany him to important events. I love her, but I don't want to end up like her." I tug her down and hold her to me.

"You don't have to."

She snorts. "Easier said than done."

"I know, but if you want something bad enough, you should fight for it." Christ, I know all about that. I'm the one wanting to take over this farm and everyone is pushing me out. Wanting me to go into the NHL, simply because I'm good at hockey. I hate feeling like I'm not wanted or needed when the only thing I want in this entire world is to be there for those I care about. It's what makes me happiest, what fills my soul with love and gratitude for all I have.

"It's different...where I come from."

I stiffen as Jesse's words come back to me, a reminder that a simple potato farmer would never be good enough for the daughter of a billionaire. "No matter where you come from, everyone has problems, Alysha. They're just different problems."

"Wait, I didn't mean that. I'm not saying my problems are important and yours are...less." She stands and walks to the window. The moonlight shines over her naked body and she shivers and hugs herself.

I push to my feet, walk over to her and wrap my body around hers. I'm still not one-hundred percent sure why she didn't want to go home for Christmas, or why her mother gave up her dance career, but I whisper, "You can't run away forever, Alysha."

"I know, but maybe for just a little while longer. Is that okay?"

My heart pounds against her back, as her words remind me that what's happening between us here has a time limit. "Yes, that's okay."

It has to be okay. What other choice do I have?

"...if you want something bad enough, you should fight for it..."

16

ALYSHA

I wake up early, the beeping sound of a plow backing up pulling me from my slumber. I check the other side of the bed to find it empty, then my gaze goes to my phone. I've yet to message Dad back, and I'd better do it soon, otherwise I wouldn't put it past him to fly here and drag me home. Maybe I should go home. Ryan is right. I can't run away forever. Maybe I should go back home and deal with things like an adult. I realize Christmas is in five days and I probably should be with my family.

But the simple fact of the matter is, I don't want to go home, and it might have more to do with loving it here than avoiding Linc. I can't even imagine what my parents would think of this sleepy farm town, and no way would they understand the beauty, peace and sense of community I feel here. Maybe Dad should come collect me. Maybe he should see that the life of a socialite, a life without dance, a life with a man I don't think I love, would smother the light inside me.

Ryan though, he nurtures that light, brings it to the surface and encourages me to let it shine. God, am I getting in too deep with him after only a couple days? I'm smart enough to know better. My heart however, sometimes it's not so smart. I push to my feet and snatch up Ryan's sweatshirt and tug it on. I walk to the window and spot Ryan in the tractor, clearing the snow that had fallen last night. He spots me and waves and my heart wobbles.

I take in the big man in the tractor, the ease at which he drives it and my damn ovaries squeeze tight. What is it about a man working heavy equipment that I find so appealing? Chatter from downstairs reaches my ears and that's when I realize how late it is. My God, the sex and fresh air are wearing me out. I never sleep until noon.

What kind of guest am I?

I tug on my clothes, finger comb my hair and hurry downstairs to find everyone getting ready for their day.

"Good morning, Alysha," Patricia says as I come into the kitchen. She walks up to the coffee pot and pours me a cup. "Did you sleep well?"

"I can't believe how long I slept." I give her an apologetic smile.

"Don't you worry about a thing. You're a guest and you can sleep as long as you want."

My phone pings again, and Patricia smiles at me. "The girls and I are headed to the shelter to drop off some scarves and mitts. Did you want to come with us?"

"Yes, sure. I should probably check with Ryan. I'm not sure if he had anything planned."

"He told me he had to run into town, some broken fence boards out back need to be replaced." An odd sense of disappointment rolls through me. What, did I really think he planned to spend every minute with me here? He's on a working farm, and chores need to be done.

"Then I'd love to come along. I'll just grab some toast, and take a quick shower."

"No hurry at all." Patricia glances at my phone. "Go ahead and take a minute to answer the message as well. We're not in any rush."

I take a big sip of coffee and give her a grateful smile. "Thanks." She disappears and I step up to the toaster and drop a slice of Patricia's homemade bread in. I've eaten more carbs in the last few days than I have in years. I'm about to turn to search for the jam when a cold set of arms wrap around me and lift me off my feet. I yelp as a chill goes through me.

Ryan sets me down and I turn to face him. The second I do, his lips close over mine and he makes a sound like I'm the best thing he's ever tasted.

"Morning," he whispers.

I try to pull away. "What are you doing?"

"I wanted to give you a proper morning kiss, and you were asleep when I had to sneak out, so I'm giving it to you now."

A bleeping sound fills the kitchen as Billy tries to squeeze between us. "Forget it, Billy. She's mine, and if I have to I'll fight you for her."

Billy bleeps and butts his horns against Ryan's legs.

"Keep it up and you're asking for it."

I laugh. "You realize you're arguing with a goat, right?"

"There's more to Billy than you think. He's a sneaky bastard that one."

I shake my head and turn when my toast pops. Ryan goes to the fridge and pulls out the raspberry jam and takes the lid off for me.

"Your mom said you had to run into town for fencing supplies."

"Yeah." He turns and pulls a spoon from the drawer. Okay, why is he suddenly acting all cagey. "Always something to be done on a farm. Summer and winter."

"Is there anything I can do to help?" I don't want to sound needy, but I really like hanging out with him.

"Nope," he says quickly.

"Oh, okay, your mom invited me along to drop some things off at the shelter, but if you need—"

"Nope." He drops a kiss onto my forehead. "Go with Mom. Tonight after dinner, we can head into town. The cider festival is going on, and so is Winterlude."

"What is Winterlude?"

"National ice carving competition."

"You say that like I should know," I say, and sip my coffee. He looks at it with longing, and I hold my cup out. He takes the mug from me and sips it.

"It's a coast to coast thing, so I thought you might have heard of it."

"I'm American, remember."

"Right, I remember." He takes one more sip of coffee and hands it back, and it's so weird. I've never shared drinks with Linc, or ice cream, or...much else. He'd be repulsed by the idea, I'm sure.

"Want to go?"

"You had me at cider festival."

"I had you a lot of ways," he whispers, his voice taking on a sexual edge that makes me smile. "And I plan on having you a lot more." A noise sounds behind us and he backs up. "So that's a yes to Winterlude?"

"That's a yes. Do we get to vote on the carvings?"

"You bet."

"I'm not an islander, though. Will my vote count?"

"I won't tell if you don't."

His words make me think back to when I took a lick of his ice cream, and that thought makes me laugh, because yeah, I've been licking a lot of things since that day.

He tugs his hat—or as he calls it, his toque—from his head and his hair is so messy my heart melts. Could the guy be any more adorable?

"What's funny?" he asks.

"I never took you as a cheater."

He grins. "I'm not, you know that."

I nod, because I do know that. But am I? Am I a cheater? The truth is, Linc gave me an ultimatum, but did I really deal with our relationship? Should I have definitively said we were over? Maybe I really should have done that before having this nooky-itis fest with Ryan. I know it's a holiday fling, but it's not really fair to Ryan if I haven't officially ended things with Linc, right? Not that I think he wants to take this relationship off the island and back to the academy.

Is that what you want, Alysha?

"I've been wondering," I say quietly.

"What?"

I want to ask him about us, what he thinks is really going on between us, and thinking something might be happening between us could very well be in my own head, so I chicken out and ask, "What should I get your family for Christmas? They've been kind enough to all let me stay here and crash Christmas and everyone is so nice about it."

"You're not crashing anything, and you don't have to get anyone a gift."

"I want to, though."

"Knit them something."

"You haven't even taught me how yet and I'd never be able to knit everyone something in five days."

"Then don't worry about it. The only one you have to worry about is me."

I take in his playful smile. "Oh?"

He wags his brow and leans into me. "I already know what I want."

"Do tell."

"I want you, dressed in my clothes, on my bed, ready for me to unwrap." Someone clears their throat and Ryan backs up.

"Are you ready?" his granddad asks.

"Yup, let me just change out of my wet pants." Ryan winks at me before he disappears, leaving me alone with John.

"Coffee?" I ask.

"Nope, I'm good thanks."

He sits at the table and starts flipping through the newspaper. I don't know why I find that odd. Maybe because back home we read everything digitally, but in this small town, things are still done the way they were years ago.

He looks over the paper. "This NHL team your father bought." His eyes narrow in on me. "They looking for a good defenseman?"

My heart jumps into my throat. "I really don't know much about it," I answer and lower myself into the chair across from him.

"Might not hurt to ask."

Unease works its way through my veins. "I'm not sure Ryan would like it if I did that."

"That boy don't know what he likes." He shakes his head. "He has this crazy idea that he has to fill his father's shoes." He sets the paper down and leans toward me, his words for my ears only. "The boy needs to play hockey. He has a gift and he needs to let go of the idea that he needs to be the man of this house."

I actually think it's commendable. "What do you think...his father would want him to do?"

"Play for the NHL," he answers definitively, without an ounce of hesitation.

"I think he likes farming," I point out, not wanting to over-step but wanting to defend Ryan.

John scoffs. "I've known the boy longer than you have. He thinks we need him around here."

"Don't you?"

He purses his lips, and fine lines form. "We can get by."

I swallow. Ryan doesn't want the farm to just get by. He's doing a degree in agriculture so he can apply new knowledge and keep the place going for generations.

I once wondered if he was too afraid to aim for the NHL, but the more I get to know him, the more I realize he carries the weight of this farm on his shoulders. But is he being fair to himself? He told me I needed to fight for what was right for me. Maybe deep down, his deep sense of responsibility is clouding his vision. His grandfather obviously knows him better than I do, and if he's telling me Ryan should play in the NHL, maybe he's right.

"Can't hurt to ask," he murmurs.

I glance at my phone on the table. Dad has been calling. Maybe when I call him back, I could ask about his new team. It can't hurt just to inquire, right? Ryan comes back into the kitchen looking good enough to eat in his low-slung jeans and big, loose sweater. John clears his throat and stands.

"Took you long enough." He eyes Ryan. "Weren't in there eating my Christmas bark, were you?"

Ryan just shakes his head and laughs at his grandfather's grouchiness, and I try to smile along, but my brain is racing a million miles a minute.

John leaves the room, grumbling under his breath and Ryan looks at me. "Are you okay?"

I widen my smile. "Yeah, why?"

"Was Granddad grouchy with you too? Accuse you of eating his bark?" He laughs. "He eats it, and forgets and then blames us. He loves the stuff and I can only get it for him during the holidays."

I laugh. "Not at all."

"Are you sure he didn't say something to upset you?"

"Positive, now go." I give him a little shove. "Before he accuses me of holding you up, or you having your hands full with me or something."

He laughs as he trots down the hall and I glance at my phone again. Just as I'm about to slide my finger over the screen, my phone rings and I nearly jump out of my socks. I answer the call.

"Hi Dad."

"Alysha," he booms, the sound of his voice making me a little homesick. While I don't like a lot of things my parents do, they're still my parents. "What is going on, Princess? Why aren't you home for the holidays? Your mother is a mess, not to mention Linc."

"What did...Linc say."

"Just that you were bumbling up his holiday plans."

My heart hurts at his words. I hurt my ankle and I'm the one bumbling up his plans, which, undoubtedly was a very public proposal. I hate everything about that. To me a proposal should be quiet, intimate, between two people. It's not about the show.

"Did he say anything else?"

"Like what?" Dad asks.

I swallow, hard. Okay, I guess Linc didn't tell him about the ultimatum, or that I didn't accept it which meant we were broken up. Does Linc still think we're a couple?

"Come home, Princess. Your daddy misses you."

"I miss you too, but…"

"No buts. You belong here, not on some ridiculous potato farm in the middle of nowhere."

I instantly take offense. "It's not ridiculous, Dad."

"Head to the airport, get on the next plane. I'll make the arrangements for you."

"My ankle," I counter weakly.

There's real disappointment in his voice when he says, "Princess…"

"You don't understand."

"No, you don't understand. You are part of the Tiffany family, and your mother is very upset. I don't like it when your mother is upset." I almost snort at that. Does he not think it upsets her when she turns a blind eye to his affairs? "I want you home for Christmas," he continues. "If you don't want to be a part of this family…you leave me little choice…" He lets his words fall off, leaving me to fill in the blanks. Does he mean he'll cut me off, or that he'll come here and collect me himself? He's a busy man. I certainly don't expect him to fly to Prince Edward Island.

"Dad," I begin, but the line goes dead, cutting off any rebuttal I might have. What the hell? I stare at my phone. Maybe he's right. Maybe I should go home and deal with things face to face. Only problem is, my family has a special way of making me see things their way. Well hell, I'm damned if I do go, and damned if I don't.

What am I going to do?

17

RYAN

Granddad casts me a glance as we drive into town in one of the pick-up trucks. "I don't see the sense of fixing up that old barn this time of year," he grouches.

"I know, but I've been putting it off and I like to keep my hands busy when I'm home."

He grumbles something again about keeping my hands safe for the NHL and I ignore it. I don't want to rehash this same debate. The fact is, I haven't been drafted, and I'm not going to get drafted. It's not the future I want, and no matter how many times I tell Granddad that, he balks at it. I really hate not feeling wanted or needed in my own family. I know they can hire help and get by without me, but I want more for the farm. I want to make it into the largest, healthiest potato farm on the island, which is why I'm at the academy.

"Too late in the year to fill the barn with sheep," he points out.

"I know. I have other ideas for it."

"Care to fill me in?"

"I'm not one hundred percent sure yet. I want to get it fixed up first and see if I can make my vision possible."

I pull up in front of the lumber mart, and we hop from the vehicle. Inside the store, I go to the back counter and put an order in for wood and nails and a few other things I need. Granddad wanders the store like he always does, and I go in search of him. I round the corner and find him talking to Owen's father, who works in the lighting department.

"Son, get over here," Granddad says, and I hold my hand out and shake Mr. Flynn's hand.

"How's the academy?" he asks.

"Great. I love it there. Learning lots. I ran into Owen the other night."

"Did he tell you he's close to being drafted?"

"Actually no, it was busy and we didn't have time to talk." I'm a little shocked by the news, actually. I hadn't heard anything about Owen getting drafted, and if he was close, he'd be shouting it from the rooftops. "Which team?" I ask, to be polite.

"Boston Bucks."

I blink once, then twice not sure I heard him correctly. If Owen was going to play on the team Alysha's father bought, wouldn't she have said something?

"Good for him. Best of luck to him."

"Which team are you going to play for?" he asks, preventing me from stepping away. I cast a fast glance at Granddad. I don't want to upset him or hurt his feelings, but I don't want to lie either.

"Not sure what's happening there yet," I say and my grandfather just nods, not upset or pleased at my non-answer.

Mr. Flynn slaps my back. "We're all rooting for you, Ryan. It'd be nice to see you and Owen on the same team. You guys played well together back in the day."

"Yeah, that would be great, and thanks." I turn to Granddad. "We should get that wood loaded."

We make our way back outside and I can tell Granddad has something on his mind. I wait for it as I back the truck up and circle the building.

"Boston Bucks would be a great team, Ryan."

"Yeah, new management can really light a fire in a team," I say.

"Not too far from home either."

I pull up to the bay, and hand my receipt over. A moment later, my order is brought over and loaded into the truck. I thank the guys and turn around to head for home. My mind is on Owen, and I know Alysha doesn't like to talk about her father owning the team, but I am curious, and not jealous at all hat if Owen plays for her father, he might see more of Alysha than me. He did, after all, seem rather interested in her at the pub.

Granddad talks about the Boston Bucks the whole way home. He's rather excited by the idea of me playing for them and by the time I reach the house, he seems convinced that it's going to happen and all I can do is let him sit with his thoughts. I don't have the bandwidth to argue it. But for the briefest of seconds, I let my mind consider it. If I did play for Boston, maybe Alysha's parents would be a little more accepting of me.

Look at me getting ahead of myself. Alysha isn't talking long term, and while one part of me is determined to sway her, there's the other part that tells me to stop being selfish, because rural Prince Edward Island is not a place she could call home.

Granddad helps me carry the supplies to the barn, and once we're done and he goes inside, I tug off my jacket and get to work on repairing boards. Before I know it, the day has slipped by and I hear my family and Alysha coming back from town.

I drop what I'm doing, pull my coat back on and head to the front of the house to greet them. My heart jumps in my chest when Alysha turns my way and smiles.

"What have you been up to?" she asks and uses her mitten to brush woodchips from my hair.

"Just doing some repairs. Did you have a good day?"

She nods and excitedly says, "We drove by the ice sculptures. Ohmigod, they are amazing. I can't wait to get a close look at them."

I give her ass a little tap after everyone disappears inside. "Let's get something to eat and then head to the waterfront."

She starts moving. "I really like your family, Ryan. They know everyone in town. We couldn't go anywhere without having to stop to talk to people. They must have introduced me to at least a hundred people. I don't remember any names, though."

I chuckle. "You don't have to. There won't be a test."

She laughs with me. "We picked up some supplies for the Christmas Eve get together. I'm really looking forward to it." Her smile briefly falls off.

"Are you sure?"

"Yeah, just Mom will be having her party that night, and she's not going to be too pleased with me if I don't show up."

"And Linc?"

She takes a quick breath. "And Linc..."

"Do you think he still thinks there's a chance you two will get back together?"

She looks down at her feet, and my heart sinks, with the sudden realization that she might think it too. "I talked to Dad this morning. Linc didn't say anything to him about us, so yeah, maybe he thinks we're not broken up."

"What do you think."

"I think we are."

"What do you want to do, Alysha?" I ask, and narrow my eyes in on her. "Stay or go back home?"

I hold my breath waiting for her answer.

"I kind of want to stay here. I really want to see the tractor races and I think the get together will be fun. We picked up all kinds of ingredients to make fun foods."

There's more she's not saying. I sense it in her. "I don't want you to get in trouble with your family."

"I don't want that either, but I'm a grown woman. I should be able to make my own choices without there being repercussions, right?"

"Right," I agree and wonder what repercussions she's talking about. She doesn't tell me instead she heads inside.

"I'm going to help with dinner."

"I'm going to take a shower." Catching me by surprise, she leans in and gives me a quick kiss. "What was that for?"

"For taking in strays."

I laugh as I head upstairs, and she walks into the kitchen, fitting right in with my family like it's where she belongs. I strip off in the bathroom and wash the sawdust from my skin. I go into my bedroom, find the bed neatly made, and tug on a clean pair of jeans, a T-shirt and a sweater. The stack of Anne of Green Gables books are on the nightstand, unread. When the hell would she have had the time to read? I've been in her bed every night.

I finger comb my hair and head back downstairs. Alysha turns and smiles at me as I enter.

"What's for dinner?" I ask, my stomach grumbling.

Alysha grins and holds up a potato that she's peeling. "Potatoes."

"I never would have guessed," I joke and grab a peeler and sit down next to her to help. Her foot touches mine beneath the table, and she rubs up my leg, looking completely innocent as she concentrates on the potato. I kind of love this playful side of her. I bet all the kids she teaches love her, because yeah, she's easy to love.

I'm not saying that I love her. That would be jumping the gun. Just like fixing up the barn for her is, but goddammit, I just want to…I don't know, I guess I just can't let her walk out of my life without a fight.

"I don't think I've ever had scalloped potatoes before. Do we put scallops in them?" I laugh and she looks at me all confused. "What?"

Mom flings the dishcloth at me. "Be nice."

"I am nice."

Mom turns to Alysha. "It makes sense that you would think there were scallops in them, but the term actually comes from an old English word collop, which means to slice thinly."

"That's all you had to say," Alysha yells at me, and tosses a peel at me.

"I actually didn't even know that."

I toss the peel back and it gets in her hair. "Oops, sorry."

"No, you're not." She fishes it out of her hair and throws it back.

"Do I have to put you both in time out?" Mom asks, as she takes the baked ham out of the oven to check it. We both laugh and go back to peeling the potatoes. Once we're done, Mom shows Alysha how to make scalloped potatoes and I sit back with a cup of coffee, enjoying their camaraderie.

As they prepare the meal, I head into the living room and reach into the wool bin and pull out the stocking I started knitting last summer. I might as well get at it again. If Alysha stays, she's going to need a stocking for the mantle. I sit and look at the tree, a sense of contentment coming over me as I knit. The guys back at the academy would probably tease the shit out of me if they knew I knitted, but I don't really give a fuck. I'm comfortable with who I am.

A short while later, Alysha comes in. "Hey, you started without me."

I pat the sofa and she drops down next to me. "Do you really want to learn?"

"Yes, and talk to me like I'm a baby with a cookie."

I laugh at that. "It's not that hard. Okay, watch me. You hold your needles like this." She nods and I continue. "Insert the needle in your right hand, into the left needle, and back." She watches, rapt, as I show her how to do it. "Form an X and hold it with your left hand. Grab the yarn with your right and wrap it around the needle. That is a knit stitch. Now watch this," I say and pull the yarn forward. "This is a pearl stitch." I lift my head and find her smiling. "What's so funny?"

"I sort of love that you knit."

"My grandmother taught us all when we were kids."

"I love that."

"I wish you could have met her."

"I'm sorry I didn't. Did she and your grandfather always live with you?"

"Yup, they ran the farm before Dad."

"What about your grandparents on your mother's side?"

"Terrible car accident. Winter storm. Mom was a teenager."

"I'm so sorry." I do a few more stitches and reach into the bin and pull out two needles. "Do you want to try?"

"I do. I'm not sure how to get started, though."

"I'll do it with you." I position the needles in her hands and put mine over them." As I sit beside her the position is awkward, so I pick her up and set her on my lap, putting her back to my chest, her legs dangling over mine.

"What are you doing?" she squeaks out.

I widen my legs and she slips between them, her backside on the sofa. "It's easier if we do it this way." I groan as she wiggles, settling herself more comfortably between my legs. Her sweet scent fills my nostrils. "Maybe that's not entirely true," I mumble under my breath.

"What do you mean?"

"It's actually hard."

"I can move."

"I'm not talking about the knitting," I say playfully and pull her against my thickening dick.

"Ryan," she squeals.

I wince as my dick presses against my zipper in very unforgiving ways. "Just stop wiggling and I'll be okay."

"I'm not wiggling," she shoots back and wiggles some more until I'm in complete distress.

I bite down on my cheek and shift so I can tug on my pants. "Jesus, Alysha, I'm dying here."

She chuckles and I move backward as far as I can, so my dick is not pressing into her back. "Do you want to do this or not?" I grumble.

She's trying so hard not to laugh when she asks, "Are we still talking about knitting?"

I shake my head. Why did I think setting her on my lap was a good idea? "You're lucky my family is here, otherwise, I'd put you over my shoulder, take you to the bedroom, tie you up with this yarn, and show you what I really want to do with you."

"Lucky?" She makes a low, distressed sound. "That's not what I'd consider lucky at all, Ryan."

She wiggles and I bite back a groan. "You're saying you want me to do that?"

"More than anything," she murmurs playfully.

Jesus...

18

ALYSHA

"You're going to have to roll me to your car, Ryan." I rub my protruding stomach and groan. I shouldn't have eaten so much, but I went back for seconds, thirds even because it was just so darn good. Why does the food taste better here? I'm convinced it has something to do with all the open space and fresh air. "I have a potato or two rolling around in here."

He laughs. "Try three."

"Hey." I whack him.

He throws his arms open. "Jump."

I consider that for a moment. I do love being in his arms, but I'm too full to jump. "No, I should walk. I need to work off all the carbs."

He bends and puts his mouth near my ear. "I plan to help you work those carbs off tonight," he whispers, his warm breath falling over my skin.

A fine shiver goes through me at the promise in his words. He grabs my zipper and pulls it to my neck and tugs the hood of the coat over the toque on my head, obviously mistaking my shiver for cold. I'm not cold. Nope, it might be single digits outside, but my body is still hot from sitting on his lap—wiggling—before dinner.

Once he has me bundled up like a mummy, he opens the car door for me and I struggle to get in. I can't take my eyes off him as he circles the car and climbs in beside me.

"Warm enough?" he asks.

"It's not like I could add another layer if I weren't."

He chuckles. "I just don't want you cold." He grips my hood and brings my mouth to his. His lips are cold as they fall over mine, but as he kisses me, they warm up. I moan and melt into him and when his tongue tangles with mine, I close my eyes wishing we were on our way to his bed. But I don't want to wish the night away. I want to enjoy every second with Ryan while I can.

Does that mean you're going home for Christmas, Alysha?

Honestly, I don't know what it means. All I know is I want to soak up every second in this town, with this man, for as long as I can. I honestly don't remember the last time I laughed or had fun, or was just....myself.

"We'll get hot chocolate," he says and starts the car.

"Nope, I want cider."

"You need alcohol to get through the holidays with me?" he teases.

"Yes," I answer bluntly. "Especially if you're going to sit me on your lap again and teach me how to knit."

"You did great." He snaps his fingers. "You picked it up fast."

I smile at the compliment and glance around as he pulls onto the main road. "Where did you go to high school? Was it far from here?"

"Not too far, but I went by bus until I could drive Gertie. We can swing by if you want."

"Sure. Are there all kinds of trophies with your name on them?"

"A few. How about you? Does your school have dance trophies with your name on them?"

"Actually, no. I went to a private school, and it didn't have a dance team." I shift to face him. "It had a gymnastics team and I was on that. I danced at a private studio, with a private teacher."

"Nice, and I guess that's why you're so good. All the one on one attention."

"Thank you." I don't know why I expected him to say something about the privilege of a private school. The truth is, I was—am—privileged, but he's not the kind of guy to belittle that anyway. "Do you think I'd be wasting that talent teaching children?"

"Fuck no," he blurts out. "You'd be wasting your talent if you gave it up." He casts a glance my way and I take in his handsome face in the dashboard light. There's a real seriousness about him when he speaks. "Promise me you won't do that, Alysha."

"I won't do that," I tell him and hope it's a promise I can keep.

He goes quiet for a moment and takes a turn into a subdivision. "Anything from Linc?"

I glance at my belt bag, which contains my phone. "No, not in a while."

He goes quiet and I take in the houses in the neighborhood as he drives past them and pulls up to a big school. I smile as I take in the grounds, and the big football field in the back.

"Nice." I smile at him. "I bet you were popular."

He shrugs. "I don't know about that. But I got along with everyone."

"It's nice that you still have close friends from your childhood."

"Do you?"

"I have friends. I get together with them when I'm home, but I wouldn't trust them with my darkest secrets or anything." I make light of the situation, but I'm really saddened by the fact that I don't have friends from home that I can call if I'm upset about something. I do have good friends at the academy, though.

He looks almost sad when he says, "If you feel the need to share your darkest secrets you can tell me. I promise I won't tell anyone." I nod. "Want to get out of here?"

I nod again and he steps on the gas and heads toward downtown. "Thanks." I realize he told me about Lexi and that was deep and dark and painful for him. Should I tell him why I'm really avoiding home? Does it even matter now that Linc and I have broken up—in my mind, anyway.

We reach the busy downtown streets, which are alive with music and people, and cute little kiosks set up selling local crafts and craft beverages.

"How adorable," I say quietly as I take it all in. For the first time in a long time, I'm excited about Christmas.

"We go all out at Christmas around these parts."

My thoughts slow as I take stock of my life, and the people in it. I'm very fortunate to have Ryan and thankful for all he's doing for me. My voice is low when I say, "I think it's really nice."

He grins at me. "Come on, let's go have some fun." I exit the vehicle and in the distance, some girl screams Ryan's name when he comes around to my side of the car.

"Who is that?" I tug my hood down, the fur no longer obscuring my peripheral vision as the girl pushes through the crowd.

He peers into the night and the next thing I know some girl is jumping into his arms and wrapping her legs around him, and no, I'm not jealous at all. "Becca," he says and spins her around. "I was hoping to run into you."

Nope not jealous at all. Much.

"How's life in Victoria?" he asks.

"I love it there. The university is amazing. You have to come out to visit sometime."

"I'd love to. I've just been busy."

She kisses his cheek. "When you're a big NHL star, maybe you'll play in Vancouver, you won't have any excuses."

He smiles and sets her down. "Sounds like a plan."

I stare at them. Why is he not telling her he has no plans for the NHL? Becca turns to me. "Oh, hi."

I take in her cute little bomber jacket and tight jeans. God, I look like I'm in a potato sack next to her. "Hi."

"Becca, this is Alysha. She's..." He pauses and angles his head. "...a friend from the Academy."

Becca puts her arm around me. "Any friend of Ryan's is a friend of mine. Now come on, let's get some cider."

"Ryan," Jesse calls out and waves as he comes over.

"I'll catch up with you," Ryan tells me as Becca drags me along through the crowd, talking a million miles an hour about the different ciders, and the band, and the sculptures.

"So, just friends, huh?"

Wait is she jealous? I glance at her and I can't quite figure out if she and Ryan were a thing and if she might still be holding out for him.

"We're friends."

She snorts. "I've known Ryan a long time, Alysha. I've never seen him look at a friend the way he looks at you."

Okay, sure we've been having sex but that doesn't mean he likes me more than a friend, right? Also, if she's known him forever and knows him well—like his grandfather—maybe she knew what she was talking about when she brought up the NHL.

"Do you think Ryan wants to play for the NHL?" I come straight out and ask when we reach the kiosk with the ciders.

She gives me a look that suggests I might be two potatoes short of a casserole. "Of course he does. He's been playing since he was a kid." She smiles. "He and his dad spent hours at the rink, until...well you know."

"You think his dad wanted him to be an NHL hockey player?"

"Every dad wants their kid to be an NHL hockey player." She eyes me. "Why are you asking this?"

"Oh, no reason." We reach the front of the line and I look at the list of ciders. "They all look so good."

"Let's start with this one," Becca suggests and points to one that says fresh and crisp. "It's made from honey crisp apples and it's delicious."

"Sounds good."

Becca orders and then her eyes go wide. "Don't look now."

I'm about to turn when she shakes her head. "It's Lexi." My stomach clenches. "I'm sure you know the history."

"Yeah."

"We used to be friends," she tells me. "Now, not so much." I slowly glance over my shoulder, and spot Lexi walking with Owen. "I'm surprised to see those two together."

I turn my attention back to the woman in the kiosk as she slides two big cups of cider our way. I reach into my belt bag, but Becca pulls out some bills and pays.

"Thank you. Next one is on me."

A warm body presses up against mine, and my heart flutters. God, why is my heart fluttering.

"What did you decide?" Ryan asks, his breath warm on the back of my neck.

"Honeycrisp," I say and take a small sip. "It's so good. Hey, Jesse."

Ryan holds his hand up to order two, and I step out of line with Becca as Lexi and Owen make their way toward us.

"Ah, why is Owen looking at you like that?"

"Like what?"

"Did you guys already meet?'

"Yeah at the pub the other night. Just briefly."

Before she can say more, Ryan and Jesse join us and we make our way toward the waterfront, where the ice sculptures are on display. Ryan stands close, his body brushing mine as we walk. I glance at his friends. Can they feel the electricity we're generating? I'm a little worried about melting the sculptures if we get too close. He grins at me before taking a sip of cider and my insides warm.

"Look at this one," Becca says and points to a huge lobster. We all walk up to it and admire the craftsmanship then we move along and admire the rest. I think my favorite might be the Canadian beaver.

"Which one are you voting for?" I ask Ryan.

"I'm partial to the beaver," he answers with a wink, and I can't help but grin. Yes, I'm well aware that Canadians like to refer to a woman's private parts as a beaver. I have no idea why and I'm not about to ask.

"Shall we vote?" He nods and we leave Jesse and Becca as they look over the sculptures again, and we cast our vote. As soon as we put our papers in the ballot box, Lexi comes over, looking worried and breathless.

"Have you seen Amy?"

Ryan and I turn to her. "No, why?" Ryan glances over her shoulder and scans the crowd.

"I don't know where she is." She nibbles her lip and searches the faces around us. "She was with me and she was, well...drinking."

"Shit, Lexi."

"Can you help me find her?"

Ryan glances at me. "Do you mind?"

"No, of course not. I can help."

Ryan glances at Jesse and Becca. "Why don't you stay here with Jesse and Becca? I don't want to drag you all over the waterfront. Enjoy your cider and I'll be back fast. I'm sure Amy hasn't gone far." I nod, but I have the strangest sensation in my gut that Lexi might be up to something. "I'll be right back."

"Okay."

I take a sip of my cider as they disappear into the crowd, and I turn to look out over the water and come face to face with Owen. He's standing so close, I yelp and nearly spill my cider.

"Whoa, you okay?"

"Yeah, you just scared me."

"Where are Lexi and Ryan off to?"

"Amy is missing. Have you seen her?"

He shakes his head. "No." He moves even closer. "I wouldn't be surprised to see those two get back together. Ryan never got over her." He snorts. "I should know. When she was with me in Quebec, he was messaging her all the time."

Okay, now that takes me by surprise and honestly, I don't think I believe him. "Really?"

"He said he forgave her and he'd go the NHL route if she wanted him to."

"Ryan wants to farm."

He snorts and laughs at me like I'm an idiot. "Is that what he's telling you?"

"It's what I know."

Owen leans into me, his body close. "Babe, he's using you. Can't you see it?"

"Using me for what?"

"Your father just bought the Boston Bucks, didn't he?" I nod, as my stomach tightens. "Did he have anything to do with you before that?"

"Well, yeah, we're in the same friend group." I glance around.

"All I'm saying is that things might not be as they seem."

My brain races. Ryan didn't correct Becca when she brought up the NHL. Why didn't he do that. I'm not sure, but I guess he has his reasons. No way is he using me to get close to my father.

"When are you back in the Hamptons?" Owen asks leaning in closer, crowding me.

"I'm not sure."

"Maybe we can get together, get a drink or something."

I spot Ryan coming my way. "What...why?"

"I'd love to see you. You're not so far from me in Quebec, and I'll be in Boston soon enough. I think you and I could be something good together."

RYAN

"What the hell did he want?" I ask Alysha as I watch Owen walk away as I approach.

She shakes her head. "It's weird. He talked about coming to see me in the Hamptons."

"What the fuck?" I glance up and catch the back of his coat before he disappears.

"I know, right? I was shocked."

"I ran into his father the other day. He told me Owen was going to be playing for your dad."

"Oh," she says and nods like it's all coming together. "That must be why he's going to be in Boston."

Rage fills me. I don't like the idea of Owen trying to hook up with Alysha. At all. Didn't I make it clear that she was with me when I fucking kissed her.

"I think he has a thing for your girlfriends."

I shake my head at that. "Lexi can have him." I slide my hands around her waist and drag her to me. "You, he can forget." A smile crosses her face, but then it wobbles. Shit, I guess maybe I shouldn't have said that. She's the one that made it clear this was a holiday hook up and there's a part of me that still thinks she's going to go back to that bastard Linc and he's going to rob her of the future she wants. "I didn't mean—"

She goes up on her toes and kisses me. "You're right, he can forget it." Her lips close over mine and soothes the savage beast inside me. I kiss her, taste the cider on her tongue. I moan and inch back.

I gesture with a nod. "Let's get another cider."

"Wait, did you find Lexi's sister?"

"Yeah, she was fine. I don't know what the big panic was all about." Alysha frowns like she might know something I don't. "What?"

"Maybe she wanted to get you alone." A strange, almost jealous look comes over her. "Do you think maybe she wants you back?"

I stare at her for a second. "What did Owen say?" Before she can answer, I add, "If he said she wanted me back, I wouldn't believe it. In fact, I wouldn't believe anything he tells you, Alysha. Don't trust him."

She shakes her head and mumbles, "That's what he said about you."

"Are you fucking kidding me?" I glance up, search the crowd, ready to go have a talk to Owen with my fist.

"Don't," she says and grips my coat to bring my attention back to her. "Can we just have fun tonight?" Everything inside me softens when I see what almost looks like desperation in her eyes. She has enough to worry about with her family, and I don't want to be adding to her troubles.

"Yeah, babe. Let's have fun."

I put my hand on her back and we go grab a couple more ciders. "Where are Jesse and Becca? This next round was supposed to be on me."

"Off having fun. We'll run into them again before the night is over. Jesse mentioned something about his family's cabin."

We grab our ciders and I take her hand in mine as we walk. We head toward the live band playing on stage, and we stand on the closed-off street where tables are set up and listen for a few minutes. Alysha shifts from one foot to the other, and I recognize the winter dance. She's cold.

I set my cider down on a table, and hold my hand out. "Dance?"

She glances around and crinkles her cute nose. "No one is dancing, Ryan."

"So."

"So, we'll make fools of ourselves."

"Did you mistake me for a guy who cared what others thought?"

She grins and shakes her head. "I guess, and I guess these people don't know me and won't see me after this week, so who cares if we make fools of ourselves."

I try not to let her words kick me in the face like an angry donkey—yes I've seen it happen on a neighboring farm—and keep my hand outstretched as she puts her drink down next to mine and holds her hand out to accept mine. I tug her to me, and slide my arm around her waist to pull her close. Her body collides with mine and she laughs as I spin her around, and numerous people turn to watch us. Sure, I'm making a spectacle of myself, but what do I care? Alysha loves to dance, and dammit, I want to dance with her.

"When you open your own studio, I'll be the first to sign up for lessons."

"Good, you need them."

"Hey," I shoot back, feigning hurt. "That's not nice, but sadly, it's true."

"You do realize you said when I open my own studio, not *if* I open one."

"That's right. You'll do it. I have faith in you." I do have faith in her, it's those in her family, I'm not so sure about and I hate that Linc never danced with her.

"Ry..."

"Yeah?"

"If you had the opportunity to play in the NHL, would you?"

Jesus, I thought she knew me better than that and I have to say, it sort of guts me that she doesn't, or doesn't believe me like everyone else I know including my own family. Before I get the chance to answer her, Jesse comes up and bumps me from behind.

"Alysha, how did you get this guy with two left feet to dance?"

"He's the one who wanted to." I let Alysha go, and she hugs herself to warm her body. "But I do love how he's trying." Her smile warms my heart. I like doing things for her. I'd like to do more for her, if she'd let me.

I turn to Becca. "Want to go grab a cider?"

She gives me a coy smile. "Actually, it's getting cold. Jesse and I were thinking of going to his cabin. Light a fire, have some drinks and play some games. Why don't you guys come with us?"

Alysha glances at me, and while I would love that, I'm going to need her alone first. "I'd love to go, but I thought Alysha might like to hang around a little longer for a few more events and she hasn't seen the fireworks. How about we meet you there later?"

Jesse slaps me on the back and grins like he knows exactly what I have in mind—what fireworks I'm talking about. "Take your time, buddy."

They take off, and Alysha smiles. "I really like your friends and that sounds like a lot of fun."

I drag her to me again, and our bodies sway together, fitting perfectly, despite how petite she is—until my second left foot gets in the way and I stumble.

"How many ciders have you had anyway?" she asks, her teeth chattering a bit as she narrows her eyes.

I laugh. "This is only my second."

"What does Becca study in Victoria?"

"She's going to be a nurse. The island is in desperate need of nurses and doctors and veterinarians."

"She's coming back here when she finishes?"

"The funny thing is, some can't wait to get off the island, and others want to come back and give back."

She frowns and looks down. "I guess there is no place for me on this island."

"Why do you say that."

She shrugs. "I mean, I want to teach dance. I wouldn't be bringing anything to the island that is really needed."

I grip her shoulders and hold her tight. "Are you kidding me? You've heard of cabin fever, right—"

"That thing we call nooky-itis?"

I laugh and shake my head. "Yeah, sort of. But the truth is, winters are long and hard here, and the arts are just as important as other services. Dancing can give kids and adults alike something to look forward to, something to help break up the long nights."

She smiles like she hadn't considered that. "I guess you're right."

Something niggles in my brain. "But this island isn't for everyone. I get that."

"No," she says absentmindedly. "I'm sure it isn't. I guess for Lexi it seemed like imprisonment, huh?"

"Yeah. She definitely wanted to escape."

She laughs, but it holds no humor. "I get that."

I angle my head, take in the hurt in her eyes, and my heart pinches tight. "Linc? Your parents? Wanting to put you in a box?"

She nods and a little noise catches in her throat. "Astute," is all she says. I pull her stiff body to me, and hold her close as others join us on the closed off road. As if wanting to shake off a conversation that brings her no happiness, she smiles up at me, her limbs loosening, "Look at you, already getting people up and dancing. Such an influencer."

"I think it's you."

She laughs. "Nah, you're the one with all the moves, and I'm not talking about just dancing." My chest puffs out as I playfully gloat, but she winks at me and adds, "I've seen you on the ice."

My jaw drops open. "Those are the moves you're talking about? I think I need to up my game…" I lean in and whisper in her ear, "…in bed."

A find shiver goes through her. "You haven't been bringing your A-game?" she teases.

"You know what I think," I say, my mind drifting as her quivering body presses against me.

"No."

I nod and look over her shoulders. "Okay."

"Um, aren't you going to tell me."

"Nah, I think I'll show you." I take her hand in mine, and we snatch up our drinks and head toward the water away from the crowd. I guide her toward the pier. The din of the crowd dies down. "Careful."

"Where are we going?" she follows me along, and we pass by numerous boats that are tied up for the winter. I stop when I find the one I'm looking for and wag my brows at Alysha. "Whose boat is this?" she asks.

"Jesse's parents." I jump on to the back of the boat and hold my hand out to her.

"I am not breaking into Jesse's parents' boat."

"I'm not breaking in...much."

"Ryan!" she says and I reach for her. I tug her toward me until I have a good grip and I haul her onboard.

"They won't mind. Jesse and I used to take the boat out all the time. I sort of alluded that I'd be using it tonight."

She eyes me, suspiciously. "You know how to pilot this boat?"

"Sure, and I know how to drive tractors, too, but we're not taking the boat out on the water."

"What are we doing on it, then?"

I step up to the door, fish the key from the hiding spot and open it. "See, not breaking in when you have a key."

I wave my hand and she steps into the spacious cabin. "Wow, this is really nice. Are you sure they won't mind us being on it?"

I step up to the heater and flick it on. I've spent a lot of time on this boat, and know it well. "Not at all, not when you needed to get warm."

She glances around the small cozy space. "Why do I get the feeling that you and Jesse used to bring girls here?"

"Because you're astute too?"

She whacks me. "Eww, I am not having sex with you on that sofa if you've had sex there with other girls."

"Whoa." I hold my hands up palms out. "Who said anything about sex? I was only talking about warming you up. Pretty presumptuous aren't you, Alysha."

Her cheeks flush, and she opens her mouth, but no words come out as I press my body to hers and back her up until she's pressed against the door.

"I...uh," she manages to get out.

"Is sex all you ever think about?" I joke but the joke is on me because my cock is swelling and pressing against her stomach.

"I just thought—"

"Fine, okay." I put my hands on the door, on either side of her head as she stares at me with big, needy eyes. "If you're so obsessed with me, I'll fuck you right here against this door."

Her quick intake of breath lets me know how much she likes that idea. "What if someone comes?" she squeaks out.

My grin holds all kinds of promises as I take her arms, and lift them over her head, pinning her in place with my body. "That's the idea, babe."

She wiggles, and the boat rocks and I bite back a groan as the movement massages my cock on her stomach. Jesus, I can't wait to get inside her. I eye her waiting for a response. Shit, is she too worried about getting caught?

Her fingers curl into mine as she grins back, and says, "I like that idea..."

Fuck yeah.

20

ALYSHA

I can't believe I'm about to have sex with Ryan, on his friend's boat, during a festival, where there are hundreds of people milling about. It's risky and scandalous, and...so much fun. Everything about Ryan is fun. He's full of life and energy and he's always lighting up a room with his presence, and always going out of his way and taking care of those he cherishes. Like he's about to take care of me right now. I can't help but wonder why he hasn't been snatched up. Okay, maybe I do know. Lexi did a number on him, and he's now afraid of commitment. I can't blame him.

His head dips, his lips closing over mine and I moan, all thoughts of those at the festival leaving my mind. Right now, all I want to think about is this man, and the way he's devouring my mouth, like he simply can't get enough of me. Dammit, I never knew that feeling until...Ryan.

Careful, Alysha.

"Are you getting warm?" he asks.

"Nope, still cold." It's a lie, but I want to see how creative he can get. "I might even have a little frostbite."

"There's only one way we can remedy that." His head lifts and his mouth is damp from pressing kisses to my flesh. "I'm going to have to get you naked and use my body to warm you."

"I mean, if that's what we have to do…"

He steps back a bit, and I instantly miss his warmth, but the view as he sheds his coat and sweater is worth it. I reach out and run my hand over his muscles, and a little sigh catches in my throat.

"I love your hands on me." I smile at him. "But I love my mouth on you more." He unzips my coat, and shoves it from my shoulders. It falls to the floor and he blows on his hands to warm them before he puts them under my sweater. I squeak. "Sorry," he murmurs. "They should warm up fast."

His hands span my ribcage and spreads his fingers, his calluses scraping over my skin in ways that stimulate the needy juncture between my legs. "You like my hands on you, Alysha?"

I open my eyes and for a second I think I spot something deep, serious and needy in his eyes before he blinks it away. "More than anything," I tell him and he takes a deep fueling breath, like my words carry a lot of weight.

"More than my mouth."

"I can't remember," I answer and his chuckle curls around my quivering body.

"Does that mean you need my hands and then my mouth on your body, so you can compare?"

"Yes, and it might take more than once for me to figure it out." I lift my arms, encouraging him to remove my clothes and he grips my sweater and tugs it over my head. A burst of cold hits my skin, but it's replaced by his big warm hands and I arch into his touch. I quiver as his mouth glides over my neck and downward, until he's pulling my hard nipple into his hot mouth.

"That is so good," I murmur as he sucks and kneads my other breast with his hand. I honestly can't decide which I like more. "Equally," I murmur, and he switches breasts, taking my other bud between his lips.

As he pleasures my nipple, he drops to his knees before me—I really do love how he always seems to get himself in this position—and unbuttons my pants. I wiggle my hips as he shimmies them, along with my underwear, down my hips, just low enough to expose my sex. With my legs bound together, I can't spread them and a frustrated moan, born out of my need for him to put his fingers and mouth between my legs, crawls out of my throat.

"Still cold?" he asks, his voice rough, and labored and full of want.

He slides a finger between my nether lips, caressing my clit, and I buck against him. Okay, that'll do just fine. For now.

"So cold," I murmur as my body quivers, from pleasure, not cold. He presses hot, open-mouthed kisses to my stomach and sides, and goosebumps break out on my flesh. The boat rocks and his finger rubs up against my clit harder, and I nearly burst around him. "Ryan," I cry out, as he manages to put a finger inside me. With my legs bound, everything feels tighter, the sensations deeper somehow. He slides his finger in and out of me until I'm a hot, squirming mess.

I run my fingers through his hair and moan and pant, and revel in the pleasure building in my core. I begin to chant his name, and I toss my head from side to side as he finger-fucks me and swirls his tongue over my clit, applying the perfect amount of pressure with the sharp blade. I honestly never knew sex could be this amazing.

He presses a second finger inside and my body quakes at the fullness. "So wet and tight," he murmurs, and the second his hot breath falls over my pussy, I let go and come all over his fingers and mouth. I claw at his hair and tug and cry out as Ryan rocks my world. He laps me up, and the second the spasms slow, he's on his feet, turning me around and putting my hands against the door.

The only sounds that fill the cabin are my gasps and his grunts as he circles my waist and pulls my hips away from the door. He pushes my pants down a tiny bit more, until their tight around my knees. His hands move urgently, needy and I don't think he wants to take the time to remove my pants completely.

The hiss of his zipper mingles with our grunts and groans and I glance over my shoulder as he releases his cock. I have never seen him quite this intense before. He strokes his cock, his eyes locked on my ass. Oh, God, he's going to fuck me up against the door like this and I'm going to love every damn second of it. I have no idea why being half dressed feels so deliciously naughty. Maybe it's the urgency in him. I don't know but my sex is growing wetter, ready for him to fuck me hard.

He grips my ass and squeezes my cheeks and I whimper as he positions his cock at my entrance. Everything about him is wild, an animal about to take down its prey, and I suck in a breath to prepare myself, until he lightly runs a finger over my back, a tender touch that reminds me this is Ryan, and it's possible that what's going on here might be more than animalistic sex.

Don't get in your head, Alysha.

"Ryan," I call out as emotions bombard me.

"Yeah, babe," he says quietly still lightly touching my back. God, he might as well be caressing my damn heart.

I want to tell him how good this feels. I want to tell him how I think I might be developing feelings, how maybe if I stayed here, we could fill our winter nights with lovemaking. What I don't want to do is scare him off.

"Please...put your cock inside me."

Coward.

But I already knew that. He hesitates for a split second and I'm about to turn to see him, when his hips canter forward and he pushes air from my throat as he powers into me, hitting my cervix with such force it nearly brings on a full-body orgasm.

"Ohmigod." I cry out as his fingers dig into my hips and he holds me tight as the boat rocks and he rocks into me. I scratch at the door, sure I'm going to leave it scarred, but I can't stop, can't get control of my body as Ryan takes me higher and higher until I'm out on open waters, going so fast the only way to stop is by crashing. I don't want to crash. Not with Ryan.

"Aly..." he grunts, pulling out and driving in so hard and fast I shatter around him. "Jesus."

He leans over me, his warm chest against my back, everything about him so tight, I'm sure something is going to snap. His mouth is near my ear, and he whispers, "I love..." He gulps and I whimper as he lets go, his cock spasming with each powerful spurt. I squeeze my legs together, milking his release and his breath is hot on my back as he grunts with pleasure. He stays over me, both of us panting, and I flatten my hands on the door, sure I've destroyed the paint and my nails.

His hands slide around my waist and he pulls me up until we're both standing, and he links his fingers over my belly and hugs me to him. I turn my head and rest it against his chest. I listen to the strength of his strong heart as it pounds against my cheek and I'm pretty sure I've never been this happy or content in my entire life.

His thumbs stroke my stomach and he buries his face in the side of my neck, just holding me tight, like he might collapse if he lets me go. I might too. I'm only standing because he's holding me. As we breathe, the noise outside reaches my ears and I begin to laugh.

He laughs with me, even though nothing about this is funny. Nope, it's intense, and profound, and is touching my heart on a whole new level. I guess it's better to laugh than cry, right?

"We should get dressed," he whispers. "I don't want you getting cold."

"Why? Don't you want to warm me up again?"

He spins me. "Babe, I want to warm you up every minute of every day, but it sounds like everyone is getting ready for the fireworks and I don't want you to miss them."

"I already saw them."

He laughs and picks our clothes up from the floor. He grabs a few tissues off the counter, and wipes between my legs, wrapping the tissues in a clean one and putting it in his pocket to dispose of later.

I tug my pants up and he does the same and then we get back into our sweaters and coats and hats and mitts. He glances around to make sure nothing is out of place, picks up the key and we both step outside. A huge gust blows over us and I swear if he didn't have my hand in his, I'd be blown overboard.

"Whoa," he says and keeps me tight against his body as he locks up and hides the key. I love the way he holds me, this strange new closeness between us. "You okay?"

"I am," I say, although I'm not really sure that's true. I might not be okay at all, especially if when we leave here and this whole fantasy world I'm currently living in comes to an abrupt end. "Are you?" I ask stupidly.

He angles his head, and his brow plows together. "I wasn't the one who was nearly blown away."

"Are you kidding me right now?" I shoot back, anger in my voice, and he stiffens, his shoulders squaring as he pulls himself up to his full height.

As he towers over me, he scrubs his face. "What would I be kidding about?"

"Are you telling me, what we did in there." I stop to point to the locked door. "Did not blow you away?"

He relaxes and laughs, and keeps hold of my hand as he jumps over the boat and lands on the dock. "Come here." He drags me to him, and cups my cheeks. His mouth is soft on mine as he kisses me and murmurs. "Everything about you blows me away, Alysha."

I kiss him back and that's when my brain clicks back into gear. Just before he climaxed he said, I love... Then his words fell off. What did he love? Oh, God, I want to know but it's too late to ask now. Not when we're no longer in the moment, and surely he wasn't going to say he loved me.

Get out of your head, girl.

"You still want to head to Jesse's cottage?"

"Yeah, I can't wait. I really like him and Becca is a sweetie." We walk along the dock and head back to the road, my body still tingling from his touch, and my orgasms. It takes us forever to go down the street. No matter where we go, someone is greeting Ryan. He's so well-known and well liked around here. "Are they a couple?"

"On and off," he says with a grin.

"Oh, like they get nooky-itis?"

He laughs. "Something like that. They dated years ago, and then she went off to Victoria for university and they didn't want to do the whole long distance thing." He pauses and glances at me. "It's hard."

"Yeah, I know first-hand," I say almost to myself. "I don't recommend it."

He nods and continues. "But I think when she comes back here, they'll probably get together. Hell, they'll probably get married. They're good to each other and for each other."

I smile. "That's really nice."

We reach the area where everyone is gathered around for the fireworks and as soon as Ryan puts his arm around me, and tugs me close the sky lights up. I lean into him, absorb his warmth as ooh's and ahhs echo around us. There's so much warmth and character to this small Canadian province. A girl could get used to it, honestly.

We reach his vehicle and he opens the door for me. I slide in and take off my hat and mitts. He negotiates the dark streets carefully and about twenty minutes later, we're outside the city and taking a long dark road hugged by trees.

"You don't have to go very far to be in the middle of nowhere," I state.

"The island is two-hundred and twenty-four kilometers long, and you're never more than fifteen minutes from a beach."

"Can you say that in English?"

He laughs. "Come on, you've been in Canada long enough to know the metric system."

I whack him. "It still confuses me."

He closes one eye and mumbles as he calculates. "I'm not great at math, but it's like one-hundred and forty miles.

I glance at the cottage as it comes into view. "Wow, it's gorgeous."

"I spent a lot of time here as a kid. There aren't many lakes in PEI, but the cottage is on one."

"Maybe we can go swimming," I joke.

He laughs at that. "I'll only go if we can go skinny dipping."

I crinkle my nose. "As much as I'd love to see you naked," I begin. "I don't want to be the one responsible for your...parts freezing and falling off."

His roar of laughter curls around me and warms my coldest parts. "If you want to get in water we can, but it's going to be hot."

"Oh?"

"Jesse has a hot tub."

"I don't have a bathing suit."

He winks at me. "We'll rig up something."

●
21

RYAN

"I'm so glad you guys decided to come," Becca says as she swings the door open and hauls Alysha inside, giving her a big hug. I grin, loving how sweet Becca always is. I'd better be the best man at their wedding. "What took you so long anyway? We were waiting for you to get here before we ordered food, but we got too hungry and put in our order. It should be here soon."

Jesse waves us in from the sofa, and I kick off my boots, and help Alysha off with her coat.

"Fireworks," Alysha says, a pink tinge on her cheeks and I don't think it's from the cold.

"How were they?"

"Mind-blowing," she deadpans and I start to choke on nothing but air.

Becca eyes me. "Do you need a drink?"

"Big one."

"Jesse, can you grab Ryan a drink?"

"You bet."

Jesse jumps up and brings over a glass with what I think is water, and I take a big swallow. "Jesus," I blurt out, and wipe the back of my mouth. "You could have warned me this was potato vodka."

"Oh, yeah sorry. I just thought you knew."

"Most people would pour a glass of water for someone who is choking."

Jesse cocks his head, a grin playing with the corners of his mouth. "But were you really choking though, Ryan?"

Fucker.

I just shake my head at the knowing grin on his face. "Yes, I was choking." Really, I wasn't. Just hearing Alysha talk about fireworks set off a storm inside me. I have to say, I love her playfulness, and the little secrets we share.

"Wait, did you say potato vodka?" Alysha asks, her nose crinkled up like that has to be the worst thing she's ever heard.

I hold the glass out to her. "Yup, here. Try."

She stares at my glass like it might contain poison. "I don't think I want to."

"You have to. When in Prince Edward Island, you have to drink potato vodka."

Jesse nods in agreement, and adds, "Just like when you're in Newfoundland you have to kiss a cod."

"Okay, note to self...do not go to Newfoundland." She shakes her head. "You Canadians have strange traditions." I give the glass a little shake. "I just can't get away from potatoes, can I?" She sniffs the vodka, and makes a face like it might have gone bad.

"Do it," I encourage, and she tips the glass to her lips, just putting a sip in her mouth. She goes quiet as she tastes it and a second later, she shrugs.

"That's not so bad."

Becca grins. "I'll get you a glass."

"Wait, are there as many carbs in that as the potato casserole I ate tonight?"

"More like devoured," I say under my breath and Alysha whacks me. I let out a loud oomph, and grab her hand, bringing it to my mouth for a kiss.

"No, not as many calories," Becca says. "And you don't have to worry about that anyway."

"Well, thank you," Alysha says and accepts the glass. We all settle in the living room in front of the fire and Becca holds up her glass.

"What should we drink to?"

"How about to our last year of college and getting on with life," Jesse says and we all clink glasses. I turn and glance at Alysha. Her eyes are narrowed, her lips tight and I get it. She's not sure what she's going to do with her life right now. I just pray she decides to dance and I'm going to do the best I can to see to it that she does.

"Alysha," I say.

She holds her glass up, her smile back in place. "I'll drink to that." She takes a big swallow and I think it's so she doesn't have to voice what's really on her mind. She turns her attention to Jesse. "Have you always wanted to be a veterinarian?"

He nods and for the next half hour as we sip our vodka—I'm sure Alysha still thinks potato vodka is weird—Jesse talks about how he's always wanted to work with animals and how he's going to be working with his parents. I relax into the sofa, my leg pressed against Alysha's, and the fire is so cozy and warm, it's all I can do not to fall asleep. Especially after our mind-blowing sex on the boat.

Something brushes up against the outside of the cottage and Alysha's eyes open wide as she shifts closer. "Is someone out there? Should we lock the door?"

I grin at her. "We're surrounded by trees. Just something brushing up against the cottage. Nothing to worry about."

"I'm not used to being in the woods."

It's a reminder that our lives are so different, but it's easy to tell she likes it here. "Do you want me to go check?"

She shakes her head. "No, it's okay."

"We can head back to the farm if you want."

"Nope." She sinks into the sofa. "I don't want to go anywhere."

"How about a game?" Becca says. "A drinking game?"

"Oh, God, I'm not much of a drinker," Alysha says.

"Then you'd better win," I tell her and give her a little nudge.

"Okay, what's the game?"

Becca taps her chin. "Hmmm, how about two truths and a lie. This will be a good way for us to get to know you Alysha so how about you go first."

"Okay, let's see. I like to write poetry. I have a sister five years younger than me, and my dad owns a hockey team."

Everyone stares at Alysha, trying to figure out the lie that I already know. "Well, I heard your dad owned a team," Becca says. "It's all Owen talks about."

"He made the team, didn't he?" I say. "I was talking to his father, who told me."

"Ah, now that makes sense," Alysha says.

I eye her. "What does?"

"The other night, Owen said something about visiting me when he was in Boston. I guess he must be playing for the team. He didn't come right out and say it, though."

I shake my head. "Strange." Something about Owen playing for her dad's team doesn't sit right, but why would he lie about it.

"Okay, who knows the lie."

I swirl the vodka in my glass. "I do, so I'll go last."

"Becca?" Alysha asks, and raises her brow.

"I think you don't have a sister five years younger."

Alysha turns to Jesse. "Same."

She turns to me. "You don't have a sister five years younger."

"You guys all won. How did you do that?"

"That means you have to drink," I tell her. She rolls her eyes and takes a small sip of vodka.

"How did you figure it out? I really thought I might have caught you up with the poetry."

"Nah, you're a dancer. It makes sense that you'd write poetry. Something you could put to music and dance too." I lean into her. "I want to read it."

"Nope."

"Hey, you looked at my photo albums."

"Still nope." She sets her glass down. "You go."

"Okay," I say, and glance at the fire. "I once won a hot dog eating contest."

"Oh, God, I already know that's true and wish it wasn't," Alysha says and we all laugh. "I can fly an airplane." Alysha nods, like she could believe that. I mean she knows I can pilot a boat, and ride tractors so she probably doesn't think that's too far out. "I can do a most excellent cartwheel."

"That," Alysha says. "That's the lie." She shakes her head as she looks over my body. "You're too...too..."

"Too what?" I ask with a laugh.

"Okay, let me just say, I think you have to be graceful to do a cartwheel and I don't think you are. I've seen you on the dance floor."

Becca and Jesse know me well, so they're both sitting there with grins on their faces as I stand and stretch out my arms and legs.

"You're kidding me."

"Oh wait." I turn to Becca and Jesse. "Which one do you guys think is the lie?" At the same time, they both say, "Fly an airplane."

Alysha puts her hands over her face and groans. "Are you guys kidding me?"

I move away from the sofa, toward the hall. "Prepare to be impressed."

I do a cartwheel down the hall, and if I do say so myself, it was pretty impressive. I stand and throw my arms out. "Flawless."

"I give it a ten," Jesse says.

"Nine," Becca pipes in. "There was a bend in his elbow."

Alysha holds her glass up. "I give it a mouthful of vodka."

"You don't have to keep drinking," I tell her.

"It's only fair."

I step into the kitchen and grab her a bottle of water, and she gratefully accepts it. "I would like to get my pilot's license one of these days, though."

"You got me with that one. I was sure you already had one."

I lift my glass to Becca. "Your turn, Becs."

"Okay, let's see. I have a pet lizard back in Victoria. I want to have four kids and two dogs." She glances at Jesse when she says that and he just raises his brow. I, for a fact, know that Jesse wants a big family too. "I'm really into jogging."

Both Jesse and I laugh at that and she glares at us. "Hey, you don't know what I do in Victoria."

"We know you don't jog."

She lifts her chin and inch. "Alysha, what do you think I'm lying about?"

She crinkles her nose, like she doesn't want to offend her. "Um, you don't have a pet lizard."

"I do," Becca says, almost apologetically and Alysha takes another swig of her vodka. At least she's taking small sips, otherwise she's going to be flat on her back...right where I want her, but I want her sober.

She glares at us again. "I might take up jogging. I thought about it." I just shake my head and grin at her. This is the girl who hid in the bathroom during gym class when we were kids. "Okay fine, jogging is stupid. That shit can give you a heart attack."

"To no heart attacks," Jesse says and we all lift our glasses and tap them. I do, however, jog to keep in shape for hockey, and for farm work, which can be tiring and strenuous.

Becca sits back on the sofa and stretches her legs out, putting them on Jesse's lap. "All right, your turn, Jesse."

He massages her feet and she exhales a satisfied moan. "Okay, pizza is my favorite food." I roll my eyes because we all know that is true. "I'm color blind." Okay, also true and too easy. He takes a big breath and lets it out slowly. "I know a guy, a friend of mine actually, who is head over heels in love."

I swallow. Shit, is he talking about me? And why the hell would he say that in front of Alysha? I'm going to fucking kill him.

"You're not color blind," Becca says and throws a pillow at him.

"Yeah, that's what I was going to say too," Alysha says. "Yay, I don't have to drink."

"What about you Ryan?" Jesse asks with a shit eating grin.

"I thought it was the friend thing." I lift my glass and take a big-ass drink just as the doorbell rings.

"That's the pizza now," he says and jumps up. I follow him to the door.

"What the fuck, dude?"

"What?" he asks as he pulls his wallet out.

I glare at him. "You basically just told Alysha I loved her."

"Oh, you thought I was talking about you?"

"Well...who else would you be talking about?"

He goes serious. "So you're saying you are head over heels in love with her?"

"Jesse—"

"Just be careful, dude." He puts his hand on my shoulder. "You're my best friend and I don't want you hurt, so be very fucking careful, and maybe start thinking about what you'd need from her, and what she'd need from you to make things work."

He swings the door open, ending our conversation, and yes, I am thinking about those things, and I'm not sure I like the answers I keep coming up with.

22

ALYSHA

Was Jesse talking about Ryan when he said his friend was head over heels in love? At first I thought he was, judging by the grin he was giving Ryan, but then Ryan got the answer wrong, so maybe it's some secret joke they share. I glance at Ryan as he eats pizza and note that he's fallen quiet. Then again, we're all quiet as we stuff our faces.

Jesse turns the conversation to Becca, and how she'll be working here at the hospital when she graduates. My thoughts jump back to our earlier conversation and my stomach tightens a bit. Everyone here knows what they want to do after college, and have laid the groundwork to accomplish their goals. I still don't have anything solidified, other than the fact that I don't want to go back and marry Linc and be at his beck and call. I want my own life. I want to make my own decisions and I want to be with someone who supports my love of dance and more importantly, encourages it.

I turn and find Ryan watching me carefully. God, when he looks at me like that, like I'm more than a stray to him and it really messes with my head and my heart. "More?" he asks as he reaches into the box for another piece.

"I am so full," I moan.

"Me too," Becca says and pushes her plate away.

Ryan bites into his piece and devours it. "I know how we can burn these calories off," he says and heat jumps into my face. He is not suggesting sex right in front of his friends, is he?

"How's that, buddy?" Jesse asks and wipes his mouth with a napkin.

"Hot tub, of course," he explains.

"Yes," Becca says and jumps up.

As everyone stands, I wipe my hands with a napkin and crinkle my nose. "I don't have a suit."

Becca shrugs. "Me neither."

"I'm liking this more and more," Jesse teases and she whacks him.

"We are not getting naked. We can wear our bra and underwear and don't worry," she says turning to me. "It's dark out there, so no one can see anything anyway. When we come in, we can wear something of Jesse's. Right, Jesse?" He nods and starts peeling off his shirt. Ryan does the same and I try not to stare at his hard muscles.

"I guess that sounds okay." I'm a dancer and I'm actually used to others seeing me in little to no clothing when changing backstage, so this really isn't a big deal. Just as long as everyone else is comfortable with it.

Ryan pulls me to my feet. "See, I told you we could rig something up."

Becca gestures with her head. "Bathroom is there. You can change and grab yourself a big towel. Actually, grab us all one."

I step into the bathroom and get out of my clothes, happy that I'm wearing plain black panties and a bra. It could easily pass as a bathing suit. With four towels in hand, I go back in the other room, and I hear a squeal as Jesse and Becca dart out the back door. I find Ryan standing in his boxer shorts waiting for me.

I grin and put my hand on his chest when I reach him. "I guess no one had a bathing suit, huh?"

"Nope and if we were alone, we'd be wearing nothing but our birthday suits."

"Didn't you already get me naked today?" I glance outside, take in the steam filling the air.

"Not quite," he says with a grin, a playful reminder that we had sex with our clothes still on. God, that was so much fun. He grabs my hand. "Ready?"

"No."

He laughs and we run out the door. The cold air whips over our skin and I shiver, but we jump into the glorious hot water and warm up quickly.

"This is amazing," I murmur and rest my head on the hot tub as I take in the stars up above. Ryan moves close and I put my hand on his leg.

"Let's get the bubbles going." Becca turns a bunch of dials, and bubbles shoot out behind me. "Oh, Jesse, can you get the bath salts."

"You want me to run back inside?"

"Please…" She says and blinks rapidly, which sets a grumbling Jesse into motion, and I have to say, I do think they make a good couple. Becca turns the jets up, and even more bubbles erupt around me. Steam fills the air, making it hard to see my new friend, or even hear her on the other side of the hot tub.

"There's the little dipper," Ryan says and points upward.

"Oh yeah, I see it." I angle my head. "I can't quite see the big dipper."

Ryan takes my hand and puts it on his cock. He leans in and whispers, "It's right here." I can't help but laugh as I tug my hand away, grateful the jets are making a lot of noise and Becca didn't hear him. Jesse comes back with a tray containing our drink cups, which he refilled, and a long bottle that must be the salts. He hands our drinks out, and pours a generous amount of salt in the water, filling the air with lavender.

"That is amazing." I breathe in the scent, and my body relaxes even more. "I might never leave."

"You guys can stay the night," Jesse says. "We can play some more games and there's more potato vodka to be drank." He holds his drink up and we all do the same.

"I can't believe I'm starting to like this," I say and set my glass in the cup holder. "Maybe I just had too much."

Ryan puts his arm around my back and plays with my hair. "Want to stay?"

"Sure, if your family is okay with that. I know they like having you home."

"They'll see enough of me when I move back here in April."

I nod, and once again I'm conflicted. Does he want to play in the NHL or not? His friends all seem to think he does, and they all know him better than I do. He drops a kiss onto my cheek and I smile at him.

"What was that for?"

He just shakes his head. "No reason."

"Maybe the cold air is freezing your brain." He chuckles and my heart does a little dance in my chest, making breathing a bit difficult as everything I feel for this man grows to dangerous proportions. I squeeze his leg, and rest my head against his shoulder, never wanting to leave this place, or this man.

What am I even saying? We live different lives, and well, I can't make a life here, right?

Okay, I suppose I could, but I can't if it's not what Ryan wants, and my family would lose their ever-loving minds. But I'm a grown up, and I should be making decisions that are best for me. I still wonder about the repercussions my father was talking about. What is he planning?

"You okay?" Ryan asks and pulls my thoughts back. I smile at him and let out a contented sigh, putting all negative thoughts behind me.

"I am. This hot water is making me tired, is all."

"Oh, in that case."

He stands and water drips off him as steams floats from his body before he jumps from the tub. He holds his hand out. "Come on."

Thinking we're heading inside, which I don't really want to do, but if it means crawling between the sheets with him, I'm game, I reach for his hand and let him help me out. But instead of heading inside, he scoops me up and darts down the grassy path leading to the wharf.

"What are you doing?" I screech.

"Cooling you off."

I try to wiggle out of his arms but his hold on me is too strong. "Ryan, don't you dare. I'll never forgive you."

"It's fun," Becca says as she and Jesse run past us and jump in the water. They both let out loud yelps after they surface and a second later, they're climbing back onto the wharf. "Hot water, cold water therapy," she tells me as she runs by. "It's good for circulation."

"More like it's good for a heart attack."

She laughs and Ryan sets me down. "You don't have to, but I'm going to." He runs to the end of the wharf and jumps in. He too squeals as he surfaces and hey, when in Rome. I'm not in Rome, I'm in Prince Edward Island and if this is what one does on the island, then I'm going to do it to.

"Here goes nothing," I scream and jump in beside Ryan. "Oh my God," I cry out as I surface, and Ryan is already climbing out and reaching for me. "You guys are crazy."

He laughs. "It feels good."

"It feels freezing."

"Come on." We run back to the hot tub and the water is even more glorious when we slip in. I dunk my head, and when I surface, everyone is watching me.

"Okay, fine, it wasn't so bad. I'm actually all kinds of tingly."

"It's good for you," Ryan says. "When there's more snow, we actually roll around in it."

A lot of the snow had melted with the warm afternoon sun. "Ah, darn. There's just not enough snow down for that. I guess I'll miss it," I joke, and Ryan gives me a smile that reaches his eyes and it's at times like this, when he does things like that, that I think we could have more. We could have a life. If I wasn't too much of a coward to go home and deal with a man who likely thinks we're still getting married.

Then again, I could be reading Ryan all wrong and dammit, I'm too afraid to ask and ruin what we do have between us.

He holds his hand out and winks at me. "Actually, it's starting to snow now. We could do it later tonight or tomorrow."

"Me and my big mouth."

He leans into me. "I like your big mouth."

Before I can respond, he kisses me so deeply and passionately, it wraps around my heart and nearly squeezes tears from my eyes. It's a good thing I'm in the water or Ryan would know what his touch does to me.

"Okay, I think I'm getting all wrinkly," Becca says and I know it's to give us privacy. I break away from Ryan.

"You don't have to go in."

"Actually, I overheat pretty quickly, so I'm going to go in, get a shower and get into some comfy clothes. I'll leave clothes in the bathroom for you."

I nod and Ryan puts his hand on my leg, giving it a squeeze. "We'll be in shortly," he says.

Jesse ties a towel around his waist. "I'll set some games up for us."

They step inside, leaving us alone in the hot tub, the stars bright overhead. "I kind of love it here," I whisper.

Ryan grabs me and I yelp as he pulls me onto his lap. I straddle him and his thickening cock presses against my center. "Fuck, I want you," he murmurs his voice deep and tortured.

"You just had me."

"Yeah, and you'd think that would satisfy me, but no, all it does is make me want you more."

I lean in and kiss his beautiful mouth, and our tongues tangle as he reaches up and cups my breasts. "I want these in my mouth later," he says. "Better yet, I'd like to slide my dick in right here." He cups my breasts to make a channel. "Can I do that, Alysha? Can I fuck your beautiful tits?" He brushes his thumbs over my hard nipples, and I'm not sure I've ever seen such hunger on his face before.

I laugh at the innocent hope in his question. "Only if I can do something."

He angles his head, his eyes wide. "Oh?"

"Wear my Anne of Green Gables hat."

He laughs hard, and I do too. "Babe, you don't need to wear that. Besides, yours is back at the farm."

"I saw one on the shelf inside," I say.

He goes serious, and cups the back of my head, bringing my mouth back to his. "When I get you alone and naked, it's you I want. No one else."

I inch back to see his face. "You know you said *when*, not *if*."

He kisses my nose, and cheeks and chin. "Uh huh, that's right," he mumbles like his mind is a million miles away. Or it could be because his blood is draining to the thick appendage between his legs.

"So you think I'm a sure thing, eh?"

He chuckles at my use of his Canadian slang. "Aren't you?"

"Yes," I murmur. It's true, when it comes to him, I am a sure thing—easy—except nothing about being with Ryan here on the island is easy, and I could find myself in real trouble if this is nothing more than a holiday hookup. Which was my stupid idea.

Well done, Alysha. Well done.

I hated leaving Alysha alone so much over the last week, but I really had so much to do to get the old barn fixed up and usable—for the future. Basically, miss time with her now, but make up for it later. Am I making a colossal mistake? I don't know, probably. But she's happy spending time inside the house with my family, and my sisters are keeping her busy by taking her places and of course, they're doing enough baking to feed the entire town, twice, tonight.

It's not like I haven't spent time with her, though. In the evenings, we always find ourselves in front of the fire, admiring the tree and knitting, and of course later, when everyone is asleep, I slide into her bed, only to leave early so my family doesn't see me. I use the few extra private minutes in my bedroom to work on the gift I'm making Alysha, which I'm giving her tonight after we hide the pickle. Still, the week has flown by and I really fucking hate that. I want time to slow down, I want to savor every second with Alysha, and while I feel I did do that, there was just never enough time.

Here it is, already Friday at lunch time, Christmas Eve and we're all getting ready for the town's festivities this afternoon. As the air grows colder, I nail in the last plank and stand back and look at my handiwork. It's not everything I wanted it to be by tonight. I did my best with what little time I had, though, and it should be enough to let Alysha envision her future—one I hope she wants as much as I do.

A moment of doubt fills my stomach and tightens it. Am I being selfish? Fuck, I really worry I am. What if down the road she comes to resent all I'm asking of her? Am I asking too much?

Fuck, I just don't know. I don't know anything anymore. I shake my head and drop the hammer. I guess love does that to a person. It messes with your brain and heart until you're second-guessing everything. All I can say is I'm happy she's still here with me. There's still a part of me that worrries her parents will convince her to go back to Linc. I guess that's why I'm trying to convince her so hard to follow her dreams. Hell, everyone wants me to play for the NHL, and I'm standing my ground, following my own dreams and that's all I want for Alysha.

"Hey, are you out here?"

Shit. I brush the dust off my coat, and hurry to the door as Alysha tries to open it, but I have it locked from the inside for a reason. I lift the lever and step out into the cold. Alysha tries to look over my shoulder, her head bobbing left and right as she scrunches her nose, but I close the door behind me.

"What are you doing in there anyway?"

"Nothing, just cleaning the place up. It had holes that needed fixing before the snow really starts falling." She looks at me like she's not sure she believes me. "What are you doing out here?"

She hugs herself and I pull her to me. "Your mom sent me to get you. It's almost time for the festivities, and I'm really looking forward to watching your sister win the tractor race."

I laugh at that. "I have no doubt she'll win."

"Actually, I'm really looking forward to the exhibition hockey game. I like watching you play. You're kind of a beast out on that ice." She gives me a playful wink. "A beast off the ice too."

I push a strand of hair off her face. "Beauty and the beast," I tease.

"You're really good at hockey, Ryan."

"Yup, I love it."

She nods her head and then glances around the vast farm and all the buildings. "You love this too."

"I love this more and a person can have two loves." I almost want to say three, and include her. "Look at you, you love dancing and eating potatoes."

She grins at that. "I don't want to have any regrets."

Okay, that's a strange thing to say. "I don't want to have any regrets either. That's why I'm choosing farming."

She nods again. "How many generations has this farm been in your family?"

"Our farm dates back to the early nineteen-hundreds. Did you know that the potato was introduced to Prince Edward Island in the seventeen hundreds?" She grins at me. "The first export was eighteen-twenty-seven."

"You need to go to trivia night with me."

"I don't think I know much about much, but I know my farming."

She goes up on her toes to kiss me. "I think you know a lot about a lot."

A door creaks on one of the potato storage barns and I glance over to see the latch has let go. Probably Billy milling about and getting into trouble. "Let me go get that."

"Can I come?"

She stands back a bit. Why the heck is she suddenly acting so strange, like I don't want her walking to the barn with me, like I have something to hide? I realize I've been neglecting her a bit, but there's a means to an end to that.

"Yeah, come on. I'll show you around."

She glances at the barn I just exited, her brows furrowed. Is she wondering why I won't let her in there? Her phone pings and when she stiffens, my stomach clenches. Shit, has Linc or her parents been pressuring her again?

I take in her paling face. "Are you going to get that?"

She shakes her head, and my heart aches at the sadness surrounding her. "Come on, let's go check that door and you can finally see the storage areas."

I take her hand and tug her to me as we walk to the big storage barn. I open the door and her eyes go wide as she takes in the mountain of potatoes. Then she crinkles her nose.

"It definitely does not smell like cinnamon in here."

"I actually love the smell." I breathe deep. "Earthy, nutty."

"Nutty, yeah, that's the word, Ryan."

I pull her to me and kiss her. "Wait, are you calling me nutty?"

She laughs and that's when my phone buzzes in my back pocket. I'd been waiting for a call from the hardware store. I'd ordered a bunch of mirrors, and they were on backorder.

I tug my phone from my pocket and check the number. "Do you mind if I get this?"

She narrows her eyes, clearly confused by the question. "Of course not."

"Just a second." I step outside so she can't hear me, and quickly take the call. She stays inside, and when I head back in, she's walking around, examining the potatoes. Her smile doesn't reach her eyes when she glances at me.

"Everything okay?"

"Yup," is all I say. I get it, she's no doubt wondering what all the secrecy is about, but she also knows she can trust me. I'm not fucking around behind her back. I really like the honesty between us, and in my heart, this is a woman who knows me and knows what I want. Even my best friends from child-hood, my closest friends like Jesse and Becca, think I'm still holding out for the NHL. A part of me can understand that. I was up at the crack of dawn every morning, tugging on skates and skating for hours. Then I chose Scotia Storms Academy in Nova Scotia over the agriculture school here, because I wanted to continue to play hockey at a high level. I love the game, it's just not my life. They can't see what's in my heart like Alysha can.

Alysha takes a deep breath. "I think the smell is growing on me."

I hope the whole fucking place is growing on her.

"We'd better get inside."

I lock up the door behind us, and I point out all the buildings on the property, explaining the process of potato farming.

"It's quite fascinating and impressive," she says, genuinely interested. Under her breath she says something about her father, and I'm about to ask her to repeat herself when Billy comes running toward us, looking for love from Alysha. I'm not sure what she was going to say about her dad. Obviously, she doesn't want me to know, probably because I wouldn't like it. If I had to guess it was most likely that he wouldn't be as impressed.

"Hey Billy, where have you been?" Alysha asks and pets his head. He bleeps and leans into her.

"He thinks he's a damn dog."

"That's understandable."

"Is it now?" I ask as she stands upright.

"He gets to come and go from the house, and he's a therapy animal. But he's even better than a dog because you get to use his mohair for sweaters and things."

"I guess when you look at it like that."

"Maybe I'll get a goat," she says with a grin.

"I don't think they're allowed in Halifax's city limits. Not sure what's allowed in the Hamptons if you move back there."

Okay, I'm fishing for information, but give me a break. I'm a man in love with a girl who just broke up with a douche bag, but might succumb to family pressure and end up with him anyway.

"Yeah," is all she says. We reach the door and the smell of freshly cooked turkey reaches my nose and my stomach grumbles as Billy takes off inside, no doubt looking for scraps. Mom really goes all out when it's her turn to host the festivities and I'm so happy Alysha is here for it.

"Is it tonight that we hide the pickle?" Alysha asks.

I grin at her. "I was just thinking about that."

She whacks me. "That's not what I'm talking about."

"What?" I glance at her like I'm shocked. "Oh, you're talking about..." I shake my head and give an exasperated sigh. "Still so obsessed with me. Fine, if you want to hide *that* pickle we can."

She crosses her arms. "Okay, if it's that much of a hardship, we don't have to. I could use a good night's sleep."

"Well that backfired," I tease and with everyone in the kitchen busy, I tug her to me, and kiss her on the lips. "Can I hide *that* pickle tonight?" I beg.

"I'll think about it."

I kiss her harder, wanting yes on her lips right now. I break the kiss and we're both practically panting. "Okay, fine, you can."

I grin and tap her ass to set her into motion and I step into the kitchen. "Look what I made earlier," Alysha says, so completely proud of herself as she waves her hand over a tray of cinnamon rolls.

"Mom shared her secret recipe."

Mom puts her fingers to her lips. "Secret family recipe, but no worries, Alysha is family now."

My heart leaps into my throat. Mom knows. She damn well knows how I feel and what I want. "You won't tell, will you, Alysha?"

Alysha slides her fingers across her lips. "These lips are sealed." Mom grins and goes back to setting sweets on a tray. Alysha leans into me. "Until later tonight, of course." My stupid dick takes that moment to thicken. "Actually, I didn't know it was a secret family recipe," Alysha says turning to Mom and I take the moment to excuse myself.

"I need a fast shower."

I dart upstairs, strip off and jump in the shower. I take my dick into my hand and debate on tugging one out, but I don't want to do anything to mess up tonight. Alysha was only planning on staying for Christmas and this could very well be our last night here on the island together and dammit, I want to go out with a bang.

I wash quickly and head to my bedroom for clean clothes. Chatter from downstairs combined with Alysha's laughter trickles up the stairs and fills my heart with home and hearth. I honestly can't imagine playing for the NHL and living life on the road. The only thing that would make that bearable was if I played for Alysha's father's team and she was there every night. But that's not going to happen, for many reasons.

I spot the Anne of Green Gables book on the nightstand, a bookmark marking the stopping place. I grin. I love that she's reading my favorite childhood books, but it does remind me that she's had a lot of spare time lately.

I just hope she's using it to think about the future she wants, not the one her family is forcing her into and honestly, I'm a little shocked that they haven't demanded she come home.

Then again, maybe they have and maybe she just hasn't told me.

I hurry back to the kitchen, and expect to be greeted by Alysha, but she's nowhere to be found. I glance at Mom who has a worried look on her face and take in my two youngest sisters.

"She had a call," she says quietly and for the first time in, ever, my sisters are quiet too. I turn and walk down the hall until I find Alysha in the living room, standing in front of the tree, staring at her phone. Her head lifts, and her face is as white as the snow falling outside.

I swallow and ask, "What?"

24

ALYSHA

My gaze goes from Ryan to my phone back to Ryan. I take in his questioning eyes, not to mention the question on his lips. I'm not sure I can find my voice, even though this turn of events shouldn't be coming as quite a shock.

"Alysha?"

"It's my...father," I manage to get out. "He's here."

"Here?" Ryan looks around like my dad might jump out from behind the tree and scream surprise. "Where?"

"At a hotel, in town."

"What the hell?"

"Yeah, I know. I mean he sort of threatened...."

His shoulders square as he pulls himself up to his full height, his entire body going stiff. "He threatened you?"

"Maybe threatened isn't the right word. He wanted me home. He said I upset Mom and he also said if I didn't want to be a part of this family...then I left him little choice..."

"And that choice was to come collect you himself?"

I shake my head. "I wasn't sure if he meant that or if he meant they were exiling me from the family."

Ryan runs agitated fingers through his hair. "Alysha, that can't happen. Family is everything. You can't be estranged from yours. I know you guys have your problems, but family..." His words fall off and the hurt from losing his dad wraps around me and squeezes the air from my lungs.

I close the distance between us and he grips my sweater tight and holds me to him, like letting me go could tear his heart from his soul. Family is the most important thing in the world to him. The loss of his father messed him up in a big way and he has this obligation, this need to stand in for his father and make him proud. It's the most important thing to him, even though I'm not sure it's the right thing. Not according to his friends and grandfather. Are they right? Does he secretly want to play in the NHL?

I don't know. All I know right now is I need to pull on my big girl panties and talk to my father.

"Let me get my coat. I'll drive you," Ryan says.

I put my hand on his chest to stop him. "You have the festivities, and the game. I'm not taking you away from that."

He touches my hair, and presses his forehead against mine. "None of that matters, Alysha. You need me right now."

My heart misses a beat, and while I know he puts himself last, doing anything and everything for those he cares about, he needs to be with his family while I summon my courage and deal with my own problems. Honestly, he brought me here to help me, and over the last week, I was beginning to worry that I was becoming a nuisance, that he felt obligated to take care of me. A part of me wonders if he's tired of me, and if Owen was right and he and Lexi were probably going to get back together. Heck, he's been disappearing for hours and taking secret phone calls, and when he leaves my bed early, I hear him moving around his room—doing something.

"I'll call an Uber," I tell him. I cup his face. "My problems aren't yours. Let me deal with my family and I'll meet you at the festivities, or the game, depending on how long this takes."

He frowns and glances down, and while I can't hear the war he's fighting inside his head, I know he's fighting one.

"I just don't want them pressuring you into doing something you don't want to do, you know."

"I do know."

He glances down as he nods and I slide my finger across my phone.

I glance back up to find Ryan inching back, and I feel not just a physical distance between us but an emotional one too, which once again brings back Owen's words of warning.

"Alysha?"

His head lifts and he looks at me through hooded eyes. "Yeah."

"Did Linc come with him?"

"He didn't say."

He nods again. "If you need me…"

"I know."

"Just…family, family is everything," he adds, and walks to the closet to get my coat.

I take the coat and note the deep concern in his eyes. When he says family, is he talking about me and mine, or that I'm a part of his? Before I can ask, his sister Lauren comes bounding into the room.

"Hey, what's up…" She pauses and glances at us. "Oh, sorry. I didn't mean to interrupt."

I pull myself together. "It's okay. I have to run. I'm hoping to see the tractor pull and game and be back here later for the potluck."

"Okay, see you there," she says and throws her arms around me, and I get the strangest feeling in my gut this is our last hug and we both know it. I call for a car, and tug my coat and boots on as I wait.

"Where is your father right now?" Ryan asks.

"He's staying at one of the hotels on the waterfront. I guess maybe he didn't know exactly where to find me."

"He probably did," Ryan says and he's probably right. I told my mother where I was and Potter's farm is the biggest on the island with signs everywhere. All he'd have to do is ask and anyone could point him in the right direction.

"Maybe he just didn't want to impose."

"Yeah, maybe."

"Is he planning on staying overnight?"

"I don't know, actually. I can't imagine he would." Ryan's eyes narrow. "I just mean that tomorrow is Christmas Day and tonight is Mom's big party, and he'll want to be back for that. I'm looking forward to watching you play tonight." Why is conversation so hard and awkward all of a sudden? Ryan and I had no trouble conversing. Everything comes easy for us, and I'm sure he's feeling this strain every bit as much as I am. But I guess I get it. He's worried about me. Worried about my future, and I freaking love him for that.

Yup, I said it. In my own head, anyway, but I love Ryan Potter.

A car comes down the long driveway. "That was fast."

He shrugs. "Nothing is too far around here."

I blink up at him. "I'll see you soon, okay?"

He nods like he's not sure he believes that. I climb into the back seat and glance over my shoulder until we round the corner and Ryan is out of sight. I exhale and play over the conversation I'm sure I'm about to have.

By the time I reach the hotel, I'm calm and ready to face my father and my future, until I get out of the car, and step inside the grand hotel and find Dad sipping coffee in a lounge chair by the fire.

"Dad," I say and he stands. I take in his perfectly tailored suit, and shoes that probably cost as much as one of Ryan's tractors.

"Alysha." He holds his hands out for a hug and I fall into his embrace.

"What's going on?"

"Sit." He gestures to the chair and raises his hand to the man behind the bar, asking for a coffee for me. I could actually use a drink, but I stay quiet.

"I guess this is what you meant when you said you leave me no choice."

He leans forward, worried eyes moving over my face, and for a second I feel like I'm about to burst out crying, but I hold it together.

"Why is it that you don't want to come home?"

I lift my chin a notch. "Linc and I broke up."

He frowns, and reaches for his coffee cup. "I see," he says after a sip. "This is news to me. As far as your mother and I knew..."

His words fall off and I stop him. "Linc was going to ask me to marry him."

He stiffens. "I didn't say that."

"You didn't have to. Mom said something a bit ago that alluded to it."

He goes quiet as the server brings me a cup of coffee and refreshes his. I blow on it, and take a sip as I let my father's brain puzzle things out.

"You don't want to marry Linc?"

"No, I don't. I really did hurt my ankle, and my friend, Ryan, really was trying to help, but the truth is, I'm a coward. I didn't want to go home and face a proposal because..."

He finishes my sentence with, "Because it's not what you want."

I brace myself, waiting for him to tell me how well suited Linc and I are and how well Linc will provide for me, but I don't want anyone to provide for me. I want someone to love me.

I want Ryan to love me.

"I didn't know you felt this way."

"I guess I didn't know either until things escalated."

"I don't want you to be unhappy, Alysha. I don't want you to end up in a relationship that doesn't give you what you need."

"Mom wants it."

He nods in understanding. "She wants what she thinks is best for you. She thinks Linc will be a good provider..."

"Dad, I don't need—"

He holds his hand up to stop me. "Your mom grew up struggling. She was a dancer, a great dancer, but it's so hard to make it big. I came along, and well, we got pregnant."

My heart lurches, because his eyes are saying what his words aren't. Mom got pregnant on purpose. My stomach tightens as that realization swirls around inside my brain. I swallow, hard. I've done the math, so I already knew they were already pregnant with me when they married. I just had no idea she'd gotten pregnant on purpose.

I fall quiet, to let him finish. "Your mom and I, we married young."

"Dad, it's okay—"

"Getting married was the right thing to do. Or at least it used to be back then." I consider Ryan and the unhappy marriage he could have found himself in. Thank God he dodged that bullet and there really wasn't an innocent child involved.

"I don't think it's ever the right thing," I say quietly, but not to hurt him.

He gives a humorless laugh. "You're smarter than all of us." He reaches out and takes my hand. "You're also the best thing about us, Alysha."

Tears pool in my eyes. My dad never talks like this, and I… don't even know how to process. "Dad," I say through a scratchy throat.

"Your mom and I, we do love each other. It's just complicated." He gives me a smile. "Now tell me about this boy Ryan who helped you."

A laugh bubbles up in my throat, partly from relief—he's not trying to convince me to marry Linc—and partly because he's so damn astute and I should have known I could never get anything by him and you know what, I don't want to get anything by him. I want him to see what I see in Ryan and in the gorgeous island.

"He's really sweet, Dad. So kind and caring, and he's a farmer."

Dad's head rears back. "A farmer you say."

"Well, his family owns Potter farms and he lost his dad when he was young and he's taken over the farm. He goes to Scotia Academy and is taking agriculture, oh and he's a great hockey player. Will you stay a little longer and watch his game tonight?"

Dad perks up at that. "A hockey player, you say."

I laugh. "Actually, he plays hockey, he's an amazing defenseman, but he's a farmer."

"How good of a hockey player is he?" He winks at me. "We're always looking for great defensemen for the team."

Once again, doubt tugs at me. Could his friends and grandfather be right? I take a moment and relive all my moments with Ryan, and see how happy he is on the farm and in my heart, I'm pretty sure they're all wrong. But what if they're not? What if he is passing up a once in a lifetime opportunity?

"I would love to hang around and watch him play." He smiles at me. "How long have you loved him, Alysha?"

My heart soars, and tears spill down my cheeks. "A long time, and I think you'll love him too. He's so good to his family and...to me. Family is really important to him."

Dad smiles. "It's important to me too, Alysha. I know I'm busy with work and commitments, but I try to be a good father." He pauses. "I need to be a better husband too."

I nod, leaving it at that. He's aware of his failings and that is his burden to bear.

"Dad?"

"Yeah."

The way he perked up when I said Ryan was an amazing hockey player triggers something deep inside me and I ask, "Do you care that he's a farmer?"

He goes quiet for a long time, so long I worry the he does care. "Farming is good honest work, Alysha. Farmers are the backbone of America."

"And Canada," I say playfully.

"Yes, of course. If this boy makes you happy, then he makes me happy too."

"And Mom?"

"She just worries about you. I'm sure she envisions a different life than this."

"Let me show you this life, Dad."

He nods and stands and I set my cup down as he pulls on his coat. We head outside and I slide into his rental car. I begin to talk about the island, telling him facts about the size and beaches and the farming. He nods and drives, and I give him directions, taking us to the center of town where the festivities have begun.

"The tractor races are beginning. Ryan's younger sister is riding one of them."

I put my arm through Dad's and drag him to an open spot on the field. I search the area for Ryan, but can't find him. Just then Owen comes up to us, and stands directly in front of me, blocking my view.

"Alysha, there you are," he says and my father smiles, about to shake his hand, no doubt thinking it's Ryan, when I quickly introduce them.

"Have you seen Ryan?" I ask. He grins, like he knows something I don't and turns and points. I follow the direction and find Ryan in a deep conversation with Lexi.

As I try not to feel jealous, try not to convince myself it was Lexi he's been secretly messaging, Owen turns to my dad.

"Mr. Tiffany, it's so nice to meet you. Alysha and I are great friends, and the Buck's are my favorite team."

My father cocks a brow. "What did you say your name was?"

"Owen Flynn." He laughs. "I'm still hoping to get scouted." He puts his arm around me, and I try to shrug it off. That's when I notice Ryan's eyes on me. "I'm currently playing for Quebec, but Alysha and I are hoping not to be so far apart in the future."

My father looks at Owen like he has no idea what's going on, but I do. Oh, I definitely do. Owen wasn't scouted for Dad's team. He was using me to get close to Dad—just like he accused Ryan of doing. Which of course, he wasn't, right?

Why the hell then is Lexi all over him, like he's about to make all her dreams come true?

25

RYAN

What the fuck is Owen doing with Alysha and her father, and why is he touching her like that? I'm going to kill the fucker. Then again, I have no claim to Alysha. Hell, I haven't even told her how I feel. I guess a part of me was always afraid to go all in, because a part of me was worried she'd go back to Linc. But Owen? I guess maybe now that he's on her father's team, he's trying to lay claim to her too. I guess he does like to go after my girls. Not that Alysha is my girl.

But speaking of girls.

"You should go talk to him," Lexi says, and keeps touching me, even though I keep telling her to stop.

"Why would I do that?"

"It's not too late to get scouted by his team, and hey, your friend Alysha could put a word in for you."

"Lexi."

"Owen told me he was going to be visiting Alysha when she returns home and he goes to play for her father."

I shake my head. Alysha mentioned that to me, but I know she didn't agree to that.

"I think we could make it work this time, Ryan. You and me. We were good together."

"Yeah, until you lied to me and tried to trap me with a pretend baby so you could force me to set my sights for the NHL. Jesus, Lexi." Saying that out loud sounds insane. Plus, we weren't good together. We were having troubles and I was gearing up to end things.

"They do make a cute couple, don't you think?"

I catch Alysha's eyes and she's frowning at me. I'm about to go to her, when Owen puts his arms around her and her father and starts walking in the opposite direction.

"Ryan," my middle sister Monica calls out. "Come on, the tractor races are about to start."

Torn on which way to turn, I'm about to hurry to Alysha and bring her to the race, but my sister Lucy, who appears out of nowhere wraps her arm in mine. "You okay?" she asks as she tugs me away from Lexi.

We start walking and Lexi follows behind.

"Yeah, I'm okay."

"Are you sure about that, big brother?"

I take a breath and my throat tightens as I let it out. "No."

She hugs my arms a little tighter. "That's what I thought."

"You need to talk to her."

"Her father...he's probably...taking her." I glance over my shoulder to see Alysha but she's gone. I look back at my sister and take in her worried eyes. "I know," I say.

"Before she leaves."

"I don't even know what she wants," I admit.

"She wants you, just like you want her." I glance at my wise kid sister. "It's so easy to see, Ryan."

"This island, I love it." I glance up and catch Lauren waving to us as she climbs into the tractor. We wave back as we approach Mom, Granddad and Monica. "It's where I belong, but it's not for everyone. I'd hate for her to regret it, you know."

"Lexi is still behind us. Want me to take care of that."

I laugh and rustle Lucy's hair. "She wants to get back together."

"And I want to put her face in the snow."

"I can fight my own battles."

"Then get fighting, Ryan, because you have a big one ahead of you." I know, realizing she's talking about Alysha and the truth is, I have been fighting, but now it's time to up my game and go all in. I'm hoping to do that tonight, after the hockey game.

I turn my attention to my sister and grin as I see Colin, the boy she's trying to impress in the tractor beside her. I count ten tractors all lined up in the field ready to go. I steal one more glance over my shoulder. Fuck, I wish Alysha was here to see this. I just hope wherever she is, she's watching, but I would have preferred for her to be here with the family.

That thought makes me snort and Lucy eyes me. This is my family, not hers, and she is with her family, just like she should be over the holidays. Was I wrong to practically force her to come home with me? Although she seemed willing to come. Eager, actually. She still hasn't told me why she didn't want to go home for the holidays, other than the fact that she'd likely spend most of it alone, and that's not right.

The tractors start and the horn blows and off they go. I start jumping up and down, cheering Lauren on when she takes the lead, and she makes some hand gesture to Colin which makes him laugh. At least she's not throwing the race to soothe his frail male ego. She's a strong-willed girl and any guy who dates her will have his hands full. The tractors kick up snow and mud, and I'm glad we're standing back.

Beside me, Lexi starts jumping up and down, and I'd forgotten she was still hanging around. I inch closer to Lucy, and throw my arm around her as Lauren crosses the finish line.

"Go Lauren," I yell and we all take off toward her. She's laughing as she jumps from the tractor into a wet slushy snow pile, and Colin circles the front to congratulate her. He picks her up and spins her around and I'm not sure I've ever seen her smile so big.

She turns to me and glances around. "Where's Alysha? Did she see me win?"

Shit.

"She's around here somewhere. I'm sure she did. She's with her father."

She frowns. "Oh, okay. Well I hope she saw me win."

It's clear my sisters like Alysha very much and her watching Lauren race was important to Lauren. Lauren puts her hand on my chest. "Okay, bro. Now it's time for you to win the game against the Islanders."

The Islanders is a team of senior locals, some who've played professionally in the past, or were in Major Juniors. The team I'll be playing on consists of college players from the island, those going to college here, and those who've come home for the holidays. It's a fun exhibition game, and no one can discount the seniors. Those men can kick ass.

I turn to head to the car to get my gear, needing a bit of time with my own thoughts. But that's short lived when I spot Alysha coming my way. My heart beats fast in my chest and a smile I have no control over spreads across my face, partly because I'm just happy to see her, and partly because Owen is nowhere in sight. He's probably getting ready for the game.

"Ryan," Alysha calls out and waves.

I start toward her, and lift my gaze to her father. "This is my father, Brian. Dad this is Ryan Potter."

"The farmer," he says, and I stiffen. His face is expressionless, like he's sizing me up as he takes my hand and gives it a firm shake. I tried to read him, but it's hard to tell whether he thinks I'm a country bumpkin because I'm a farmer or not. I get it, I'm not rich and powerful and successful like him. Nor do I want to be. I'm happy with who I am, but could a man like him be happy to have a guy like me with his daughter?

My stomach tightens. "It's nice to meet you, Mr. Tiffany," I say and he doesn't correct me, doesn't tell me to call him Brian. Alrighty then. I turn to Alysha. "Did you see the race?"

Her smile widens. "Yes, we watched from over there." She points down the field. "I didn't want Dad to get snow or mud on him." I can understand that. He's in an Armani suit after all. "Lauren was amazing. Don't you think so, Dad?"

"Yes, amazing," he says, his brows pulled together like he can't for the life of him understand why anyone would race tractors.

"Are you coming to the game?"

Brian—or rather Mr. Tiffany—lights up. "Can't wait. I hear you're a pretty good hockey player."

"I'm okay."

"And Owen Flynn. Apparently, he's one I should be watching too."

Too?

I'm about to ask what he means by that. Isn't Owen already on his team, and why would he be watching me? Alysha mouths the word, *later*. Okay, something strange going on here, and I guess I'll find out later. As the field begins to clear, her father clears his throat.

"Should we make our way to the rink?"

For a second, I think Alysha is going to go up on her toes and kiss me. Instead she gives an uneasy finger wave. "Good luck." We stand facing each other for a second, a strange awkwardness between us.

"Thanks." They walk away and I grab my bag from the car and follow the crowd to the rink. I spot Lexi making her way inside, running to catch up to Owen. If he cheated on her, why the hell is she always talking to him? I shake my head.

Not my business, but it does make me wonder if they're up to something.

There's lots of shoving and razzing going on in the locker room, but my stomach is in knots and I don't join in. I honestly felt like her father was scrutinizing me, and I'm not sure he liked what he saw. Is he here to watch me play? If so, why?

What the hell did he and Alysha talk about?

Owen comes into the locker room and drops his bag down next to me. "Hey, I saw you met my new boss."

"Yeah." I tug on my gear, not wanting to make conversation.

"I'll probably be seeing a lot of Alysha when I play for her dad."

I shake my head. Is he trying to piss me off?

"She's headed back tonight, huh?"

I glare at him and while I suspected she would be going back, I didn't know for sure. "She should be with her family for Christmas."

"Someday I might be a part of that family."

I turn to him, ready to punch him in the face, but he's just not worth it and I kind of think he wants me to start something. Maybe he wants me to play a shit game in front of Brian. I have no idea why it would matter to him.

We all file out of the locker room and onto the ice, and we get a standing ovation. I search the crowd until I find Alysha and she waves to me. Beside me, Owen waves back. What the fuck? I wish he was on the opposing team so I could shove his head into the boards.

We get into position and the ref drops the puck, and after a scrap, Owen wins it. The crowd claps and I work to focus on the game, and not Alysha.

A big ass defenseman on the seniors team body checks Owen and snags the puck. It gets passed around until the opposing forward gets it and skates around our left winger. I move back, timing his moves and positioning myself as he comes my way.

He stops aggressively and does a cross over and he leans in on me as I reposition. I move quickly, and before he can do another cross over, I push the puck with the tip of my stick and send it down the ice. The crowd cheers and I smile up at Alysha as she claps for me.

The game continues, and the seniors give us a run for our money and by the end of the game, I'm sweaty and exhausted but happy, because I saved a lot of goals. Only one got past me and into the net, but Owen scored two, so the young guns win. We all played a great game, but we'll razz the seniors about it later tonight at the house when they come for the potluck.

We make our way off the ice, and I jump in the shower, anxious to get outside and see Alysha. I hope she comes to the house, not just to say goodbye before she goes home for the holidays, but because I have a gift I want to give her. A gift that will show her exactly what she means to me.

Outside, she's nowhere to be found. Maybe she's already on her way to the farm. A wave of panic grips me. Maybe she's already on her way to the airport. She wouldn't leave without saying goodbye, would she? Her stuff is still at the farm.

I drive back to the house, and the only other car in the driveway is a rental. My heart jumps into my throat. Alysha is here. I jump from my car, and spot her father in the driver's seat of the rental. Did he not want to come in? He has his head down, so I hurry inside the house and find Alysha by the fire, looking at the stocking I knitted for her.

She turns when she hears me, and has tears in her eyes. "Is this for me?"

I smile and nod. "Yeah, I was sneaking out of your bed early every morning so I could work on it in secret."

What looks like relief moves over her face. "Oh, is that what you were doing?"

I angle my head. "What did you think I was doing?"

"Doesn't matter. Thank you, though. I love it. It's the most thoughtful present anyone has ever made me." She frowns. "I'm going back."

"Owen told me."

Her body stiffens. "Oh." A beat of silence and then, "I have some things to take care of. Dad and I talked..." She looks down for a second, a deep frown on her face like she's battling an internal war.

"What's going on, Alysha?"

"I have a Christmas present for you, too."

I step closer, and take her hand. "Oh? Does it involve you in my clothes, in my bed?"

"No, actually." She hesitates for a second, and looks almost nervous. "Dad thought you were a great player. He's going to send a scout to the academy. He said the team could use a strong defenseman."

I swallow—at least I think I'm swallowing—as my world collapses around me. I stare at Alysha, hardly able to believe what I'm hearing. My heart pounds so hard against my ribs that it reverberates in my ears. My head spins as I run her words around in my brain over and over again. The room closes in on me as I break out in a cold sweat as I take a small step backward.

"I…think…you should go."

"What?" she asks her eyes wide. "Ryan. If this isn't what you—"

"Of course it's what I want." I shake my head at my lie. After all the time we spent together, all the talking we did, she still thinks I want to play hockey? Or maybe she doesn't and maybe me being on the team is the only way a man like her father could ever accept me in his daughter's life. I guess a farmer just isn't good enough for a girl like her, and she must think the same if she just put that offer on the table. But you know what, family is everything and while I'd fight tooth and nail for this girl to be mine, I can't—won't—come between her and her family.

"What the fuck, Alysha?" is all I can manage to push out.

She reaches for me and I flinch. "Ryan, wait. Is it Lexi? Is it true? Are you getting back together with her?"

"No, I'm…why the hell would you think that?"

"It's just…Owen…Lexi…" She shakes her head, clearly flustered and unable to string her words together.

"What about them?"

"The things they said, about you using me."

"Things I thought you didn't believe." I run agitated fingers through my hair. "But I guess I was wrong because suddenly you're thinking all kinds of things about me, aren't you?"

"I don't...I didn't."

"Want to know what I think?" She nods and blinks up at me, her lips quivering. It takes everything in me not to pull her to me and tell her I love her. I hate seeing her like this and I don't want to hurt her but if she needs me to be something else—something other than a farmer—before she can be with me, much like Lexi did, I can't be with her. "That you shouldn't keep your father waiting."

26

ALYSHA

The house is beautifully, professionally decorated, and music blares from the surround-sound speakers, but I don't feel any Christmas cheer. All I feel is cold inside. The kind of cold I'm not sure I ever felt before. It's almost numbing, and I actually wish it was because what I'm feeling hurts so badly, I'd rather be numb.

"Darling, is that what you're wearing?" Mom asks as she glances at me, giving me a once over with disapproving eyes.

"It's a simple black dress, Mom."

"Well maybe you can put on something a little brighter, you know, for the pictures." I really, really hope she's not talking about engagement pictures. Ryan might not want me anymore, but that does not mean I'm going to run into Linc's arms and beg forgiveness. I might have only spent a week with Ryan, but it changed me in profound ways, made me realize what I want, what I don't want, and injected me with a voice and courage.

On the way home, I texted Linc and told him we needed to talk. If he has it in his head we're still together, I need to set the record straight. In the past he never showed up for Mom's elaborate Christmas Eve party, and if he did, it was just a quick hello to show his face to the important people and off he went again. I sometimes wondered if he had a secret family. But no, his love is his work and that's what comes first.

Mom pinches my cheeks, and I flinch away. "Ow, what did you do that for?"

"You're so pale."

"It's winter."

"Maybe you should have gone to one of those tanning beds."

"Do you have any idea how bad they are for you?"

"But darling, you need to look your best."

"Yeah, how well do you think I'll look if I get skin cancer from one of those things."

"Stop being so dramatic."

I shake my head and walk up to the tree. It's gorgeous with its blue and white balls, but it definitely lacks character. "Where are all the ornaments I made in school?" I ask.

"Oh Alysha, what has gotten into you." I turn to face Mom and take in her too-thin body draped in a wraparound dress embedded with jewels. She tucks a strand of dark hair behind her ear and tsks. "You never should have gone to that...that place with that boy."

"The place was Prince Edward Island and the boy, Ryan Potter, is a man."

"Linc is a man," she corrects.

"Have you ever heard of hiding a pickle on a Christmas tree?" I'm so sad that I missed out on doing that with Ryan. My mother looks at me like she might march me straight to a hospital for a brain scan.

The doorbell rings and Mom claps her hands. "Straighten up, guests are arriving."

"Yay," I say under my breath. God, am I acting like a spoiled child here? I live a privileged life, I know that, but dammit, it's been a very unhappy life too. I don't want this for my future. I don't want to throw fake parties for fake people.

"You're back."

I spin and find Linc walking into the room like he owns it, and my heart jumps into my throat.

"You're here," I respond. He comes toward me like nothing happened, but something did happen, something big and important. I fell in love with another man, who told me to go home, and right now this house doesn't feel like home. Tears prick my eyes, because all I want to do is go back to Halifax, and lock myself away in my apartment, or maybe cry on one of my friends' shoulders.

"We never should have broken up over text," I tell him. "It was not the way to handle the demise of a four-year relationship."

He grins at me, like he holds all the cards and I'm caving to him. "I'm home, here tonight, because I wanted to talk to you, face to face."

He comes closer and puts his hand on my shoulder and it sends an uneasy feeling through me. How did I waste so much of my life with a man whose touch I don't really like? Not that he ever really touched me a lot, which is why I craved it so badly with Ryan. God, the way that man touched me...

Stop.

"You want to put that foolishness behind us. I understand."

"No, I wanted to tell you to your face that it is over, Linc. You and me, it's not working out."

His face scrunches up and I swear to God he looks like a three-year-old about to have a temper tantrum. And why wouldn't he? I don't think he's ever been told no before.

"It's not over, Alysha. We're not over."

My God, the way he says that with conviction, like he is in total charge of my life infuriates me. It shouldn't, though. It's my fault. I've gone with the flow, let things happen and sat back and played the dutiful 'practically engaged' girlfriend for a while now. But I'm not that girl anymore.

"Listen," he begins. "I get it. You and the farmer." He snorts out a laugh. "I guess you had to sow your wild oats." He snorts again. "Get it." Rage goes through me. "He's a farmer, Alysha. Don't tell me you want to be with a guy like that."

"A guy like that!" I blurt out. "You have no idea what kind of guy he is."

He holds his hands up palms out. "Fine, go to him then." There's a challenging look in his eyes, like he knows more than I think he does and I'm guessing he talked to my father. I didn't tell Dad much when Ryan sent me home, only that I never wanted to set foot on Prince Edward Island again. And of course, I cried all the way to the airport, and cried all the way home on Dad's private plane. He's a smart man. He figured it out.

What I haven't figured out is how I could have been so stupid.

"I'm not going to him."

He straightens his shoulders, everything about him smug. "We can move past this, Alysha. You had some fun."

"Really, Linc. You're okay that I was with another guy?"

"We were broken up, weren't we?"

"In my mind we were, but you didn't even tell Dad."

He shrugs. "I didn't see the sense in dragging him into anything, and I assumed we'd be getting back together."

I glare at him, and that's when it hits me. "You were with someone else, weren't you?"

"None of that matters now."

I step back, my stomach swirling. "Linc, in your head we were still together, but you still slept with someone else?" I honestly don't care that he was with someone else, but it's the whole fact that he wanted me back—assumed we'd be getting back together—and went and slept with someone anyway. Is that love? Hell no. This man doesn't love me. He never has. He wants to be part of the Tiffany family.

I calm myself down and in an even voice I say, "It's over Linc. We're over. We've actually been over for a while now. I was faithful to you when we were together. I didn't start anything with Ryan—"

He snorts and cuts me off. "A fucking farmer."

A part of me wants to tell him everything Ryan is, but I stop myself. He's not worth my breath. I know who Ryan is, despite him accusing me of knowing nothing about him, and I can understand why he said that.

"I didn't start anything with Ryan until we were broken up."

Mom's voice rings out in the hallway as she greets guests. "Let's not make a scene."

"I'm not."

He pulls a velvet box from his pocket and I nearly swallow my tongue. "Really?"

"Come on, babe. Think about it. This Ryan guy doesn't want you. Well, he got what he wanted from you and now it's over. We make a good team. Your mother is expecting this. You don't want to disappoint her, do you?"

"Actually, I do. I want to disappoint everyone." I've disappointed myself greatly, so why not bring the whole family into my big stupid disappointing life.

"You're talking silly."

"Silly, that's me, like my dancing. Everything is silly." Okay, now I'm worried I might be getting a bit hysterical, but I did just lose the only man I've ever loved, and I lost his family, and a goat named Billy, and a Clydesdale named Sugar Bear and...a future I wanted.

Mom peeks her head into the room. "I'm not interrupting anything, am I?" She gives Linc a hopeful smile and he glares at me. "Alysha, you need to pull yourself together."

"Pull this together," I say and offer him my middle finger, showing him I am indeed silly. I walk away, and find my father sipping whisky at the bar in the other room.

"Honey," he says, as I walk up to him.

"I'm not feeling well. I'm going to go to bed." He nods. "I'm going to head back to Halifax in the morning. I just need some quiet time." He nods and I turn, and head up the stairs, locking the world out and myself inside. I fall onto my bed, and when my phone pings I scramble to check it, hoping it's Ryan. But no, it's Linc, giving me one last chance, which makes me laugh hysterically.

I think I might be losing it.

I crawl into bed, and the next thing I know morning is upon us and I'm shocked that I actually slept. I guess all the crying and exhaustion finally took over. I check my phone, but still nothing from Ryan and while I want to text him, I stop myself. He does not want to hear from me, not ever again. I have no idea how we're going to function in our friend group. I guess we only have a few months left before graduation. I can probably hide out until then.

I force myself to get up, and head downstairs, a very disappointed mother greets me. I love how she cares more about image and me marrying a professional guy like Linc over my well-being. At least Dad understands, and I'm very grateful for that. But he doesn't want me disappointing Mom either. Apparently, he does enough of that himself.

I go through the motions of opening the lovely gifts under the tree, and apologize profusely that I didn't have anything for them. My mother kindly tells me an engagement would have been the best gift and that's when I know I have to go.

I get myself together, kiss my parents goodbye and call an Uber to take me to the airport. I'm flying commercial. I don't want to take Dad's pilot away from his family on Christmas day. Hours later, I climb from my ride home and stand on the curb and stare at my place.

Home sweet home. For now, anyway. I still have no idea where I'll live after graduation, or what I'll be doing but I have to figure that out, and soon.

I head inside and change into a pair of pajamas, wishing they were Ryan's—but that thought makes me cry—and climb into bed, where I stay for the next few days, only getting up to eat, or go to the bathroom.

Before I know it, it's the thirty-first and I'm sure all my friends—who have no idea I'm even home—will be having a big party tonight. I walk into my living room and pull open my curtains, but as soon as I do, I spot Daisy and Brandon on the sidewalk. They both stop and turn, staring at me with slack jaws and I can't blame them. I don't know when I showered last, and I've been in the same clothes for a week. I am so pathetic.

They come up to my door, and I hesitate, but it's too late to go hide in my bed now. I pad down the hall, open it and they take one look at me and shake their heads.

"Alysha," Daisy says. "What is going on?" She looks at my clothes, and I'm sure I have chocolate on my face.

"I messed up," I blurt out and fresh tears begin to fall. Here I thought I was all cried out.

"Oh, girl." She puts her arm around me and walks me to the living room.

"I'll make coffee," Brandon says. He knows his way around the place because Daisy used to live here with me.

He heads to the kitchen, and Daisy sets me on the sofa and sits on the coffee table facing me. "How long have you been home?"

I sniff. "I came back on Christmas Day."

She shakes her head. "Why didn't you call?"

"Because..." I sniff. "Have you heard from Ryan."

"No, what happened?"

"I messed up, big time."

She grabs a tissue from the box and hands it to me and I blurt out everything that happened in Prince Edward Island, and everything that happened when I went home Christmas Eve.

She sits there stunned, absorbing my rushed words as Brandon brings us each a mug of coffee.

"Thank you," I say, blow in it and take a sip.

"So your dad offered him a position on the team?" Brandon says and sits beside Daisy.

I nod. "Something like that...I asked him to consider him, and I thought." I shake my head. "I don't know what I thought. I mean his mother, grandfather and friends... I thought they all must know him better than me, and they got it in my head that Ryan wanted to play in the NHL"

"He doesn't," Brandon says.

"I know, and I did know, and now... I don't know anything."

"Do you know if you love him?" Daisy asks gently.

A hysterical laugh bubbles out of my throat. "That I do know."

She exhales and takes a sip of coffee looking confident when she says, "Okay, then this can all be fixed."

I snort and nearly spill my coffee. I set it on the table. "Nothing can be fixed. I actually even sort of accused him of using me, because Lexi and Owen got into my head. He's never going to talk to me again."

They glance at each other, because they clearly have no idea what I'm talking about.

"Ryan is a proud guy, Alysha."

I nod, understanding that. "He said I didn't know him at all."

"I think, and I could be wrong, but I think because you come from a pretty important family, that by asking your dad to consider Ryan for the team, maybe he thought you thought he wasn't good enough unless he did something impressive."

"Farming is impressive," I say, coming to Ryan's defense. "He showed me everything and he's even getting an agriculture degree to make improvements to the farm. What he does is important work."

Daisy gives my arm a squeeze. "Maybe you need to tell him that."

I bury my face in my hands. "I didn't just accuse him of awful things, I insulted him, didn't I?"

"I think you might have."

"Oh, God, I need to fix this."

"Yeah, you do," Daisy and Brandon say at the same time.

"But how...?"

RYAN

It's later in the afternoon, and the town's big New Year's Eve party is on everyone's mind. Everyone's but mine. Jesse keeps messaging me to get me to go out tonight, but I'm not much in the mood. Nope, not much in the mood for anything these days, and I'm also not looking forward to going back to Halifax and running into Alysha.

Fuck, man, I still can't believe she talked to her father about getting me on the team. Did she not listen to me; not hear anything I was saying to her about farming? I thought she knew me way better than that. I swallow against a tight throat as Billy nudges me, as if he too misses Alysha.

"Sorry, Billy. She's gone." She's gone because I told her to go. Jesus, I really wish Dad was here to talk to, to give me advice.

I finish brushing down Sugar Bear and close the stall. Billy follows me to the door, when it opens and in walks Granddad.

"Hey," I say. "Sugar Bear is taken care of."

"I'm not here to see Sugar Bear."

"Grandad," I begin, to cut him off, much like I've been doing to my entire family all week. I don't want to talk about it. Judging from the look in my grandfather's eyes, I'm not sure he's going to let me walk away this time.

"Your father isn't here to talk to, Ryan, but I am, and if you'll take the advice of a stupid old fart, I'd like to give it."

"You're not a stupid old fart."

"Yeah, actually I am. I think what happened between you and Alysha is all my fault."

"How can it be your fault?"

He takes his hat off and rubs the bald spot on the top of his head. His fingers are aged and gnarled, and it reminds me again of how much work he does around this place, and how much I can take off his hands.

"Your mother and I...we know the responsibilities you put on your shoulders."

"It's not like that. I love this farm, you know that."

"I know you do, but after your father passed, you did everything to be the man of the house, to take care of everyone around you. It's commendable, Ryan. But your mother and I, we don't want you here—"

My fucking heart jumps into my throat. "Jesus Christ," I blurt out. Is this week all about hurting me?

He shakes his head and holds a hand up. "Not like that. Let me finish." I lean against one of the stalls, my legs a bit shaky. "We don't want you here out of some misplaced obligation to your father and family. We want you here, of course, but we also want you to do the things you love."

"I love this." Why can no one see that?

"Your father wouldn't have wanted you to give up a career in the NHL for this."

"I'm not giving up anything," I tell him. "I get more from this farm…" I pause and put my hand over my heart. "…than I get from any game. Farming is in my blood, hockey isn't. It's a fun pastime for me. That's all it is, Granddad."

He nods and frowns, and my chest constricts when I see the tears in his milky blue eyes. "Granddad," I say, and put my hand on his shoulder. He's had loss too, and he hurts just like I do.

"You playing hockey was never about me," he tells me. "It was about you, and I always pushed simply because it was my way of letting you know that no matter what you do, we'll always love you and respect your decisions."

"I know that."

"I just want you happy." I snort, because right now I'm the opposite of that. "And you won't be happy until you go get back that girl of yours."

I shake my head. "Not going to happen."

"It's my fault," he says again. I'm about to correct him but he stops me. "I asked her to do it. I planted the idea in her head. I told her I knew you better than her, and I did it because I'm a stupid old fart who thought that once the option of playing in the NHL was on the table, you'd examine it, and really think about it, and maybe put yourself first for once. A part of me thought you secretly wanted it, and once it was a possibility, I thought maybe you'd realize that you didn't always have to shoulder the responsibility for everything around here."

"Granddad," I say quietly, my heart racing a million miles an hour. It wasn't just Granddad who put that in her head, she said Owen and Lexi did too, and then there was Becca. I didn't correct her when she said once I was in the NHL I could visit her in Victoria. Actually, I told her it sounded like a plan.

Fuck me sideways.

"I honestly don't think she ever believed you wanted to play. She defended you, told me as much."

"Fuck."

"Language," he says and then softens and mumbles, "Fuck is right."

"I love her," I simply state.

Granddad smiles. "She's a keeper."

"Her family though. I don't think they want her with a guy like me."

"A guy who is smart, and funny and kind and caring? Yeah, why would they want her with a guy like that?"

"They won't see that, Granddad."

I glance down and kick at the hay on the floor, my mind and heart racing. "Jesse once said something to me, that maybe me staying here on the farm is selfish."

"I don't understand."

"He once said I needed to start thinking about what Alysha would need from me, and what I'd need from her to make things work." I begin to breathe faster, a new sense of panic invading me. "I was only thinking about what I needed from her. Jesus. I wasn't thinking about what she needed from me."

My granddad nods, like he fully understands. "Jesse is a wise man. Now tell me, what is it she needs from you?"

I try to breathe past the sense of urgency racing through my veins, not to mention the growing lump in my throat. "I have to go. I have to go back to Halifax, right now."

Granddad steps to the side, and when I see who's standing behind him, the world drops out from beneath my feet. The look on my face, the shocked expression I'm no doubt wearing causes my granddad to turn.

He clears his throat and nods. "If you'll both excuse me."

He steps around Alysha, and I stare, unable to find my voice as she stands in front of me, all bundled up in obviously new and proper winter clothes, a glass casserole dish in her hand.

"What...what are you doing here?"

"I made a potato casserole."

I shake my head, completely confused. "Why?"

"Um, a peace offering, I think."

"I want to play for your father," I blurt out, and she stumbles a bit, her jaw falling open in surprise.

I reach for her, take the casserole, and set it on a bench in the barn.

"You do?"

"Yes. If that's what it takes for us to be together." If this is what she needs from me then I'm going to damn well give it to her. Later, when my playing years are over, and even off season, I can come back to the farm, if that's what she wants.

"I was being selfish. I was thinking only about me."

"What are you talking about?"

"I love you, Alysha. I wanted you to stay here, in Prince Edward Island with me. I was going to show you all that on Christmas Eve, but well, things went pretty bad." I put my hand on her shoulder. "I was just about to get in my car and drive back to Halifax to tell you that."

"You were coming to get me?" she asks quietly. "I wasn't sure you ever wanted to speak to me again." She takes a gulping breath. "I...I never meant to hurt or insult you with the offer to play hockey. I understand my mistake, and I hurt you and I don't blame you for being mad. I just thought..."

"I know what you thought. I'm not mad at you. I love you, Alysha."

"I love you too."

I grin like a fool, unable to help myself. As long as we have love, we can figure the other shit out after.

"I don't understand. You don't want to play hockey. I know that. I've always known that. Why are you saying you do?"

"If that's what it takes for us to be together."

"You would do that, Ryan? You would give up everything you love here, to play hockey for me?"

"If it's what it takes and I don't want you to lose your family over me."

"My father doesn't care that you're a farmer, by the way. Even if he did, I'm not sure that would have stopped me from coming here. My mom, well, she'll just have to get over it." She laughs as my heart pounds against my ribs. "You don't have to play hockey. It's not what it takes for us to be together, Ryan. Not at all. But..." She puts her hand on my chest. "The fact that you said you would means the world to me."

"I realized I was being selfish, wanting you to give up everything to be here with me. I wasn't sacrificing anything."

"You are the least selfish man I know and I want you to know, you never asked me to give up anything. You're very supportive of everyone."

I swallow. "I need to circle back to something." She angles her head and waits for me to speak. "You love me?"

She laughs and I throw my arms around her, pick her up and spin her. My lips find hers for a deep, soul-searing kiss.

"I need to tell you something. When I came here with you, it was because I was being a coward."

"I don't understand. I knew you didn't want to go home but I wasn't sure why. You never told me."

"I want to tell you now." I fall quiet. "Linc was going to propose."

"Oh," I say and shrug. "I guess I shouldn't be surprised since you guys were 'practically engaged'. You didn't want that?"

"Practically and engaged are two different things, and it scared me. I was a coward. I came here with you, to avoid dealing with him. But I had to go home. I had to deal with it. I...I didn't tell you how I felt because again, coward. I wasn't sure what we were doing, and I didn't want to do or say anything to end it."

"I was a coward too, and I'm glad you came back. Since we're being honest, I think I was afraid to go all in and tell you how I felt because a part of me thought you'd go back to Linc."

"I kind of thought you were worried about that."

I roll my eyes. "I mean how many times did I hear that you were 'practically engaged, right?"

"A lot."

I go serious again. "How did he take it?"

"Not well. Neither did my mother, but I have to live my own life, the life I want." She taps my chest. "I think a wise man once told me that." She turns and looks around the wide expanse of farm. "I fell in love with you here, Ryan." She glances down. "Actually, I think I fell in love with you back home, the night you slept on my sofa."

"I've been in love with you since I first set eyes on you," I admit and she grins.

"I'm sorry I accused you of going back to Lexi. I just...I don't know. I think they were feeding me lies, working together. He was pretending to like me to get in good with my dad. I don't know how she was in on it. Maybe he promised to take her with him if she broke us up and I went for him, and got him on the team. Like you said, she'd do anything to get off this island."

"It's not for everyone, and I don't know what those two were up to. But that's all in the past. Let's forget about them and think about the future."

"I want to spend my future on this gorgeous island with you. I love it here, Ryan."

"Are you sure, Alysha?" I cup her face, my gaze moving over her pink cheeks. "Is it what you really want?"

"I have never been more positive about anything in my entire life. Wait." She reaches into her bag and pulls out a card and hands it to me.

"What's this?"

"My business cards with my name and number. I'm going to give a card to your sisters, your mom and granddad. Free dance lessons. It's their Christmas present." She shrugs. "I don't know where or how, or when, but I'm going to open my own studio someday."

"I know how."

Her brow pulls together. "What?"

"You never hung around for my present." Excitement races through my blood, anxious to show her what I'd been working on.

"You made me a stocking."

"There's more." She eyes me. "Remember when I said I was going to show you on Christmas Eve that I loved you?"

"I wasn't sure what you meant by that."

I take her hand, and we head to the barn, and when I swing open the doors and turn on the lights and heat. When she sees the dance studio I made for her, she gasps and then starts to cry.

"Babe," I say and pull her to me.

She sobs into my chest, and my own eyes water as I hug her trembling body and absorb her tremors. "I can't believe you did this for me?"

"Actually, it was me being selfish again."

She snort-laughs and makes a fist and lightly pounds it against my chest. "You are not selfish."

"I wanted to keep you here, but then I was worried that might have been wrong of me. But I really wanted to surprise you with this, and support all your dreams. I thought...you could teach, right here on the farm."

"You are the sweetest man on this planet, and I'm the luckiest woman."

"I'm the lucky one," I say and cup her face. I brush her tears away with my thumbs and brush my lips over hers. "Dance lessons will bring so much joy to this community, especially during the long, cold winters."

"I can't wait to get started."

"This does mean you'll marry me, right?" I ask and her eyes go wide.

"Did you just ask me to marry you?"

"I'll do it proper, on one knee with a ring, just as soon as I can get one. But I want you to be my wife, Alysha, and I promise, I'll spend every day trying to make you the happiest woman in the world."

"You already do, Ryan, and that's a yes, I will marry you."

"So we can officially say we're engaged. None of this 'practically engaged' bullshit."

That makes her laugh and the sound warms my heart. "We're engaged," she says and I kiss her again.

"Tonight." I tug her to me and hold her so tight I'm a little worried she might not be able to breathe, but I can't get her close enough. "Will you kiss me when the ball drops tonight?"

"Only if we can do something."

"Oh, and what is it you'd like to do?"

She goes up on her toes, closes her eyes. "Start now."

Instead of kissing her, which nearly kills me, I back up. Her eyes open, confusion clouding them. "Wait, do you feel that?" I ask.

"What?"

"Your body. You're shivering."

"It's cold out here."

"No, that's not it." Confusion clouds her eyes and I examine her. "Your skin, is it tingly and sensitive?"

A small smile curls the corners of her mouth as understanding dawns. "Now that you mention it, it is."

I take in the dark smudges under her eyes. "You haven't been sleeping, have you?"

"Not well."

With the new dance studio warming, I pull her zipper down, and put my hand over her heart. "High heart rate," I say and frown, feigning worry.

"Nooky-itis." She shakes her head. "What can you do?"

"You," I say. "I can do you, over and over and over."

She grins and throws her arms around me. "I love you, Ryan and I really love nooky-itis."

I grip her hips and pull her against my hard cock. "Just for the record, the cure isn't a no strings hook-up. It's a lifetime of lovemaking."

"And potato casseroles," she adds with a laugh.

"Right, and potato casseroles," I agree. "Now let's burn some calories so we can go devour the one you made."

I kiss my gorgeous fiancée with all the love inside me as her sweet moans curl around my heart and hug tight. Wait, did she just bleep?

I inch back to see her as Billy comes running in between us, nearly knocking me on my ass. I shake my head as Alysha bends to hug Billy.

I shake my head in disbelief. "Cock blocked by a fucking goat..."

I glance around my dance studio and take in all the kids stretching. As they chatter, my heart soars with happiness. I honestly had no idea a person could be this blessed in life. There's this constant bubble of happiness inside of me. Then again, it could be a bubble of indigestion, which I've been suffering from greatly this last week. I turn and look at myself in the mirror. My hand goes to my protruding belly.

"Why is your belly big?" one of the little girls asks. She wasn't here when I told the class last week.

I laugh and want to tell her it's from eating too many potatoes, which I totally do, but instead I say, "I'm going to have a baby." I'm only four months pregnant, but my frame is so small it looks like I'm seven months along.

Her eyes go big. "A boy or girl?"

"We don't know yet." Ryan doesn't want to find out early. He likes the idea of the baby's sex being a surprise, and I agree. What I don't like the idea of is giving birth to enough kids to fill this dance studio. Ryan and I probably should have discussed that before I agreed to be his wife last year. That thought makes me laugh. He could have told me he wanted to have a hundred kids and I still would have married him. I do like the idea of filling the big farmhouse with kids, though. There's so much love and laughter in it now, a bevy of kids can only add to the happy chaos.

Dressed in dirty coveralls, Ryan walks by the open door and I blow him a kiss. The kids see me and they all do the same which makes me laugh. It's summer, and Ryan is pretty busy farming, but that's okay. I'm busy building my business, but we fall in bed together every night, where we talk about our days and dreams and hopes, and most nights make love.

Things have been great so far here on the Island. We moved here right after graduation, but I haven't done a winter here yet. Ryan worries about me, but with him by my side, I know I'll do just fine and he's an expert at curing nooky-itis, so that's a plus. My phone pings and I glance at it. I smile when I see the message from my mother checking up on me. When I said she'd have to deal with Ryan being a farmer, I meant it, and she did.

She came here for the wedding in April, right after our graduation, and while she could never live here, she understands my draw to the country's smallest province. Ryan was so charming, and so was his family, that there was no way she couldn't fall for all of them. In the end, I think like Dad, she wants me happy and they're pretty excited about having a grandbaby. They're constantly sending me toys and blankets and clothes and the little one isn't even here yet, but it's good to know how loved our child will be.

As for Linc, the last I heard he married some senator's daughter, and I hope they're happy. I really do. He still works for

Dad, but I don't hear about him anymore. Ryan is still playing hockey, for fun, and I still love watching him. Many of our friends now play in the NHL, and according to Sawyer, who is the daughter of Scotia Storm's hockey coach, there's a bunch of new rookies at Storm House who are tearing up the town. What did she say they thought they were? Oh right, a bunch of warriors. I'm sure they can't be as bad as all that.

Speaking of Sawyer, I do miss my friends, but they were all here for the wedding at the end of April, and we're all planning another reunion for next year. Kennedy and Matt even brought sweet Madelyn, who was my flower girl. I also loved seeing Sawyer and Chase, Piper and Beckett, and Brandon and Daisy. They all found their happily ever afters, just like Ryan and me. Cheddar and his new girlfriend weren't able to make the wedding due to other commitments, but they'll be coming to the reunion. Apparently he fell in love over the holidays and we've yet to hear his story, considering they barely surfaced for air during our last semester. I'm sure it's going to be a good one and when he comes to the reunion, I have no doubt we'll hear all the sordid details. How could they not be sordid? This is Cheddar we're talking about.

One of the girls in the class stands up and sticks out her belly. "Am I having a baby too?"

Oh God.

I clap my hands. "Okay, time to dance."

I turn on the music and for the next half hour with a warm summer breeze blowing in, we go over the routine, and I'm so proud of my kids. I can't wait for the end of summer recital. Cars soon pull into the driveway and I clap my hands again.

"Okay, time to tidy up. Your parents are arriving."

The kids go about their routine of putting things away, and I walk to the door to greet the parents. In the distance, I spot Lauren with Colin and I grin. I guess she impressed him when she won the tractor races. I talk to the parents as they come to collect their kids and once I'm alone, I turn the music on, put my hand on my belly, and sway in front of the mirror.

I glance up as footsteps echo on the floor and smile at my husband, who is filthy dirty, as he comes toward me. I turn, and throw my arms around him.

"I'm going to get you all dirty."

"I like dirty," I tease and I hug him tighter as he laughs.

"Why are you so obsessed with me, Alysha?"

This time I laugh. "What are you doing in here anyway?"

I want to show you something."

"Oh?"

He shakes his head, his lips quirking. "My god, is sex all you think about?"

"Yes." It's the truth. I don't know what it is about being pregnant, but my hormones are going crazy. "Don't tell me you don't." He puts his hand on my belly. He's a little afraid of sex now, but I've been reassuring him it won't hurt the baby, but it's simply in his nature to care for those he loves and being one of those people is the greatest feeling in the world.

"Sex after. I want to show you something first." He takes my hand and we walk outside. He leads me into the farm house and starts taking me to the bedroom.

"I thought you said sex after."

He pushes open the bedroom door, and I stop in my tracks when I take in the very old, antique cradle. "What's this?"

I turn to him, and he swallows as a few tears build in his eyes. He swipes at them and my heart aches because I think I know what I'm looking at.

"It was Dad's," he says quietly, like he has a lump in his throat and it takes effort to speak. He shuts the door and locks it, giving us private time.

I take Ryan's hand and squeeze it, knowing what his father means to him. I tug on his hand and we walk to the cradle. I give it a little push and it creaks as it swings back and forth.

"I found it in the back of the attic the other day when I was searching for something. Mom didn't even know it was there." He narrows his eyes. "Is it weird to think Dad somehow guided me to it?"

"No Ry, not weird at all." I put my hand on his heart. "Your father is with us, always watching out for us. I truly believe that."

He nods. "I think he is too. I wish you could have met him."

"I think there is so much of your father in you, Ryan, that I have met him."

He touches the cradle, lightly rubbing his fingers over the aged wood. "Do you like it?"

"I love it."

He looks at me with such hopeful eyes, my chest tightens. "Do you think we could clean it up, paint it, get some nice bedding and use it for our little one?" His shoulders lift and fall slowly. "I mean I know it's old, but—"

"It's the most perfect cradle I've ever seen. I want to clean it with you. I want to work on it together." I take his face into my hands, and see all the love in his eyes as his gaze goes from the cradle to me. "Your dad would love this, Ryan, and this way, he can be a part of our baby's life. All of our children's lives. I mean you did say you wanted an entire dance troop, didn't you?"

He laughs at that as tears fall down his cheeks, and I start crying with him. "Thank you," he says as he buries his face in the crook of my neck.

"Thank you," I say in return. "Thank you for loving me, and giving me an amazing life, and for finding a way for your father to be part of our family."

I inch back to see him. He grins.

"What's so funny?"

"I was just thinking about Dad, and there was this incident..."

"Not another incident." I move to the bed, sit and pat it for him to join me.

"Oh, there was an incident, but can I tell you later."

"Okay sure, if you want." I smile at him. I love all the emotions this man has no trouble showing.

"Good, because right now I want to make love to my beautiful wife."

"So obsessed with me," I tease."

He grins, and presses his lips to mine, and I fall back onto the bed with the man I love so much today it hurts, but know I'll love him even more tomorrow.

***

Thank you so much for reading Alysha and Ryan's story. I hope you enjoyed it as much as I loved writing it. Please read on for an excerpt of Fair Play, book on in my End Zone Series

Fair Play

Ella

"What does this button do?"

I smack my best friend's hand away from the football's team brand new camcorder, and give her the evil eye. She knows better than to play with it, which makes the shocked looked on her face all the more amusing. But the fact is, I've been entrusted with the very expensive device to record the Falcons' first home game. Since I can't afford to replace it, I can't let my friend go around poking at every shiny knob and possibly breaking something.

"What?" Peyton says, blinking dark lashes over big innocent eyes. "I'm just asking a question."

"No. You're pushing buttons you shouldn't be pushing. Now sit there before I send you to the bleachers with everyone else." I point to the bench to the left of us and raise a warning brow.

She gives a light laugh, brushing off my threat. "You'd never do that. You love me too much." She's right. I wouldn't. Peyton and I have been best friends since kindergarten, and for the last three years we've been college roommates choosing apartment-style living over a sorority house. She's here for a degree in social work, and I'm here because I want to be a filmmaker. Yeah, working in Hollywood, behind the scenes, has been my dream since childhood.

Beside me, Peyton gives a very big, very happy sigh and takes in the football field from our perch—only the best, first class seating for the camera woman. "I do love the perks of being your best friend," she says as she admires the football players warming up. A few are so close we could practically reach out and touch them if we wanted to. I don't.

"I really can't understand the fascination," I murmur. "A bunch of guys in tight pants chasing a ball."

She crosses her arms, and waggles her brows at me. "What's it called again when a player passes the goal line with the ball in his hand?"

"Winning," I say, giving her a look that suggests she might be dense, but when she breaks out laughing, I crack a smile. Yeah, I get it. I'm the one who's dense. It's true, I know nothing about football, but I need this fourth-year credit to complete my cinematic arts degree and really, do I need to understand the game to record it for the team to analyze later? That would be a big fat no. I hope.

"Well, at least you know how this thing works," Peyton says, once again scoping out the buttons on my camcorder. "How about this knob? What does it do?"

"Peyton, cut it out." I slap her hand again and laugh at her childish antics. How we remained friends all these years when we're so different is a mystery. But we love each other like sisters. Sisters? Wait, that's not right at all. I'm an identical twin and my sister Ivy and I go together like hotdogs and Ferris wheels. Peyton and I, however, no matter how different, we just work.

I stare at her. "Don't you have football players to drool over?" Unlike me, she knows every player, and doesn't hold the same kind of grudge against them as I do.

I adjust my ballcap to shade the sun from my eyes as I glance out at the football field. I catch sight of my sister Ivy as she kicks one leg out and flirts with one of the players, trailing her finger over his chest. Blonde and bubbly. That's Ivy. We were raised by the same two parents, yet we're so different, and I wouldn't be caught dead in a cheerleading outfit that barely covered my ass. That's her business though, and I don't judge or interfere in her life, just like she doesn't interfere in mine.

I'd like to think when push comes to shove, she'd be there for me, just like I'd be there for her. At least, I think she'd be there for me. We might not hang out, but we love one another and have each other's best interests at heart. Of that I'm certain. It's funny really. Ever since we were young, we fell into certain roles. The extrovert and the introvert, the outgoing one and the quiet one. I always stood in the shadows and let her have the limelight. Pretty Ivy, the theater student who lights up a room with her smile and flamboyance when she enters. Which of course, makes me the introverted smart, quiet one. We both easily fell into those roles and have yet to stray.

Peyton gives a low, slow whistle. "I don't know what you have against tight pants. Look at all those cute butts and luscious muscles. Talk about slurpalicious." She rakes her teeth over her bottom lip. "Don't you want one little nibble, one taste?"

I give her a playful shove to move her away from the camcorder. "No. No nibbles. No tastes." I'm a virgin with no plans to change that anytime soon, and as my best friend, she damn well knows it. I take up position behind the camera, and look at the world through my beloved lens. I exhale a contented breath. This is where I belong. This is where I feel most at home.

Okay, yeah, so it's true. I'm the world's biggest nerd. Do I care? Nope. Not one little bit. I'm happy to stand in the shadow and view the world through my camcorder lens. As I do, I catch sight of Ivy again as she shakes her ass for the boys on the field. Truth be told, I actually hate football players. Back in high school, they bullied my friend Jacob until he ended up taking his own life. Terrible hazing went on at our school. The bullying was torturous and cruel, and no matter how hard Peyton and I tried to help Jacob, get him help, the bullying continued, and actually increased the more we tried to stop it. A stab of pain sears my heart at the painful memory, and I suck in air to breathe through it. I know I shouldn't lump all jocks into one category, shouldn't label them all as egotistical bullies, but a single player has yet to prove me wrong. Arrogant assholes. What more can I say?

I check my watch, as my stomach growls. "Hungry much?" Peyton says. "Maybe you'd like a nibble after all?"

"Really, Peyton. Did you just meet me?" I tease and reach into my backpack and grab a granola bar, all the while trying to cleanse my brain of football players and their tight asses—one player in particular. Peyton holds her hand out, and I place a bar in her palm. Granola bars and juice boxes on the go. The life of a busy fourth year student—or that of a toddler.

She tears into her wrapper and looks me in the eye. Her brow is furrowed as she examines me like I'm a bug under a microscope—a new kind of species no one can figure out. "You really don't find any of those guys attractive?"

"Nope, not a single one of them." A little white lie never hurt anything, right? "I prefer brains over brawn."

"That's a pretty blanket statement don't you think? I bet a lot of them are smart." Peyton doesn't hold the same grudge as I do. She figured it was a few bad apples on our high school football team who persecuted Jacob until his suicide, not every jock in the world. I don't forgive as easily. Maybe it's the social worker in her. She sees the world through a different lens, and that's her right.

"Yeah, probably." I shrug. She's right, but it doesn't matter. I'm not going to hold it against her if she wants to date a player.

She grins. "What about Landon Brooks?"

A chunk of granola lodges in my throat and I try not to react, try not to let my eyes bulge out of my brain as I choke. Reacting will only fuel her ridiculous fantasy that Landon and I would be good together. She's wrong, a million times over. A trillion, even.

I snatch a juice box from my backpack, rip the straw open and jab the foil opening. After a big sip, I roll my eyes. "Oh, Please, Landon's ego is as big as—"

"His cock?"

Ohmigod.

My granola bar jumps back into my throat and I take another huge sip. In my calmest voice, I stare at her and say, "That is not what I was going to say. I mean, come on. I have no idea how big his...his thing is, and I don't want to know."

"His *thing*." She laughs. "Oh, come on, Ella. You can say cock. I know you've watched porn before. We've watched it together, for God's sake. We all have fantasies, and that's normal."

Flustered, I say, "Okay, fine. His cock. That's the last time you're going to hear that word on my lips, and the last time I'm going to think about it." It's possible that's a lie. I might actually think of it tonight—when I watch porn.

"His cock is going nowhere near your lips then?"

I plant one hand on my hip and glare at her as she teases and twists my words. "How many ways do you need me to say it, Peyton?"

She braces her hands on the bench behind her and leans back, lifting her face to the sun. "I can tell you like him."

"I do not like him."

"What do you have against him anyway?"

Oh, other than the fact that he's living rent free in my head, nothing. "He's an asshole, and wait, why did you say his ego was as big as his cock. How do you know that?"

She gives me a slow grin that says she knows me too well. "Ah, look at that, you are thinking about his *thing* again." She wags her dark brows. "You know, they just don't call him Torpedo because he's lightning fast, on the field. It's because he has a big—"

"Stop," I say. I take a fast breath. *Do not think about Landon's torpedo.* I'm two seconds from demoting her to the bleachers, when she sits up straight, her mouth gaping. "What?" I ask, my blood draining to my toes even though I have no idea what's going on. I only know that look on her face and it's bad. So very, very bad. She looks past my shoulder and points her finger.

"Uh..."

Ohmigod. I mouth the words, "He's behind me, isn't he?"

As she gives a slow nod, I spin around. Landon is adjusting his helmet as his gaze moves over my face. He's not smirking, or showing any sign that he overheard us. Thank God!

"Hey," he says and my stupid ovaries quiver as my gaze lands on his brutally handsome face. He's not typically handsome, with a square jaw, perfect skin, perfect features. No. He's a bit harder, his face scarred from fights, and football. It only makes him hotter.

"Hey," I squeak out.

He smiles at me, then looks past my shoulder to Peyton when she clears her throat. "Hey, Peyton."

"Landon," Peyton says. "Looking good out there."

He turns his attention back to me. "Coach wants to know if you've got this thing all figured out." He gestures with a nod to the camcorder and I try not to react to his sexy Texas accent. "You know how to work all these buttons?"

"Yes, I do," I say, and while I get that he has no idea how to use the camcorder, there are plenty of buttons this guy knows how to press. Yes, I'm talking about the buttons between a girl's legs and the ones on the end of each breast. I've heard the rumors, and have zero intentions of ever finding out if they're true. I'd have a better chance of landing an assistant director position with Spielberg right out of college than this guy has of landing a position between my sheets. Not that he wants that, but chances of either of them happening: zero.

His gaze rakes over me, and my goddamn legs nearly give out as those dark eyes ignite my blood from simmer to inferno. What the hell is wrong with me? I do not like football players. I do not like Landon.

Yeah, you just keep telling yourself that, Ella.

"Wait, am I seeing double," he asks, and looks from me to Ivy and back to me again.

"Ivy is my twin," I say with an exaggerated sigh, and steal a fast glance at her across the field. As if feeling my eyes on her, her head lifts, and she stares at me. I can't see her expression from where I'm standing. I can only imagine she's in shock to see me talking with Landon. Not because I don't associate with football players, but because a nerd like me would never be worthy of his attention. She has nothing to worry about. He's all hers.

Have at him, sis.

"How come I've never seen you around before?" He shifts from one foot to the other, and I become acutely aware of his height, and of the way his muscles fill out his uniform. Does he even need all that padding? The fresh scent of soap, fabric softener, and something uniquely Landon fills my senses. It's not a bad scent. Nope, not bad at all. Which really sucks.

"I hang in different circles," I tell him and like the nerd I am, I snort, and tap the camcorder. "Cinematography."

"Oh yeah?" Dark eyes leave mine to steal a quick glance at the camcorder, and for a second he almost seems truly interested. "You're one of those audio/visual students?"

I nod and resist the urge to roll my eyes, because honestly, the fact that he doesn't know what my major is called isn't his fault. I don't know a thing about football, and I kind of get the sense he's trying to be nice, although for the life of me I can't figure out why. I'm pretty sure he's not trying to lure me to the locker room so the team can beat the crap out of me, like those boys in high school did to Jacob.

"You mean nerds?" I ask, with a raised brow, and Peyton kicks my ankle. I whimper, but don't take my eyes off Landon. God, he's so alluring, his face brutally interesting, I'm not sure I can.

Something passes over his dark eyes. A hint of sadness? I'm not sure why I suddenly feel like I've bruised him somehow. Jeez, I'd never purposely hurt anyone, whether I liked them or not.

"I never said that. I just mean..." He shrugs one of those broad shoulders and it's all I can do to keep my gaze from dropping...from admiring all his muscles. "You, uh, you like movies, huh?"

"Yes. I like movies," I respond, and resist the urge to walk through the door he just opened. Once someone brings up movies, I could go on and on about films, rambling about what I like, what I don't like, but I don't want to bore him to death. He has a game to play, women to impress.

He rubs a scar beneath his eye, and it flares red. "Seen anything good lately?"

How did he get that? Football, or something else? "Yes," I say again, and he smiles.

"Any recommendations?"

Porn.

What. The. Hell.

Get yourself together, girl!!

"Depends on what you like." I say, trying for casual when my stupid brain is conjuring up all kinds of unwanted images. Landon on top of me, underneath me...

"You should come to the party tonight." He gestures to the field with a nod. "I'll show you what I like."

Holy shit, no. He is definitely barking up the wrong tree here. I am not one of his groupies, bunnies, cleat chasers, or whatever the hell they call women who sleep with footballers. Wait! My brain takes a moment to catch up, alerting me that the guy everyone calls torpedo—and not just because he's lightning fast—invited me to a party. Did I just enter the twilight zone or something? I think I might have heard him wrong.

"I'm busy," I say.

This time his smile is cocky, full of brazen confidence, and I get it. I really do. I get why women hand their panties over. "Come on, you can't be too busy to celebrate our win?"

"Pretty sure of yourself," I say in a bored voice, even though there's a storm going on inside me.

He cocks his head. "Attitude is half the battle, don't you think?"

"You don't want to know what I think," I mumble.

He grins, and despite myself, my stupid lips twitch. God, why am I acting like a dim-witted moth around him? Yes, he's a shining star and has his own gravitational pull, but I am not into egotistical football players. My only goal is to keep my head down, finish my degree and get a job in Hollywood. Why I'm suddenly on this guy's radar is beyond me. Did he lose a bet or something? Have to talk to the nerdy girl? If not, and if there's something about me that appeals to him, he should go after Ivy. We look alike, except she dyes her hair blonde, and he could have her with a snap of his fingers.

"Her name is Ella," Peyton says. "She'll be at that party."

I spin, and give my former best friend the death glare. She studies her nails, like she doesn't have a care in the world. From across the field, a whistle blows, and I nearly jump ten feet in the air when a big, strong hand lands on my arm. I spin to face Landon, and he snatches his hand back.

"Sorry, didn't mean to touch without permission." He holds both hands up, palms out. "I just ah, I gotta go. Coach is calling." He pauses for a brief second.

"What?" I ask as I reposition myself at the camcorder and reach for the record button. Wait, why is it on? Rattled, and pretending not to be, as Landon continues to stand there, six feet of sex in a football outfit, looming over my small frame, I flick the record button off, and close my eyes, hoping when I open them again, he'll be gone.

"Aren't you going to say good luck?"

Nope not gone, and goddamn that cocky grin of his. I'm going to give my traitorous body—one spot in particular—a good hard lecture when we get home. With my vibrator.

"Good luck," I murmur, sounding uninterested.

He backs up an inch and I can almost fully refill my lungs again. "See you tonight, Ella."

"Not going to be there," I say.

He pauses and I sigh as I look at him. Why won't he leave already?

"How about this? If I score a touchdown, you come, if I don't...then it's my loss. In more ways than one."

His loss? Okay, I really am in some alternate universe. Football players do not flirt with me, and that's the way I like it.

"Why would I bargain with you? What could possibly be in it for me?"

"Come tonight." He flashes perfect white teeth. "Find out."

"We'll be there," Peyton says, finality in her tone, letting us both know it's going to happen and the conversation is over.

"We will not be there," I clarify through clenched teeth. We have a better chance of getting snow in Southern California this late September evening. Not. Going. To. Happen.

"See you tonight, Peyton," Landon says. "See you too, Ella." He points to the camera. "Now you'd better press record. You don't want to miss my touchdown."

My God, could the guy be any hotter...I mean, cockier. Yeah, cockier, that's what I meant. The guy is *not* hot. Nope not hot at all.

Much.

If you want to find out what kind of trouble Ella and Landon get themselves into check it out here **Fair Play**

ALSO BY CATHRYN FOX

Scotia Storms

Away Game (Rebels)

Warm Up (Rebels)

Crash Course (Rebels)

Home Advantage (Rebels)

Shut Out (Rebels)

End Zone

Fair Play

Enemy Down

Keeping Score

Trading Up

All In

Blue Bay Crew

Demolished

Leveled

Hammered

Single Dad

Single Dad Next Door

Single Dad on Tap

Single Dad Burning Up

Players on Ice

The Playmaker

The Stick Handler

The Body Checker

The Hard Hitter

The Risk Taker

The Wing Man

The Puck Charmer

The Troublemaker

The Rule Breaker

The Rookie

The Sweet Talker

The Heart Breaker

In the Line of Duty

His Obsession Next Door

His Strings to Pull

His Trouble in Talulah

His Taste of Temptation

His Moment to Steal

His Best Friend's Girl

His Reason to Stay

Confessions

Confessions of a Bad Boy Professor

Confessions of a Bad Boy Officer

Confessions of a Bad Boy Fighter

Confessions of a Bad Boy Doctor

Confessions of a Bad Boy Gamer

Confessions of a Bad Boy Millionaire

Confessions of a Bad Boy Santa

Confessions of a Bad Boy CEO

Hands On
Hands On
Body Contact
Full Exposure

Dossier
Private Reserve
House Rules
Under Pressure
Big Catch
Brazilian Fantasy
Improper Proposal

Boys of Beachville
Good at Being Bad
Igniting the Bad Boy
Bad Girl Therapy

Stone Cliff Series:
Crashing Down
Wasted Summer
Love Lessons
Wrapped Up

Eternal Pleasure Series
Instinctive
Impulsive
Indulgent

Sun Stroked Series

Seaside Seduction

Deep Desire

Private Pleasure

Captured and Claimed Series:

Yours to Take

Yours to Teach

Yours to Keep

Firefighter Heat Series

Fever

Siren

Flash Fire

Playing For Keeps Series

Slow Ride

Wild Ride

Sweet Ride

Breaking the Rules:

Hold Me Down Hard

Pin Me Up Proper

Tie Me Down Tight

Stand Alone Title:

Hands on with the CEO

Torn Between Two Brothers

Holiday Spirit

Unleashed

Knocking on Demon's Door

Web of Desire

ABOUT CATHRYN

New York Times and *USA today* Bestselling author, Cathryn is a wife, mom, sister, daughter, and friend. She loves dogs, sunny weather, anything chocolate (she never says no to a brownie) pizza and red wine. She has two teenagers who keep her busy with their never ending activities, and a husband who is convinced he can turn her into a mixed martial arts fan. Cathryn can never find balance in her life, is always trying to find time to go to the gym, can never keep up with emails, Facebook or Twitter and tries to write page-turning books that her readers will love.

Connect with Cathryn:

Tik Tok: @cathrynfoxwriter
Newsletter https://app.mailerlite.com/webforms/landing/c1f8n1
Twitter: https://twitter.com/writercatfox
Facebook: https://www.facebook.com/AuthorCathrynFox?ref=hl

Blog: http://cathrynfox.com/blog/
Goodreads: https://www.goodreads.com/author/show/91799.
Cathryn_Fox
Pinterest http://www.pinterest.com/catkalen/